Mehbub Gulley

Mehbub Gulley

Short Stories from India

Elizabeth Kottarem

PARTRIDGE

A Penguin Random House Company

To order additional copies of this book, contact
Partridge India
000 800 10062 62
orders.india@partridgepublishing.com

www.partridgepublishing.com/india

This book is dedicated to my father.
He was funny, kind hearted, and handsome.
He played the game of life with courage –
And he never gave up!
Love you Dad. You were the best!!

CONTENTS

Volume I

Volume II

VOLUME I

UNTOUCHED BY HAND

Nurse Shaila Oomachan was of good and honest peasant stock. Her family was Syrian Catholic and had owned fertile farming land in Iranjalakuda for more than fifteen generations. Her father owned five acres of rubber estates. His father before him had had thirty-five acres. But then he had sired seven sons. Shaila had four younger brothers. Her father decided that he would send her to be trained as a nurse and arrange for her to go to the Gulf. It would be the way out of the family's monetary difficulties.

Shaila had a pretty, brown face and she wore a small gold nose ring in her nose. Nose rings were in fashion then. She also wore a red stick-on bindi in the middle of her forehead, though she was a Christian. She tied her curly, black hair in a tight bun, on which her nurse's cap perched saucily. She had a lithe figure with curves in all the right places. She did half an hour of exercises every morning, when she had no night duty. She creamed her face every night with a deep cleansing, moisturising cream and wore no make-up. She got up early every morning and went to mass. Since there was no Syrian Catholic church nearby, she attended mass at St. John's church at the Fifth Cross Road in Bangalore.

She also wrote a letter home every week which hardly ever varied in its contents. It read –
"Dear Amma and Appacha,
I am well here. The work is interesting. The food is good. Yesterday we had chicken curry in the mess for lunch. I will be trying for admission to the B.Sc. nursing course since such girls are paid much higher in Muscat, where my friend Sheena is working in the government hospital. Hope Baji, Saji, Veeji and Shaiji are well and studying properly. Nothing else to add.
Your dutiful daughter, Shaila."

The letter arrived every week without fail and Shaila's mother opened it with trembling fingers each time and read the identical letter, as though it was something precious. They had ascertained that Sheena was getting fifty thousand rupees every month in her Gulf job. Shaila's parents' mouths watered at the thought of Shaila getting fifty thousand rupees every month. It would be enough to get Baji through his engineering. Presently they were always behind in paying the fees. Shaila's mother could also fulfil her ambition of making Saji a doctor. He was sitting for his pre-degree examination that year. If Veeji could become an IAS officer and Shaiji a police officer, then they could die in peace, Shaila's mother told Shaila's father, as they sat together at the kitchen table, poring over Shaila's letter.

Shaila would also rebuild the Tharavad, keeping only the porch and the verandah with Mangalore tiles. The rest of the house would be a modern RCC structure. They would have attached bathrooms, with western style commodes, in pastel colours. One toilet would have to be the conventional, Indian, squatting latrine, because Shaila's father said that he would never be able to do his morning ablutions in an English commode. Presently they only had a latrine outside the house. It had walls of matted palm leaves, instead of brick walls and a loose palm mat door. The entry to the house would be grand with a big carved wrought iron gate, with pillars in black granite. The gate would have the name *John Paramukkhill*, printed in gilt lettering on the granite pillars, just like their neighbour Avrachan's. His son was a garage mechanic in the Gulf and had improved the family fortunes. Avrachan's house was now the envy of the neighbourhood, a magnificent three storey structure.

Of course they would marry Shaila to a good accountant or teacher in the Gulf when she was twenty-nine – not too old, but after she had done her duty by her family, who had brought her so close to this stupendous good fortune. In fact Sheena was already thirty years old but her parents had not still found a suitable groom for her. Sheena's monthly remittances of thirty thousand rupees had rebuilt the family house and she had set up a printing press for her younger brother Polton, an idler who had not completed his tenth standard. Sheena's parents hoped to get him married soon for a fat dowry, to a nurse in the Gulf who would take Polton with her – who knows they said, if his stars were bright, he might even get a job as a shop assistant there.

There was consternation in the family when for the first time Shaila's weekly letter did not arrive. When

there was no letter for three weeks, Shaila's mother told her husband to go to Bangalore and see what had happened. But before he could leave for the long train journey, there came a note from Bangalore. It was addressed to Shaila's mother and the ink had run with tears. There were only four lines. It said:
"Dear Amma,
I am with child. It was a doctor. I don't know what to do. I will be dead by the time you get this.
Your sinful daughter, Shaila."

Shaila's old parents took the journey to Bangalore by bus. It was the cheapest way and train reservations were not available at such short notice. They found her body, cut after the post-mortem and the police case, in the hospital morgue and they took it home with them in a hospital ambulance. They had to pay a thousand rupees a day for the ambulance service. Fortunately her face was not disfigured. No one spoke to them. Shaila's friends were silent about what had happened. None of the doctors were available. All of them were either on duty or out for the day. The Matron was tight-lipped and looked accusingly at Shaila's parents, as though it were *they* who were responsible in some way for her death. The old couple came back home to the village. People stood around in knots, at the village tea shop, gossiping in undertones, about Shaila's death. All those who had envied Shaila's family for their impending good fortune when Shaila would go to the Gulf, now looked down on them scornfully. The family had been giving themselves too many airs just because their daughter was a nurse in Bangalore, the neighbours said.

No one attended the funeral except Shaila's own family. The coffin was not placed in the church but just outside the door because it had been a suicide. The body was buried in the separate area outside the main cemetery – the *themmadi kuzhi*, marked for those who had lead sinful and debauched lives.

જ જ જ

Young Doctor Innocent was not so very innocent. His name set the hearts of the lady medical students in the medical college in Manipal aflutter. His father had bought him a 'payment' seat in the medical college there, since he had scored only seventy percent in his pre-degree as against the ninety-six percent marks needed for a 'merit' seat. He was always seen wearing his goggles and leather jacket, with some of the bolder girls hugging him from the pillion seat of his motorbike. He also visited the Nurses' hostel where he was entertained by some of the lonely, young nurses who longed to hear someone speak in Malayalam. The nurses liked his witty conversation and expressions of ardour for all of them. But they sent him off after a cup of tea in the parlour. He was not successful in seducing his fellow female students either, since they all wanted to marry a good doctor and set up a clinic of their own. But he managed to do some heavy petting occasionally, after an ice-cream soda in a café.

His first introduction to sex had been through a passionate housemaid, at their farm in Changnasheri. She was two years older than his seventeen years and when she had got pregnant, there had been a great to

7

do in his family. His mother had said that boys after all would be boys. It had been for the maid not to lead him on. His mother had doted on him and hidden his every misdemeanour from his father. It was left to his father, Patros Vattakara, to hastily arrange for the marriage of the maid, Mariakutty, to a farm labourer, on the payment of a hefty sum to the man. Thankappan was also given a small hut, in the farthest field. Patros was incensed by the talk in the village tea shop. He strode around the house compound angrily, with his hands behind his back and bellowed that his son was to keep his hands off the working women or else he would give him a hiding the next time he was caught.

It was when he was posted as an intern at the Newness Hospital, in Bangalore, that Casanova Innocent began skirt chasing in earnest. The young trainee nurses were bowled over by his rakish, good looks and his general air of prosperity. He never missed the opportunity of holding a trainee nurse's hand, while checking a patient. He also looked deep into the eyes of the sweet, young things when he sat having his coffee in the pantry with one of them. They all wanted to hook a young doctor. Some of them fell for his promises of marriage and consented to sleep with him. He often took a cute trainee sister to the King's Arch hotel and entertained her in a room there.

Dr. Innocent had first seen Shaila when she sat counting the packets of I V needles and tubes in the nurses' room and entering them in the register with her lips pursed. A small curl had escaped her cap and hung tantalisingly on her cheek. Dr. Innocent passed by and pulled the curl. Shaila jumped up startled and saw a handsome, young face, with twinkling black eyes full of mischief, smiling at her. She smiled back. 'S. Oomachan,' Dr Innocent read from her name tag on her starched white uniform. 'And what is S?' he asked.

'Shaila, doctor,' she answered softly. Dr. Innocent looked at the day book and pretended to check the entries with a frown on his brow. He found out a few pointless mistakes and asked her to correct them. He then walked away, looking quite disinterested. Shaila felt unaccountably down cast that he had not waited to talk to her, like he usually did with the other young nurses. Perhaps he found her unattractive, she thought sadly. She did not have a fair complexion like some of the other nurses. The next day she wore a little light make-up, when she dressed. She was assigned the female post-operative ward. But Dr. Innocent did not appear there for three days. He was seen at the far end of the men's ward doing rounds with the Sister-in-charge, Sister Sylvia – a Mangalorean. He had scarcely looked in Shaila's direction.

Shaila was surprised when Dr. Innocent came and sat down next to her at lunch in the canteen one afternoon, instead of sitting on one of the tables reserved for doctors. He asked her how she was getting on in the hospital and about her parents and family back home. But he didn't volunteer any information about himself. Shaila soon found herself chatting to him quite artlessly every time that she saw him, as though they were from the same village. In fact when Dr. Jaswant Singh saw them talking together, Dr. Innocent told him, 'She's from my village back in Kerala.' To this Dr. Singh had replied with quiet sarcasm, 'Aren't they all?' But Shaila didn't hear that. She was flattered that Dr. Innocent had lied that they were from the same village. It made them conspirators together of a sort.

One afternoon, Innocent met Shaila in the ward just as she was coming off duty. He suggested that they have a masala dosa for lunch in the Sri Krishna Udipi. That was when her room-mates, Molly and Indu warned her about Dr. Innocent. 'He has already fooled many girls,' they told her, 'Don't get taken in by him.' But she was sure that they were jealous of her success in attracting the attentions of a handsome doctor. Dr. Innocent had never suggested the smallest impropriety when they had their ice creams at the park or even later when they went to the theatre. But he had snuggled up comfortably against her. On the way out, he held her hand to steady her on the steps of the exit out of the darkened theatre. Weeks later as they sat on the last row in a corner seat in a half empty theatre, he put his arms around her and kissed her. A little gasp escaped her lips. But he stifled her protests with a kiss that smothered her breath. Shaila was confused by the pleasurable feelings that she had when he caressed her. She sat with her head on his chest, her arms around him, wishing that the delicious sensations that made her feel so delirious, would never cease. But the three magic hours in the theatre were over all too soon. They met thereafter at cinema halls or in a deserted park. He dropped her back late at night a little away from the hostel gate. She tried to avoid her companions as she came up the stairs, on the way to her room. But sometimes she met the girls going out for night duty. They looked at her scornfully and she passed by them with downcast eyes. She stopped speaking to her workmates.

In a few months, Dr. Innocent went away on leave. No one knew for sure where he had gone. Shaila did not dare ask, in case she was teased. The Matron speculated that he had gone home to 'see' an eligible girl. Shaila was unhappy. She did her work quietly, completing her allotted tasks mechanically. She sat in her room in her off duty hours, staring at the wall, a bruised feeling in her heart. Dr. Innocent came back to the hospital two weeks later. He did not make any move to meet her or speak to her. Shaila was jealous, certain that he was engaged to be married to some heiress.

She pretended not to see him when he walked by in the hospital corridors and held her head averted and high. One Tuesday afternoon when she off duty, she went out shopping. She had run a ladder in her stockings and she also needed a new pair of shoes. As she was waiting for a bus at the bus-stop near the hospital, Dr. Innocent came by on his scooter. He stopped in front of her and asked softly, 'Why are you avoiding me *mollu*? Come I'll give you a ride to town.' He soon persuaded her to take the daring step of sitting behind him on the pillion, for all the world to see. She felt rather reckless, as she sat behind him holding on to him. He suggested that they stop at the park on the way. The park was quite deserted since there was a circus in town, which had attracted the young children who played there regularly. At the park, Innocent sat under the shade of a tree, plucking at the grass. He was very quiet and looked tortured. She looked at him, her young and trusting heart melted with grief for him and the words slipped out of her mouth, as she voiced the thoughts that had been whirling in her head, 'You went away without telling.' He pulled her towards him and said thickly, 'Couldn't you understand, that I couldn't just meet you anymore? You are so innocent.' They said nothing for a while. Then he said that he wanted to talk things over with her. He would take her to a quiet place he knew.

Shaila sat on the scooter with Dr. Innocent, her heart fluttering like a dove in a cage. They drove some distance out of town and he stopped at a small motel. He walked into the reception and the clerk nodded and handed him a key. They entered a shabby room, with a single bed in it. Shaila sat at the edge of the bed, twisting her pallu in her hands. Innocent slowly took hold of her hands and held them in his. With infinite tenderness, he kissed her willing lips, and she succumbed to the sweet temptation that followed. Gently he unhooked her sari blouse and undid the strings of her sari petticoat. Shaila made small, coquettish, murmurs of dissent. But she did not resist the surge of passion that overwhelmed them both. He felt a thrill of exultation, as blood stained the sheets. The little minx was a virgin after all.

The reception clerk telephoned to say that their one hour was up. They got up languorously, their bodies heavy with spent passion. Shaila washed the sheets clean and hung them in the bathroom. She washed herself thoroughly and wore her sari with the pallu covering her shoulders. She felt guilty and sad. The motel clerk had a leer on his face as they checked out. Innocent dropped her wordlessly at her hostel. He took her to the same motel, the next three Sundays. Each time she was filled with ecstasy and later with self-loathing and fear. They avoided each other during week days. But Shaila waited with a beating heart every Sunday morning for his call over the intercom from the hostel reception desk.

Dr. Innocent's internship at the hospital came to an end the week after Shaila and Innocent had met at the motel for the fourth time. Innocent went the following week for his interview for a job in a hospital in Dubai. He was selected for the position. He did not see Shaila after that. Then she missed her period. She had a sinking feeling, as she felt her abdomen increase in girth with each passing week. But she was afraid to consult her work mates or the Matron who would surely give her marching orders. Sister would not want the hospital to get a bad name. When Shaila could no longer hide her belly, one night she took an overdose of sleeping tablets. She was found cold and dead in her room by the staff nurse who was sent to find out why she had not reported for morning duty.

જ જ જ

Doctor Innocent joined the super speciality hospital in Dubai. He won recognition as a brilliant doctor and a hard task master. He received higher responsibilities each succeeding year. He sent home large sums of money, which were dutifully deposited into his account by his father, who was relieved that his son had at last settled down to a serious career.

His mother wrote him that there was an heiress from Kanjirapalli, who would be just right for him. She wanted him to get married, when he next came on home leave. Much to her surprise, Innocent promptly agreed. It was good fun chasing the hospital nurses, taking them out to dinner and seeing them crumble under his irresistible charm. But now a small, unmistakable bald patch was beginning to grow on Innocent's crown. It was time to settle down, he decided, as he combed the thinning mass of hair. On his next trip home for the holidays, he went to the girl's house for the bride viewing. He was thirty two. The girl was only seventeen. She was pink as an unfolding rose bud. Innocent had been particular about that. She should be so young that no man could have looked at her, he had told his mother. These days with pills and condoms available at every corner pan shop, it was so difficult to ensure that you got a virgin bride, he guffawed with his friends over beer. Never mind that she was an undergraduate, he wrote his mother. She could complete her studies after their marriage. He looked at her pictures and chuckled at her chubby baby face. 'She's untouched by hand!' he chortled to his friends at the hospital, 'I'm a lucky man!'

Nirmala and Innocent were married at the village church. Nirmala wore ten gold chains, beginning with a necklace of diamonds and ending with a long *kash mala* that went down to her navel – a long strand of gold coins entwined with gold threads. She wore twenty-four bangles, twelve on each arm and a ring on every finger of her hands. Patros Vatakara spent a lakh of rupees for the firecrackers that were burst after the wedding ceremony. There were a thousand guests for the wedding. A special pandal had to be erected outside their house and the cooks who were engaged for the marriage feast had wrought magic with the chicken biryani and the payasam.

Innocent returned to Dubai with Nirmala. She graduated in Geography by a correspondence course from Osmania University. They had a son. But then Nirmala got bored. So Innocent got her a job as a teacher at the Champion English High School in the lane of the Four Nightingales. The school was owned by a wealthy Sheikh.

Early one morning as Innocent sat in his room in the hospital, the air conditioning failed abruptly. There was an unexpected power failure. The generators sprang into life. But when the power failure lasted over two hours, the hospital declared an emergency. Ward boys and technicians crowded around the canteen. The operation theatres had not been fumigated for the day's operations. New patients were turned away at the gates by the guards.

A decision had to be taken urgently about the serious, emergency operations which could not be postponed. The Hospital Chief Administrator, Masood Ali was a suave Harvard man – an Arab with an American accent. Innocent strode hurriedly into the C.A's room with a perfunctory knock on the door. He found the Malayali office stenographer sitting on the Arab's knee, being kissed passionately by the CA. The woman was thirty-five, married to one of the hospital technicians and had two young children.

Innocent left the room wordlessly and almost ran to his car. He drove at a furious pace to the lane of the Four Nightingales and rushed into the school compound. He found Nirmala in the staff room and pulled her out by her hand. He handed her a piece of paper. 'Here, sign your resignation letter,' he told her brusquely. They went back home in silence after she had handed in the letter. She was stupefied, as he led her to the kitchen and told her that from now on she could employ herself teaching their son and cooking up delicious meals for them. Soon the news trickled home. Everyone in Changnasheri was impressed about how much Innocent had cared to protect his wife's purity. He had bid goodbye to the very handsome salary drawn by his wife, just so that her honour was protected. He was a real family man, with sound Christian values, they said.

Innocent made his fortune in the Gulf and he came back home to savour the sweet fruits of success. He purchased fifty acres of fertile land near the family land in Changnasheri. Innocent walked barefoot in the rich, red earth and as his feet sank into the soil, he was filled with a heady feeling of joy. He grew rubber and cashew nut and fragrant spices – cardamom and black pepper. He watched them grow in luxuriant abundance.

He constructed a large hospital in the town near his village. He called it the Sevaanjali Nursing Home. The hospital kept him busy twenty-four hours a day. His two sons were doing well at an engineering college in Madras. But it was his wife, Nirmala, who was dissatisfied. There were enough servants to look after the house. She hardly had any work to do to keep her occupied. She drank endless cups of tea and watched three Malayalam movies a day on Asianet, Surya and DD Keralam. She slept the entire afternoon. She was unable to sleep at night. Strange desires kept her awake, she was only thirty-five. Innocent snored heavily beside her, oblivious of her plight.

Early one morning Nirmala sat up in bed, sleep eluding her. She gazed out of the window. It was four o'clock and a few stars lit the sky. The air conditioner had stopped. Another spell of load-shedding had made the heat oppressive. Outside a little breeze rustled the coconut trees. She saw a small lantern light moving in the cowsheds across the courtyard. It was the cowman Jonkennedy, Thankappan the old farmhand's son. Thankapan had long been dead and the maid Mariakutty was now a virtuous, churchgoing widow. Thankappan had been an admirer of the late American president. Jonkennedy's handsome face had always looked vaguely familiar to Nirmala. It reminded her of someone she had met somewhere. But she couldn't quite remember. Jonkennedy had not studied beyond the eighth standard. He had learnt to work as a cowhand instead. She remembered how he had whistled impudently as he walked past her in the backyard, his red checked lungi jauntily bunched up above his knees. He had not lowered it to cover his calves out of respect for her, like the other farm hands did. Instead he had flung her a careless remark – 'Kochamma the cow feed is over. We have to buy some

17

more today,' and had gone his way, without waiting humbly for her reply.

Nirmala stole softly to the cow-shed and stood at the doorway watching Jonkennedy milking the black cow. He sat on a stool, bare-chested, with the black, matted, hair curling on his strong, brown chest. He wore a blue checked lungi loosely from his waist and he sat with his feet pressed on the floor firmly, the muscles on his arms rippling as he effortlessly milked the cow. When he became aware of her gaze, the milking stopped. He took in the sight of her, with her bright eyes and curving lips, her black wavy hair tumbling over her shoulders and the top buttons of her flimsy nightie undone. He got up slowly, his eyes crinkling with laughter. He knew that she would come to him. He strolled up languidly and held out his arms. She walked up to him and he held her close. The odour of sweat from his body and his milky hands enveloped her. Moments later he led her to the pile of hay, at the far end of the cowshed. He reached out and switched off the light of the hurricane lantern.

ॐ ॐ ॐ

Dr. Innocent went into the village shop to get a new battery for his torch. As he got out into the afternoon sunlight, a straggle of small boys followed him at a distance. They looked at him and set up a chant, 'Why does Nirmala anty have hay in her hair? Why does Nirmala anty have hay in her hair?' He looked around and shooed them away before getting into his car. Strange, how children were now a days, he thought. They should be occupying themselves with their lessons, if they want to get ahead like me, instead they occupy themselves with silly chanting games, he mused. He gave a self satisfied grunt. Now, the new extension wing to the Sevaanjali nursing home was coming up, with an entire ward for a government approved abortion clinic. There were so many indiscreet liaisons these days. It would do very well indeed.

ॐ ॐ ॐ

A TREAT FOR THE ORPHANS

It was a lovely day in the first week of June. It had rained the whole of the week before and there was a smell of wet earth in the air. The sun shone brightly after the week of rain. It was four in the evening and we were on our way to Naomi's house. It was in the Jewish quarter of Cochin. Naomi's family was one of the few that had not migrated to Israel. The tall coconut palms that lined the narrow streets, swayed in the breeze, the leaves spraying droplets of water everywhere. The small lane that we turned into was cobbled and neat. There were little pools of rain water on the road. We picked our way carefully, so that we did not wet our feet. The houses on either side of the lane, had dull orange moss lined Mangalore tiled roofs and white-washed walls of red laterite stone. In one of the houses, an old crone sat on a verandah wall rocking herself and singing a Jewish folk song in singsong Malayalam, as she cleaned and winnowed rice on a bamboo *morram*. A rooster and a brood of hens scratched in the compound.

We turned into Naomi's gate. It was a small yellowing wooden gate that had once been white. Now it hung loose with rusty hinges. We entered the front door, which led straight into the front room. The house did not have a verandah. Its windows were shut tight. The room we entered was dark and gloomy. An old wooden clock ticked away the minutes and the hours on a wall which had plaster peeling. There was a sofa with a torn green rexine cover, at one end of the room. Across it were two arm chairs that had bright patches of new rexine, over the worn out areas of the old, green cover. Three wooden straight backed chairs stood in a row against another wall. There was a small wooden teapoy near the sofa, with an embroidered cross-stitch tablecloth on it, with designs of Mistress Mary, quite contrary, watering her flowerbeds. Naomi had done it for her craft class in the ninth standard. A beautiful crystal vase, filled with wilting red roses stood on the teapoy. There were faded yellow half-curtains for the windows strung on taut springs. But the windows were shut.

Naomi was small and fair, with brown eyes and straight black hair, which she wore long up to her waist. Her heart shaped face had a fragile look, as though a word might crumble it. We took special care of Naomi. She was the only girl from a Jewish background, in our rough and boisterous class of thirty students. She lived with her uncle and her two brothers. Her parents had died in a car accident when she was ten. Naomi had called us home as an unusual treat. It was a sort of farewell for our gang of five before we sat for the Board exams. We had never been to her house before. There were three girls – Annu, Raji, and I and two boys – Partha and Kannan. Naomi asked us to sit down in the front room.

We sat on the hard chairs, feeling shy all at once in the strange surroundings. She went inside. We heard the clatter of vessels and the sounds of a wooden cupboard being opened. Naomi was making the tea. She came out of the kitchen bearing the teapot on a tray with cups and set them in the next room, which was the dining room.

A bald man in a yellowing vest and faded pyjamas came down the stairs that lead to the rooms on the first floor and looked at us through thick glasses.

'Noami's friends,' he grunted and went into the kitchen. He had a string of keys in his hand. A lock turned and squeaked in the kitchen.

'Bring the plates Naomi,' shouted the old man.

'Yes uncle,' Naomi's voice came subdued from the dining room. It was not her lilting school voice. She went into the kitchen bearing six china quarter plates.

She brought back the plates two at a time. The plates were laden with cream cakes, bright orange fat juicy jangris and namkeen of fried puffed rice and lentils. Naomi guided us into the dining room. It was a long room with a meat-safe at one end and dusty shuttered windows. We all trouped in and sat down on the round wooden chairs. The backs of the chairs extended into arms. They were etched with a design of clubs on the seat. We each had a pretty china plate with a pattern of pale yellow and mauve flowers on it. As we munched the cakes, we laughed and teased each other. Naomi was withdrawn and distant. She glanced now and then at the door and then at her plate. She did not eat the pastry or the namkeen. Suddenly her eyes were fearful. We looked up at the doorway. Two young boys had crept silently down the stairway and now stood staring wistfully at us from the last step, right near the entrance to the dining room. We fell silent. Naomi's uncle looked up and a deep frown crossed his face.

'Moses, Isaac come down from there,' he shouted. They moved forward slowly and stood near the door.
'Come here and say hullo to Naomi's friends,' he commanded. They came to the table and stood quietly near the old man, their arms by their sides, their eyes to the ground.
'Go and get your plates,' he barked after a long silence. The boys shuffled to the kitchen and came back bearing two dented aluminium plates.
'Here,' he said. The boys held out their plates like lepers receiving offerings outside a mosque. He placed a jangri and a pastry each on their plates and put in three careful teaspoons of namkeen.
'Got, no?' he said, 'Now eat and don't speak to the neighbours after Sabbath day prayers at the synagogue, that you don't get any of the good things to eat in this house.'

The boys stood against the wall, slowly masticating the food. We stopped eating. Naomi sat with her head slightly bent forward. Her face was puckered up and a tear trembled on her eyelid. We all got up one by one and pushed back our chairs. We helped Naomi clear up. She kept the uneaten food in the meat-safe in the dining room and locked it and handed over the key to her uncle.

We said, 'Thank you uncle,' in small voices, and left hurriedly. Naomi looked at us wordlessly, as we went out of the dark and dank front room. Somehow the sun was not so bright anymore and the sound of the koel was low and plaintive. We walked home listlessly. Partha kicked a stone and said, 'I hate that bloody uncle of Naomi's.'

ॐ ॐ ॐ

MEHBUB GULLEY

Mehbub Gulley – or Lovers Lane, was not a romantic tree lined avenue in Hyderabad. It had just a few dry, Gulmohor trees. And it was not named after any lover, but after a local bigwig – Nawab Mehbub Amin Rahimatullah Khan, who had owned large estates in Hirekund before they had been squandered away on wine, women and horse racing by his only son and heir Nawab Mir Bux Khan. Mehbub Gulley was dusty and crowded with street vendors who advertised their wares in a loud, noisome clamour. There was horse dung and urine everywhere. The horses were hitched to Tongas, in which people rode to the old Charminar area. Flies swarmed around the dung and the food stalls. Stray dogs sniffed around the food stalls for a bite to eat and the beggars who sat around in groups, scratched their sores and whined whenever they saw a well dressed person walk down the road. They called attention to their blindness, or missing limbs or other deficiency in their body which nature or the underworld dons running the beggary racket, had given them, until the harassed victim dropped a coin into the outstretched palm of the mendicant.

Stefan Hoffman parked his cycle outside the stylish 'Book Nook' in Mehbub Gulley and entered the air-conditioned shop selling books, magazines, cassettes and compact discs.

'Blasted, dirty city,' he muttered under his breath as he entered the shop, running his fingers through his soft, brown hair in exasperation. His hair was tousled and his Bermudas looked crushed. He was irritable. The heat and dust in Hyderabad had made him bad tempered. He had had the misfortune of stepping into a patch of horse dung on the street, when he had got down from the bicycle which he had rented from the corner pan shop near his hotel. The pan shop keeper had charged him thirty rupees an hour instead of the usual ten, because he was white.

A brown girl, with a small, round face and a snub nose on which rested a pair of large spectacles, seated at a table in the corner of the bookshop, looked up sharply from the book that she was browsing, entitled *Dream Spires*. It was about churches in Europe.

'What do you mean dirty city?' she demanded aggressively, tossing her shoulder length hair, 'Then why did you come here? It's a beautiful city.'

'What parrt is clean and what parrt is beauty fool?' he asked her, surprised by her vehemence. She shut the book and explained that Hyderabad was a very ancient city. The old Charminar area was no doubt very crowded but it had a charm of its own and the city centre was modern. Some of the old monuments were priceless, she said.

Stefan introduced himself. He said that he was a tourist from Vienna. He had come to see India and imbibe some of its age old culture. He felt that the East had profound knowledge and a depth of understanding of the meaning of life, which had eluded the West – which had alas, become so selfish and consumerist. Stefan was embarrassed that he had been apprehended so unexpectedly by a brown nymph with hazel eyes, while giving vent to his irritation. He remembered (too late) that the travel guides issued by the Travel and Tourism department of his native land, had advised travellers going abroad against complaining about their host country. The books had also dwelt on the stringent consequences in some countries, such as a public flogging or even castration by the moral police authorities, for attempting to become friendly with an attractive woman resident.

Of course such laws were fortunately not adopted in India, he reflected . . . India was a free, open country in which there were elections held every five years and sometimes even oftener and motorists did not feel abashed in driving through a red light and tipping the constable who accosted them. Some people also believed in their unfettered freedom of expression – to set trains and buses on fire, ransack museums, demolish ancient mosques, or even break heads or body parts in order to express their disagreement with those who had written plays, novels, historical books, painted pictures or shot motion pictures expressing ideas that were not in harmony with those of the protestors. The mosque breakers preferred cucumber shaped roofs on places of worship over onion shaped ones. 'Those who collide against us, will become part of the mud,' they shouted fiercely, as they moved through the streets brandishing their swords and choppers. Such actions resulted in no more serious consequences to those who indulged in these freedoms, than in tut tutting by beleaguered and over burdened courts. People (most often 'outsiders') who wanted to protest about the protestors, mostly refrained from doing so. They were fearful in case their faces were blacked by boot polish or their limbs broken by the protestors (who were 'insiders' and sons of the soil). It was of course undisputed that the feelings and sensitivities of 'insiders' were more delicate and important than those of mere 'outsiders' – those vastly inferior beings, who were in a minority and whose voices and votes did not matter.

It was all not quite clear either. Though castration was not officially prescribed, the public display of affection for the opposite sex or sending them valentine cards was frowned upon by a part of the populace (though at present somewhat in a minority). He had read in the local papers of an earnest policeman – Inspector Bunglae, who wanted to keep his motherland pure and free from all evil polluting western sexual activity. Bunglae hence took to patrolling his beat, armed with a hockey stick and personally intervening with the assistance of his hockey stick and dissuading young men and women from holding hands and walking together in the evening, in secluded pathways in Bandra or Khar. Of course private moments of affection could not be prohibited, in the interest of protecting women's virtue and purity, even by Bunglae. The escalating population graph was an eloquent testimony to these private moments ... Bunglae was removed and put away in an administrative post after people made known their disapproval of his tendency to carry a hockey stick with him on his evening walks. Stefan had also heard that there were groups of young and not-so-young men in baggy khaki shorts, also armed with hockey sticks, who took matters in their own hands and trashed any young woman found consuming alcohol in a pub, as they saw in such public consumption of alcohol by women, yet another threat to women's purity. A little confusing, thought Stefan, better to be careful . . . Hockey sticks seemed to be rated as the favourite article of accoutrement for men having a higher-than-the-average sense of moral outrage in India.

So he talked on at length about the mysticism of the East, all the while noticing that though the nymph presently had a steely look in her eye, she had a naughty dimple and the most winsome, sparkling teeth. It was when she frowned, with her black eyebrows almost meeting each other, that he was terrified. She reminded him of his headmistress at junior school. His interrogator frowned when she asked him whether he was a student and he replied that he was not an student. The frown deepened when she followed it up with a question as to which firm he worked in and he was forced to admit that he did not work in any firm but that he was an art collector by profession. She looked as though she was not impressed, as though she did not think that 'collecting' anything could be a reasonable profession for a man. He glanced diffidently at her book and asked her deferentially whether she had visited Europe. She said, 'No, I've never been abroad. But I do want to go to London for my masters.' She said that she was reading for her degree in History from the Nizam's College. She then asked him whether he knew anybody in Hyderabad. When he admitted, looking a little forlorn, that he had no friends in the city, she decided that she needed to take charge of this bleating lamb. She volunteered to take him around the city. They arranged to meet the following morning at eight at her house which was in Mehbub Gulley, a little away from the book shop. It was after she had left on her moped that Stefan realized that he had not asked for her name. As he found out later, her name was Qudsiya – the Pure One.

He arrived at her house at eight fifteen the next morning. He hired a taxi instead of riding his cycle, so that his freshly laundered shirt and trousers did not crease. The taxi driver (who felt that at last some good luck had come his way) had smiled superciliously when Stefan hesitantly looked at the sheet of paper in his hand and read out the address of his destination – *81, Zeeenath Mahell Meehbooob Golly*. A poor spirited Mehbub, the cabbie muttered under his breath and used the opportunity to take Stefan there in a roundabout manner. Stefan knocked at Qudsiya's door feeling a little nervous.

A servant woman opened the door to him and had a round eyed look of wonder when he asked for Qudsiya. She let him in and gestured towards the *dewan* in the sitting room. 'Bait ja-i-ye' she muttered, motioning him to sit down. He heard a small commotion of voices in the household. His arrival had evidently been the cause of some discussion. He waited in trepidation, wondering whether strong men would shortly enter and despatch him outside the house. But no one came in.

He looked around the room. There was a sofa at one end of it with broad teak arm rests and rich red and black tapestry on it and a Kashmiri teapoy of walnut wood, delicately carved with a design of vine and leaves. A broad swing with cushioned seats adorned the other end near a closed balcony door. There were miniature paintings on the walls – battle scenes with warriors seated on horses and elephants, a lady adorning her hair, Radha-Krishna in embrace and a Grand Mogul, rose in hand.

The servant woman came back after a while and offered him a glass of water which she served with her hands cupped in a gesture of service. Grateful for the cool draught, he sipped the water slowly. A little later, Qudsiya's mother Nusrat Begum walked into the room. She was a tall, thin, woman, with an aquiline nose, on which she wore a diamond nose stud. Her head was covered by her sari pallu which she held in place with her right hand.

'Salaam Alaykum!' she intoned, her head bent slightly forward, her right hand leaving the pallu momentarily was raised twice in greeting. Stefan jumped to his feet and said, 'A very goot morning to you Madame!'

'Please sit,' she commanded him. She enquired of Stefan whether his hotel accommodation was comfortable and she asked why he had thought of visiting India. Soon they were chatting together in easy fashion. The servant maid brought in tea on a tray. Nusrat Begum served him the tea herself, pouring out the milk and stirring it with two lumps of sugar, after asking him how much sugar he usually had with his tea.

He was describing the grandeur of the Austrian Alps when Qudsiya came in. She looked at him quizzically, rolled her eyes and said, 'Oh you've already made a friend of Ammi!' She was dressed in jeans and a long t-shirt and as they were leaving she wore a large pair of goggles that made her face disappear. Qudsiya said that they would travel on her brother's scooter. It would be cheaper than hiring a taxi. He agreed. He was impressed by her eye for economy. She set off at a pace that left him alarmed. He clutched the steel handle of the pillion seat for dear life. This would never have happened in Vienna where he lived, he thought.

Qudsiya first stopped at the Charminar. 'This was a monument built by Sultan Muhammed Qutub Shah in memory of his beautiful Hindu wife Bhagmati. The Qutub Shahi kings ruled this area in the sixteenth and seventeenth centuries AD,' she explained as they stood near the massive granite walls. He took photographs of the tiers of balconies and the four minarets that soared into the sky. He took some pictures of people getting into Tongas near the bazaar, as crowds of people walked by, unmindful of the ancient monument. Qudsiya took Stefan past the jewellers' shops in the Lad Bazaar surrounding the Charminar. The jewellers sold pearl necklaces and bangles. They were persistent and held out the strings of pearls and let the glowing beads run through their fingers.

'This rate is very cheap rate Saab,' they said. Stefan bought a few strands of pearls to take back home. No, she didn't want any pearls, Qudsiya said businesslike, when he asked her whether she'd like some. Instead

Qudsiya suggested that the Sallar Jung museum was something he would want to see since he was interested in Art.

They rode to the museum on her scooter and Qudsiya manoeuvred through the unruly traffic in an expert manner that left him gasping in admiration. In a few minutes they reached the museum near the banks of the Musi River. While Qudsiya paid the parking attendant, Stefan bought the museum entry tickets. He admired the Nawab's collection of paintings, sculpture, carpets, clocks and rare manuscripts and he made notes in his notebook of the details of each piece. "Nawab Mir Yousuf Ali Khan Salar Jung III (1889-1949), former Prime Minister to the seventh Nizam of Hyderabad, spent a substantial part of his income over thirty five years, to make this priceless collection" he wrote painstakingly in his beautiful handwriting.

They stopped at an Udipi eating house. The cashier sat at the entry to the cafe, behind a counter shielded by a glass half partition. He had a white u-shaped caste mark on his forehead. On the wall behind the cashier there was a picture of the black god, Sri Murugan covered in garlands, with his third eye in the middle of his forehead. They found two empty chairs at a marble topped table and sat down. Qudsiya treated Stefan to a fifteen inch long "paper" masala dosa. He followed her lead, attacking the dosa from the middle with his fingers, scooping out the delicious potato filling, wrapped with a sliver of dosa and gradually peeling off the ends and wrapping them with potato filling. The waiter brought them hot filter coffee in small steel dishes, placed in little steel tubs. He watched with interest as she cooled the coffee, pouring it into the tub and then back into the small dish. He thought it a novel way to cool the coffee and studiously cooled his coffee likewise and then drank it in appreciative sips.

A fat man in a tight red T-shirt and a white dhoti sitting at the adjoining table, looked at them curiously as he noisily slurped his own coffee. When he leaned forward and looked as though he was about to enter into a conversation with them, Qudsiya got up abruptly and paid for their snacks to the bored, middle aged cashier and walked out of the cafe. Qudsiya looked over her shoulder at Stefan and said that they would go to the Hussain Sagar Lake and look at the statue of the Buddha before it got too dark to see it clearly. Stefan was able to nimbly hop on to the pillion seat just before Qudsiya started the scooter and they went racing off – at what seemed to be the speed of light. Stefan felt exhilarated, as though he was riding a new kind of roller coaster.

Qudsiya was back home at five in the evening. She spent three more days showing Stefan around Hyderabad. They visited the Golconda fort. They gazed at the inscription which said that it dated back to the 13th century, to the rule of the Katkatiyas, who built a mud fort and that it was later built in granite by the Qutub Shahi kings. They had lunch at a little wayside dhaba which served hot nans and spicy chicken curry. The boy who waited on them had a greasy towel on his arm. He brought them a dessert of sweet creamy kulfis.

The waiter wrote out the bill. He placed it on the table between them. Stefan reached for his wallet. But Qudsiya had already paid for the meal.

'This is not goot. In our konthry, the man always makes the payment,' he protested.

'My father said that you are a guest in our country and he gave special instructions that you must not pay for any food. We say in our country *Athithi Devo bhava*. That's Sanskrit and means – *a guest is divine*.' Stefan looked wonderingly at her and murmured to himself, 'Aatiti devo baava'.

After the third day of sightseeing, Qudsiya said that she had college to attend and that she could not take him to see any more of the places but that they had seen most of the main attractions of Hyderabad. He thanked her profusely and gave her a bracelet of multicoloured gemstones that he had bought at Lad bazaar. 'This is mark of my gratitude for all the troubles you have taken for the education of this unknown stranger,' he told her self-consciously. Qudsiya thanked him with her dimpled smile and Stefan then felt a strange stirring in his heart. He suddenly wished that the three days could have stretched on endlessly.

Qudsiya's family invited him to a farewell dinner the night before he left for Delhi. Stefan sat in the sitting room in Qudsiya's home, talking desultorily to Qudsiya's father, as the evening shadows lengthened. A Meena work brass lamp in deep red and blue and green, occupied a corner of the room and its light cast a soft glow around the room.

Stefan felt unaccountably welcome and happy. Qudsiya's father, Sadiq Ali, was a senior official in the Archaeological Survey of India. He had a thin, gaunt face and wore round spectacles in a black wire frame. He looked dignified in his formal, black sherwani and white chooridars. Sadiq Ali wanted to entertain the young foreigner and make him feel that he was not among strangers. He wondered what would be of interest to the Austrian tourist. Ah Yes! He was a tourist, and so naturally interested in tourism! Sadiq Ali took down what was most precious to him – his collection of rare black and white photographs of ancient Indian monuments, and showed it to Stefan, explaining the significance of the architecture of each edifice. Stefan was intrigued by the photograph of the goddess Parvati sitting on the god Shiva's lap in the Hoysaleshwara temple at Halebidu. Apparently there was no equivalent of Inspector Bunglae in India in those ancient times, to prevent this sort of expression of affection, Stefan astutely concluded.

'This temple is over eight hundred years old, carved from a single rock,' Sadiq Ali said, 'Notice the engineering expertise even eight hundred ago!' Stefan was suitably impressed and decided to alter his tour itinerary to include Belur and Halebidu.

Nusrat Begum gave him a cool drink of red Rooh Afza in a tall glass and Qudsiya handed around small quarter plates of roasted cashew nuts and almonds. The inviting smell of baking Indian bread wafted into the room from the kitchen. They went in to dinner in the long dining room. It was a dinner to remember – Hyderabadi biryani with murg masallam and kulfi with falooda and raisins for dessert. Nusrat Begum heaped food on his plate and coaxed him to eat just a little more. Not since he was a little boy had so much fuss been made of him. He remembered his stout and affectionate mother and the delicious strudels she made. His eyes misted over at her memory. She had struggled to bring him up after his father had died at thirty-five of cancer. She had worked as a typist in a large firm that dealt in sanitary fittings. But she saw him through his university education. She had wanted him to become a doctor like his father. Instead he had become an art collector. Now she was no more. A dutiful son, he visited the cemetery where she was buried and laid flowers at her grave every year.

Qudsiya's father was curious to know about his family.
'How many brothers and sisters have you?' he asked Stefan.
'None,' he answered, 'I am zee only one.'
'And your parents? What do they do?'
'My father was a doktor – a paediatrician. Both the parents are dead.'
There was a sound of pity and a respectful silence before the next question. Was he married?
'No,' he answered. 'In Austria many people do not marry.' There were surprised looks. 'But some people do marry. The others live with companions.'

Qudsiya's sixteen-year-old brother Salim giggled at the shocked look on his mother's face. Her outrage struggled with curiosity – did Stefan have a companion? But decorum forbade a frontal enquiry into the matter. Stefan asked about Indian customs and in particular the Muslim customs in their family. Marriages were arranged and girls rarely fell in love since they were traditional folk, Qudsiya's father told him. Then Stefan on his own, without any prompting or prodding, said that since he was a church going Roman Catholic, he did not believe in the notion of having a live in companion.

They discussed the customs in various cultures. Sadiq Ali was an ardent believer in Sufism. He recited from Rumi –
'A moment of happiness, you and I sitting on the verandah, apparently two, but one in soul, you and I.
We feel the flowing water of life here
You and I, with the garden's beauty
And the birds singing.'

And Stefan, much to the delight of his hosts, quoted from Khalil Gibran –
'I would not exchange the sorrows of my heart for the joys of the multitude,
I would not have the tears that sadness makes, to flow from my every part, to turn into laughter.
I would that my life remained a tear and a smile.'

The evening was over all too soon and they bid him goodbye. Sadiq Ali gave Stefan a present of a book of poetry by Khalil Gibran, taken down from his own shelf of books.

The next morning, Stefan dropped by Qudsiya's home on his way to the railway station. He was leaving for Delhi by the Rajdhani Empress. The hotel had secured him a good seat in a second class AC chair car compartment of the train. Qudsiya opened the door to him and looked surprised to see him. Her face was small and pinched and her eyes had dark shadows under them. She looked a little guilty as she led him inside. She said that her mother had gone out to the bazaar. They sat down self-consciously on the divan in the sitting room. Stefan felt his heart booming. He looked at his hands. They suddenly seemed to have become too large. He put them behind his back, but then changed his mind. Perhaps it looked too aggressive and dominant sitting in this manner? In any case Qudsiya did not look at him. She looked at the Persian carpet on the floor instead. They were silent. Then after a few moments, she looked up and smiled a smile that was at once shy and tremulous. He said that he was there only for a few minutes, to say goodbye. He had to leave by the morning train for Delhi. He was so thankful at the kind treatment of a stranger, by her family. She said that it was the custom in their family to help those in need of help. 'Athithi Devo Bhava,' she said. 'Ah yes, a guest is divine,' he murmured.

Then it was time for him to leave or else he would miss his train. He got up awkwardly. He had wanted to take down her telephone number. But he now forgot about that. His head seemed to have become light. There were no coherent thoughts in it. Only a vast emptiness. He shook hands with Qudsiya. She opened the door to let him out. Panic overtook him as he felt destiny slipping away, eluding his grasp. Then as he looked at her face, he thought that he detected a quiver in her lips, as she looked up at him. The dancing eyes were clouded over.

41

When he said, 'Bye bye Queedsiya,' she turned her face away to gaze at the blue sky outside her doorstep, and inclined her head mechanically, rather like a broken doll. A tear rolled over her nose.

He was disturbed. So unlike Qudsiya. She was so much better being bossy and commanding. The passage was dark. Stefan decided that destiny was what we make of it, after all. 'Queedsiya,' he said, in a husky voice as he gently shut the door. He wiped away the tear with his fore finger. He took her face into his hands and suddenly his brain cleared.

'A moment of happiness, you and I sitting on the verandah, apparently two, but one in soul, you and I,' he murmured.

'Stefan!' she whispered.

It encouraged him. He kissed her lips, slowly, experimentally and then as her eyelids fluttered and she clung to him, her lips parted. His tongue explored her mouth. It tasted sweet and innocent. He lingered to taste its sweetness. She wound herself around him. He kissed her face and her neck. He ventured lower, his fingers went to the buttons on her kameez. He struggled unsuccessfully with the difficult-to-undo small eyelets, inserted by an overzealous tailor with high moral values. Suddenly the sitting room clock clanged. Damn! The unavoidable train! He tore himself away.

'Queedsiya I weel be back,' he said in a strangled voice. He kissed her one last time and left the house. Qudsiya's face was radiant. She floated on a joyous ribbon of light as she glided back to her room. Quite suddenly she had become a woman.

Stefan reached Delhi the next day. He spent the afternoon at the Jantar Mantar and the Red fort, dutifully drinking in the sights. The next morning he took a car to Fatehpur Sikri. But his heart was not in it. He felt listless. He was pursued by a gaggle of small boys selling souvenirs and tourist guides who saw in his open, generous face, some scope for their personal enrichment. They ran behind him, offering him unasked for information.

'Expot guide surr, expot guide surr, faboolus informashun on creaking old monoments,' they shouted. He gave them some coins, including a few shillings and cents that were in his pockct and they scampered away, nudging and jostling each other for the booty.

Stefan returned to Vienna. But a small, round, brown face with a dimpled smile constantly intruded into his thoughts. He could not forget the grace and the warmth of the welcome that he had received in Qudsiya's house. The fragrance of the biryani still lingered in his memory. It would be wonderful to live in a family like that, he thought. It would be marvellous to hold Qudsiya forever in his arms! It was then that he thought of the answer to his anxious longing. Of course! It was so simple! He would marry Qudsiya!

Qudsiya went back to her B.A History classes at Nizam's College. 'At least now he knows something about our ancient culture,' she said stoutly when Salim teased her about her 'feringee aashiq', as she checked the post every day for a letter from Stefan. One morning at eleven, the postman brought a letter addressed to Sadiq Ali. It was a marriage proposal for Qudsiya from Stefan, written in black ink in beautiful calligraphy, on hand made paper.

Stefan wrote:

"Honoured and Respected Sir,

I have admired your family atmosphere and sacred connections and ties. I ask for the hand of your accomplished daughter Qudsiya in marriage. I offer her a comfortable six-bedroom home, in a separate building of its own, in a garden of perfumed flowers, beautiful surroundings in Vienna, itself a city of culture and renown. I have good income and can have good care of your daughter. The marriage can be conducted in Vienna. If this proposal has your blessings, I will be coming to attend on you and take Qudsiya and the family of Qudsiya to Austria for the matrimonial ceremony.

With sincere regards,

Stefan Shrider"

Qudsiya's family were astonished at the proposal. They examined her closely. Had she had a love affair with the stranger when he was visiting Hyderabad? Had she encouraged him to think that he could marry into their renowned family? Qudisya was silent. However, she did not stand with her head hanging down, a picture of remorse, twisting the ends of her chunni in her hands. Neither did her eyes flash outrage at her friendliness being so mistaken by a crass foreigner, who did not understand their ancient customs and culture. Instead, she answered the cross questioning of her elders with a beatific smile, and a look of supreme happiness in her sparkling eyes.

Her relatives were mystified. Why would a twenty six year old Viennese art collector want to marry their Qudsiya? For one thing she was no beauty, not at all fair like Nusrat's brother Sultan Ahmed's daughter Shirin. Not even wheat complexioned. Just about walnut coloured maybe. Qudsiya's uncles talked privately among themselves. It was all due to these modern views of Sadiq Ali. Allowing his daughter to escort a male tourist around Hyderabad. Really! Unheard of! It was in vain that Sadiq Ali argued that the male tourist in question was more like a Bakrid goat, ready to be sacrificed to the whims of cunning shop keepers and the heartless auto-rickshaw drivers of Hyderabad. Not a wicked schemer at all! The uncles shook their heads in disapproval. They re-read the letter and the eldest uncle decided to call a family council.

Uncles and aunts, grand uncles and grand aunts assembled in the long dining room specially cleared of furniture for the event. *Shatranjees* were spread on the floor and soft mattresses were laid on them, with bolsters to lean against. Eighty five year old grand uncle Hameed presided over the meeting. Qudsiya's mother first served them tea and dry fruits with some namkeen. The letter was read aloud by Sultan Ahmed. It was passed around. The elders appreciated the educated handwriting and the respectful tone of the letter. The younger uncles appreciated the quality of the scented paper and made a mental note to find out where such paper could be obtained. It would be useful to impress prospective grooms when a marriage proposal had to be sent for their daughters.

'It is clear that he wishes for an honourable marriage and not a partnership or companionship as some others in his country have a habit of,' Sultan Ahmed said.

'He has put forth the facts clearly and honourably like a man,' another uncle said. There were murmurs of approval.

'But do we want our girl to marry a non-believer?' said the fiery Granduncle Mohamad Fakir, who was also a priest at the green mosque in Rani Baug.

'But he belongs to the religion of the book,' said Qudsiya's mother's cousin Imran, softly since he was a mere forty-eight.

In the end it was decided that a team of uncles and aunts and Qudsiya's parents would visit Vienna and see the home of the suitor to assess whether he was really unmarried and the owner of such a fine home as he had claimed and also make discreet enquiries about his character and sources of income. Brawny Uncle Bismilla Noor Muhammed who was inclined to swashbuckling and braggadocio, ordered a dozen hockey sticks from a leading sport goods shop, for their use (if the opportunity arose) when they visited the suitor in Vienna.

Stefan received the delegation with warmth and hospitality. He was a little alarmed to see that each of the male members of the team carried a hockey stick. He felt queasy but he masterfully quelled the slight tremble in his chin and insisted with a deadpan face, that the visitors stay at his home and not in an hotel. He showed them the valuable ancient paintings he had collected. He also gave them copies of his income tax statement. He took them to dine at elegant restaurants. Stefan accompanied them to the local church, where the padre assured them that he was a regular worshipper – a fine straight boy, without any vices. Stefan bought the matrimonial inspection delegation of prospective relatives, lavish presents of suits of fine cloth. And he bowled over the pepper tongued Mohamad Fakir with a gift of the Koran bound in leather, decorated with gold and red lettering, in beautiful Persian script.

The relatives returned to India. They forgot their hockey sticks in Stefan's house. He had in any case taken the precaution of putting them away in the loft, when the delegation was dining off the twelve course meal that he had arranged for them. Their verdict was unanimous: Stefan and Qudsiya were united in marriage. Qudsiya wore a lacy, white gown for the wedding. And she had a charming crown of white, satin flowers studded with pink and white pearls, with a long white veil on her head. Precocious fifteen year old Shirin, deftly caught the bouquet of flowers tossed by Qudsiya at the end of the reception.

Soon after the festivities, Stefan and Qudsiya flew to Paris for a bewitching honeymoon that lasted a whole fortnight. They of course only dined at the cheaper sidewalk cafes as Qudsiya's sense of economy prevailed over any instinct of extravagance in Stefan. But they saw all the sights with zeal. Quidsiya photographed Stefan holding the Eiffel Tower in his palm. Stefan carefully made out notes in his notebook about the height of the Eiffel Tower and how many years it had taken to make it. They saved a tolerable amount of money which Qudsiya stowed away in her large practical handbag. The day before they left Paris Qudsiya used the money to buy a beautiful set of crystal bowls and two exquisite crystal flower vases. Stefan carried the precious cargo carefully in their hand baggage in the aircraft and as they settled into their seats they looked at each other triumphantly.

Stefan and Qudsiya lived a happy life thereafter. Stefan proved a dutiful, reliable husband. He had eyes only for Qudsiya. And Qudsiya looked after Stefan. He needed a lot of looking after, since he was always misplacing his glasses, his watch, his cuff links and his pen. Qudsiya learnt German. She found her dead mother-in-law's recipe book in a box in the loft and she learnt how to make strudels. Qudsiya became comfortably plump and wore skirts and blouses. She grew to have an uncanny resemblance to Stefan's mother.

Stefan was happy. The empty house now rang with the sounds of six children squabbling over who would have the last piece of strudel. Alas, Stefan had to restrict the intake of sweets and savouries in his diet. The doctor had warned him that he would have to control the diabetes which he now had. He sat reading the paper in his rocking chair in the study, while Qudsiya comfortably chatted about the day's events. Once a year they went back to Mehbub Gulley, to be embraced and cosseted by Nusrat Begum and eat her delicately flavoured biryani. They stood under the shadows of the Charminar and breathed in the warm, generous, bright colours and noises of Hyderabad. Their children looked on wide eyed and cajoled them for one more ride on a Tonga with a sleek black horse, which passed by with its bells jingling merrily.

ॐ   ॐ   ॐ

AUNT EMILY'S GARDEN

Emily Coelho stood outside the Fatima church in Hadapsar, in suburban Poona, where a small East Indian community congregated every Sunday for morning mass. She was dressed in her second best, printed silk dress, which went a little below her knees. It had a narrow strip of pink lace at the collar, which matched the pale pink and grey flowers, on the off white silk dress. The dress, with its gathered skirt, hung loosely over her as she had gone thin since the last year, after a long bout of flu. She wore open toed sandals, with sensible low heels and in her hand was her small black handbag of artificial leather, which held her prayer book and black rosary in it.

The whitewashed church embellished with twin curvy spires that rose into the sky, had a massive front door and broad steps on which parishioners stood talking.

'Hie Aunt Emily!' hailed a neighbour. Emily turned around and peered to see who it was. Joachim from the ground floor flat next to hers smiled at her and waved from the far end, near Our Lady's grotto.

'Joachim! I want you to come for my barbecue today at seven in the evening,' Emily said warmly, her eyes twinkling, 'You weren't at home when I telephoned on Friday.' Joachim was always wanted at parties. He was funny and good at mimicking people – ponderous Father William who had a pot belly that wobbled, or the headmaster at the local English medium school Mr. Raunak Pandurang, who always talked in a British accent, which occasionally slipped to say 'test' instead of 'taste' and 'jeero' instead of 'zero'. Joachim promised to come, provided Aunt Emily made her famous sorpotel, in addition to the pig that would be roasted at the barbecue. Emily nodded her head. 'Of course,' she said and waved at a few more of her friends before she said, 'Well, I must be going,' and turned to the cemetery for her customary visit to Sophie's grave.

The tombs were spread out over grassy knolls in orderly rows. Most of them were old, with marble slabs, but there were a few wooden crosses to mark the newer graves, over mounds of earth. Some were inscribed with messages about the good nature of those who had passed on and others just bore terse dates that conveyed the births and deaths of those interred in the graves. Emily walked up to Sophie's grave. Her little Sophie who had died of a fever twenty years ago. The grief was as fresh as on the day that she had lost her youngest child. The small marble edifice had the words *"Sophie Coelho. Born on 14-10-74. Called to the Lord on 1-7-78. In Heaven we will meet our Darling Angel."* Emily bent her head in prayer for a few minutes and then moved on. A soft breeze played around as she walked through the grass and a dandelion flew in the air. Emily remembered playing in the park with Sophie, chasing dandelions. Sophie had loved dandelions. Emily almost heard her gurgling with childish delight. She seemed to be saying, 'Don't worry ma, I'm still around.'

Emily deftly caught the dandelion for Sophie. 'Lucky to catch a dandelion, Baby,' she murmured to Sophie. Just then Orchid D'Cruz came up and loped her arm into Emily's. 'Let's go home together,' she said, 'I'll help you with the cooking.'

They walked to the nearby Sarowar Apartments where they both lived. Emily had three flats on the ground floor. James had bought them after he had returned from the Gulf fifteen years earlier. There would be one for each of their three children, he had said. But the children grew up and went away, in the manner of all children.

James merged the three flats into a single apartment. The three ground floor flats had entitled them to the ownership of the open area around. Emily had green fingers. The open space was soon transformed into a lovely garden with a hedge of honey suckle and a handkerchief sized lawn that shimmered like an emerald. They planted two trees – a sapling of guava and another of mango, at each corner, at the back of the garden, so that small boys would not steal the fruit from near the front gate. A spreading *champa* grew near their bed room window and the fragrance of its small mauve, flowers filled the air. James watered the lawn and every season Emily planted beds of flowering plants and shrubs. There were flocks, gerberas and daisies. Along the wall, she planted lovely dahlias and bright red gladioli. She remembered the time when her dahlias had won prizes for two consecutive years at the local flower show held by the Rotary Club. Emily entered her garden gate and Orchid left her. 'I'll come in half an hour,' Orchid called over her shoulder.

The garden was no longer orderly now. It was full of wild growth. A large, yellow lizard with beady eyes stared at Emily from its perch on the guava tree. Emily shooed away the lizard. Only the other day, she had strained the milk from the saucepan to find a dead lizard in it. They had just escaped being poisoned. She had chided the servant Gangoobai for being so careless. 'You did not even bother to cover the milk. We'll die one of these days of lizard poisoning and our children won't even know that we are dead,' she scolded.

Emily walked into the kitchen meditatively. She planned her menu for the evening. The meat had been bought and the spices had been ground fresh by Gangoobai and kept in the airtight plastic container on the kitchen shelf. She had bought fresh cucumber, tomatoes and spring onions on her visit to the bazaar the previous evening. The flour had been already kneaded into firm dough for the parathas. Gangoo would come in the evening to roll out the parathas. Orchid would also help. She must ask James to get the ice cream, she thought.

James lay in the easy chair in the garden in the sun dozing, his mouth slack and open. 'James – James,' she called softly. 'Get up,' a note of reproach creeping into her voice. 'No Sunday mass and sleeping so late in the morning.' James rubbed his eyes guiltily.
'Nat sleepin,' he said, 'Just dozed off, the sun was so warm.' He moved in languidly.

' Wot yu cooking?' he asked.

'Your fav,' she answered, 'sorpotel and roast pig, biryani and parathas. Just call at the corner store for ice cream.'

James shuffled off to do her bidding. He was no longer as sprightly as he was when the children were around. They had fewer parties now. Ten years ago the house rang with laughter, as the children teased each other and threw the ball through the basketball net on the post that stood at one end of the garden. The post was now rickety, the wood rotting at the base. The dark brown piano in the sitting room stood silent, a coat of dust on the top, with the sheets of music untouched for so many years. They had spent so many happy hours singing songs of an evening –

My Bonnie lies over the o-shun,
My Bonnie lies oh-ver the see,
My Bonnie lies over the o-shun,
My Bonnie lies oh-ver the see,
Bring back, O bring back –
O bring back my Bonnie to meee!

Last night as I lay on my pil-low,
Last night as I lay on my bed,
Last night as I lay on my pil-ow,
I dreamt that – my Bonnie was dead.
Bring back – O bring back –
O bring back my Bonnie to me – to me!
O bring back my Bonnie to mee . . .

The house was silent now. They missed the children and the happy days gone by. But today there was an air of merriment. It was Stephen's birthday and they celebrated it just the same as if he were right there with them and not miles away in Ottawa. Stephen was working on his Ph.D. on 'Nutritional Deficiency and Delayed Cognitive Skills in Korku children of Melghat.' He had met a white girl at a discotheque and married her in the Lutheran church that he attended. Emily's eyes smarted with tears at the memory of the marriage of her first born. No invitation card in white and gold, no dinner reception. She had so looked forward to a grand wedding at the Church hall, with her best grape wine and Father Fio's witty toast to the bride and groom. Emily wiped her tears with her kerchief and looked out of the sitting room window. She saw James, his head bobbing above the garden hedge, walking along the road. She watched him till she could no longer see him.

James reached the cold storage with its lurid picture of roasted chicken and a live fowl, on the sign board at the front of the shop.

'Give me two party packs of ice cream,' he told the store boy, Chotu.

'What flavour Uncle?' asked Chotu.

'Chocolate,' said James. As he stood at the store, James suddenly felt sick, a dizzy feeling over took him and he gripped the service table. Perspiration beaded his brow.

'Uncle! Uncle! Are you ill?' Chotu called out in alarm. He helped James to the back of the shop and made him sit on a bench there and got him a glass of water. He called up Emily. She came in a taxi, dressed just as she was when she got the phone call from the shop – in her faded home clothes. James smiled wanly when he saw her.

'Just feeling a little queer, old girl,' he whispered.

"Now James! You're going to be right as rain! You can't get sick just now,' she scolded, her face looking strong and dependable. James lay gratefully with his head on her shoulder in the taxi as they took him to the Sassoon Hospital. But on the way James slumped forward and Emily caught him with a stifled scream. His head lay on her shoulders till they got to the hospital. She was too stunned to cry when the doctors came out of the ICU and told her that they had been too late. She sat silent and still, fingering her rosary, clinging to it like a lifeline. James was dead, she told herself. How would she live without James? Orchid came to the hospital and took her home.

The neighbours and relatives came and sat in Emily's tidy front room. They lit a candle at the altar with the picture of the Sacred Heart of Jesus and hastily cleared the room of furniture. A long, wooden table was placed in the centre of the room, with the brown wooden coffin in which James lay peacefully. Two lit candles were kept at the head of the corpse. They sat praying, saying the rosary, the prayers for the Dead – *Eternal Rest Grant Unto Him O Lord and Let Thy Perpetual Light Shine Upon Him* . . . . They sang hymns of grief and hope, *Lord I'm coming Home* and *Lead Kindly Light*.

Orchid phoned the boys at Ottawa and Philadelphia and Rose at New Jersey. The children came home – first Rose and then Stephen and Cajetin. They sat by their mother, holding her frail hands, as Emily lay in bed, dry eyed and numb. She was unable to come to terms to a home without James to be taken care of. Cooking his special Sunday lunch of chicken curry and fried fish. He had liked his evening rotis hot from the tava with the vegetable curry and just two sausages grilled. And bless him, he never worried her by drinking more than was good for him. He just had a glass of whisky for company at Christmas and Easter . . .

For a few days the house was filled with the sounds of people moving and talking. Rose took over the kitchen and boiled endless cups of tea for the visitors who streamed in. But after the funeral and the seventh day's memorial mass, the children went back. They said that they could not get more leave of absence from their jobs in America. A father's death entitled you to a week's leave, no more. Americans were workaholics and had no time for their parents. Most of them put their parents in old age homes anyway and didn't even visit them at Christmas. The children urged Emily to accompany them to America. But she demurred. She dreaded the thought of living as a dependant with her children. She preferred the golden sun in Poona. The one time she had visited Rose in New Jersey, her arthritis had got more painful during the long, cold winter.

The garden now went completely to ruin. Weeds grew and there were no flowering plants other than the wild roses and the bougainvillea. The grass in the garden wore a dull, yellow, dry look in the summer months since no one watered the lawn any more. Sometimes Emily pulled up an old wicker chair and sat dozing in the sun, her head shaded by a straw hat that her grand children had bought on a trip to Goa and left behind. Her eyesight was fading and she no longer read the papers. She sat at times in the evening before the TV hearing the world news about bomb blasts and hijacks and the worsening Arab-Israeli crisis. She was alarmed at the news of a Sikh mistaken for an Iraqi and being attacked by right wing Americans in New York. Her heart beat with anxiety for the safety of her children lest they be mistaken – with their brown complexions, for Arabs and attacked in the streets. She wrote letters in a shaky hand to her children every month.

"Dear Stephen," she wrote, "Do take care and lock the door safely at night. See that the children are safe. Hope they are studying well." Rose replied to her letters and sent her a present of two hundred dollars every month. The boys remembered her at Christmas and sent her five hundred dollars each with their greetings. They promised to send her a return ticket provided she was ready to cross the seas and be with them. But she refused to be persuaded.

One night Emily shut the fine mesh front door which kept out mosquitoes and had her lonely supper of bread and a chicken curry. She said her prayers and retired to bed, switching off the bedroom light. Then she heard a low hissing sound. It emanated from the window which overlooked the garden. The sound unnerved her. There was a soft slithering noise and she prayed to Archangel Michael who crushed the serpent and St George who destroyed dragons and all kinds of evil. She didn't sleep a wink that night. As the first streaks of the grey dawn gave way to the morning light, she got up in bed and looked around fearfully. At the far end of the room, near her writing desk, coiled on the leg of her chair, was a fat black cobra that looked at her with malevolent, red eyes. She stepped out of the room slowly, softly, in bare feet, backing out of the room, her eye on the serpent.

'Joachim, Orchid,' she called in her high, quavering voice and they came out hurriedly, alarmed at the sense of urgency in her voice. Joachim asked his two sons to come down and they came armed with sticks. The snake had moved away to a dark corner under the bed. When they poked at it with a long broom, it stood up with its hood flared out and darted out angrily at them. They beat it and killed it.

'Unlucky to kill a snake, its mate will come back and seek its revenge,' muttered the watchman Vikram Singh, who had come along to watch the spectacle.

Orchid kept her company for a few nights thereafter. But Emily was tired of her large apartment and her garden. She called an estate agent and asked him to look for a buyer for her home. She bought a small flat, which had fortuitously just fallen vacant – on the first floor of Sarovar Apartments. Her new home had a single bedroom, a small kitchen and a little sitting room in which to entertain her few visitors.

Emily's three flats were bought by a prosperous Gujarati joint family – old Mr. Kishanchand Mehta and his wife Saritabehn and their three sons, their daughters-in-law and their six grandchildren. The Mehtas owned a large textile shop in the city and the house rang with the merry laughter of the six Gujarati children. Emily called the children upstairs to her flat sometimes and gave them a chocolate each from the chocolates that her children sent her in parcels with visitors who were going home to India.

The new Gujarati owners employed a young mali who planted large dahlias and chrysanthemums in the earth along the wall, with separate beds of daisies, flocks and gerberas. He planted a fresh layer of lawn grass and assiduously watered the lawn every evening. The green grass glistened with drops of water and the smell of wet earth wafted up to Emily every evening, as she stood at the window watching the mali at work. She saw the garden bloom once more. It warmed her old bones to think that there was beauty and laughter again in the apartment that she and James had lived in and raised their children. The lonely, empty feeling in her heart was assuaged a little.

ॐ   ॐ   ॐ

TWO FATHERS

Sumathi was the Senior Manager Advances, in the State Bank at Balligunge in Calcutta. She was sitting one afternoon in the Madras Coffee House at the corner of the Subash Chandra Bose Road in Balligunge and had just ordered a cup of coffee for herself. She had not got her tiffin that day and so she thought of having a snack at the coffee house. Just then Ravindran walked in. He was an officer in another branch of the bank, at Tolligunge. Ravindran recognized Sumathi and smiled. He introduced himself and they shared the same table, since the house was crowded and had very few empty seats. They had met earlier at the Officers' Training course, a few months back at the Training College in Bombay.

Ravindran lit a cigarette after asking her, 'Do you mind?' in a voice, which did not expect her to mind. She grimaced but waved her hand and said, 'OK'. The coffee house was full of smoke and the smell of dosas, wadas and sambaar and the high roar of a hundred people all talking together at the same time. Sumathi and Ravindran continued the discussion on the topic of 'Customer Relations' that had been the theme of the training programme. Most of the public believed that they had got better service when the banks had been private. Nationalisation had made the bank staff just like government clerks – rude and lethargic.

While discussing customer satisfaction and the frenzy of the year ending efforts to attain the targets for deposits, Ravindran had been covertly admiring Sumathi's lovely, long, black hair, dressed in a single braid and her beautiful profile. She was light brown – the colour that the Sunday matrimonial page advertisements referred to as 'wheat complexioned'. And she wore a pair of tiny diamond earrings in her ears that flashed like rainbows every time she turned her head. He paid for their coffees, though she protested that she would pay for her own coffee. The man at the cash counter with the picture of Sri Murugan behind him gave Ravindran a covert wink and said, 'Best luck,' under his breath. Ravindran scowled at him and looked anxiously at Sumathi. But she gave no sign that she had seen the wink or heard the cashier's good wishes. Relieved, he smiled and asked Sumathi whether he could drop her to her office on his scooter. She said, 'No thank you,' in a soft voice that meant just that.

They parted to go their mutual ways. But he called her up at the bank after a week. He had a small problem, he said apologetically. A friend was getting married and he just did not know what he ought to buy for the wedding gift. Would she accompany him to Park Street and help him to pick up something suitable? She agreed hesitantly. They met at Firpo's. They had a cup of tea together before they bought the present from the Cottage Emporium. Then there was nothing else to keep them together. Ravindran prolonged the visit to the shop by looking at sandalwood carvings and pointing out interesting Tibetan masks and brass chimes to Sumathi. But an hour later Sumathi looked at her watch and said that it was getting to be late. Ravindran jingled the change in his pocket and asked her in a voice cracked with anxiety, for her telephone number at the hostel, just in case there was anything he had to ask her. Fortunately she gave him her number without demur. Ten days later he telephoned Sumathi.

'There's a movie at the *Apsara*, this evening,' he said, 'Would you like to see *The Poseidon Adventure?*'

'Who else is coming?' she asked.

'My friends. Tommy and Gracie,' he said briefly.

They met in the foyer of the *Apsara*. She was introduced to Tommy and Gracie who were from Kottayam and had married after a short courtship in the Tolligunge office of the State Bank. Many movies later with Tommy and Gracie dutifully in tow, Sumathi and Ravindran at last went for a film by themselves. Ravindran proposed to Sumathi and she shyly accepted.

They were married at the local registry office. Ravindran explained that his parents were not quite prepared for his marriage, since his elder brother, Rajeevan already thirty-five, had not yet married. Rajeevan suffered from a *chova dosham*, the black mark in the horoscope that predicted trouble in life. It was difficult to find him a partner with an identical risk in her horoscope, which would cancel out their mutual bad luck. Sumathi said that her parents were conservative and would also not approve of a love match. She was apprehensive that her two brothers who were in the army would oppose the marriage. They both felt that it was better not to inform either of their families about the wedding.

Ravindran and Sumathi had a reception for their office colleagues at St. George's high school auditorium in Tollygunge. Sumathi entered Ravindran's quarters at Park Circus, wearing a traditional two piece off white *mumdum nereyatha* with a red and gold border, holding the lighted lamp in her hands. She wore a long garland of fragrant jasmine flowers in her hair and they both wore thick white marriage flower garlands interwoven with tinsel threads, on their necks. They posed for one last photograph outside the entrance of their new home and then they began their domestic life quietly and without any fuss.

They wrote home informing their parents of the marriage and that they would be coming home shortly to seek their blessings. Sumathi got no response to her letter. Ravindran's younger brother Ananthan wrote on behalf of his parents, expressing their happiness. He urged his brother and sister-in-law to come home as soon as it was possible for them.

Sumathi had a small sense of apprehension, as she packed their bags for their visit to Ravindran's home in Mankuzhi. Ravindran's parents were simple village folk. The old man had a large farm. Actually it was his wife's property. In the old *Marumakkattayam* days, the groom was only a visiting husband. He lived with his own sisters in their ancestral house and managed their property. The family line descended through the woman, in the Nayar *Tharavads*.

The old family house stood perched on a hillock on which rough stone steps had been hewn. The house had a high ceiling, with polished teakwood rafters. The wooden shutters in the windows kept the rooms cool. There were narrow wooden stairs that lead to the upper storey which had four bed rooms and a long verandah in front of the rooms, near the stair case. There was a large brass oil lamp on the ground floor verandah, hanging from its own brass string. It shone like gold. It was the evening hour when they reached the house and Sathi, Ravindran's youngest sister, had just intoned *'Deepam Deepam'* and placed a lighted oil lamp on the verandah floor.

Ravindran's father came running out into the courtyard as soon as he heard the sound of the tourist taxi, like a latter day father of the prodigal son. He clasped Ravindran affectionately. Ravindran hugged his mother. Ravindran's sisters welcomed Sumathi warmly. There was a small bustle as the coffee was got ready. Ravindran's mother had fried sweet banana fritters and made steamed jackfruit dumplings. There were salty banana chips and tapioca sweetened with jaggery, taken out from large aluminium tins. They discussed old times and exclaimed on how brown Ravindran had got.

'How is Kulkatta?' they asked Sumathi, 'We've heard that the floods in the monsoon are unbearable.' Sumathi murmured that there was a prolonged holiday when it rained very heavily. Ravindran explained how cool it was when it rained. They soon took out the gifts that they had selected in a hurry the day before they left. A shirt for father. A *mundum nereyatha* with

67

a green border for mother from Kairali. Lac bangles from the Rajasthani emporium for the three small sisters-in-law and a pair of jeans for Ananthan. The gifts were exclaimed over. The girls emitted cries of delight at the delicate pink and gold and red and gold designs on the lac bangles. Then Ravindran's mother, Sumangali, went to her rose wood box, embossed with strips of shining brass, in which she kept her few belongings. She took out an old, gold, snake-shaped bangle. The snake's head had small, red, ruby eyes. It had been her Grandmother's.

'Take this, daughter,' she said, 'I had kept it for you.'

Sumathi wore the ornament and smiled shyly, overcome by the spontaneous affection she had found in her husband's family. A little later they all had an early dinner and went to bed. 'You must be tired after the journey and you know we always sleep early,' Ravindra's father remarked.

The next day Sumathi got up at the crack of dawn. But although it was not yet light, her mother-in-law was already up. She had fed the cows and milked them. And she had coffee brewing on the wood fire. She was now kneading the dough for the rice hoppers.

'I thought you'd like to eat Iddiyappam and potato istoo,' she remarked pleasantly, as Sumathi entered the dark kitchen. Above the brick hearth, blackened with years of curling smoke and soot, the rubber sheets lay drying. They were moulded every morning by Muthu the farmhand, from the milk that dripped from the barks of the rubber trees planted in the northern field. Sumathi brushed her teeth and hurried to help her mother-in-law. Soon everybody had the first round of early morning black coffee. It was only with breakfast that they would have coffee with the rich creamy milk from Mylanchi, the brown cow. Later Ravindran's father sat in the verandah, in his long easy chair, reading the day's news in the *Mathrabhumi*. Ravindran sat on the verandah wall, sipping a glass of steaming coffee, talking to his father desultorily about the state of the farm and the cows. They discussed village politics. The village Panchayat Chairman, Tommychen modalali had been beaten up by the villagers the previous evening, for usurping the money earmarked for macadamizing the main village road. They remarked on the instant justice delivered by the people's court in their village of Mankuzhi.

A goat (christened *Cutlet* with macabre humour by Ananthan) came into view, led by a goatherd. 'Let's have Cutlet for today's lunch,' Ananthan suggested truculently and went off to the village to find the local butcher, while Cutlet, unaware of his own fate, placidly chewed the jackfruit leaves that the goatherd threw before him. Ravindran's father did not object to their newly acquired city ways of eating goat's meat and chicken, though he didn't touch the meat himself. But the servant had to cook the meat in an outhouse, far away from the kitchen, so that the sanctity of the kitchen hearth was not polluted.

The idyllic days sped by and they almost forgot that they had to go back to their life in Calcutta. Then, there were only three days of leave left. Sumathi told her husband that they must visit her father and mother before they returned to Calcutta. They packed up their belongings and Ravindran's parents bid them farewell. His mother sobbed silently as she hugged Ravindran.

'My son I know not whether I will be alive, when you are next able . . .' Ravindran's father's voice trailed away as his voice broke with emotion. Tears streaked the old man's face.

'Oh father you've got many more years yet in your bones,' Ravindran said heartily, to cover his own emotion.

A taxi had been hired for the eight-hour journey to Sumathi's house at Velumili and it was evening when they reached. Her parents had a house on the main road. Sumathi's father had retired as the village post-master. As the taxi stopped, a grey head peeped out of a window in the rear end of the house and then the window banged shut. No one opened the front door. They alighted from the taxi and took out their belongings and rang the doorbell. They had to wait a long while before someone drew open the wooden bolt of the front door. It was Sumathi's mother. She looked thin and gaunt and grey with worry. They greeted her with a hug. She looked at them quietly.

'Mother, where is father?' Sumathi enquired.

'Shhh,' her mother admonished, and added in an undertone, 'He's saying his prayers. You know how he hates to be disturbed when he is reciting the puranas.'

They tiptoed into the dark kitchen. Sumathi's mother switched on the light. It gave a thin orange glare that fell in uncertain streaks on the new wooden furniture. They sat uncomfortably on the yellow laminated chairs. Sumathi's mother went to the kitchen and made them some watery tea. She took out a few Marie biscuits that had gone soft and musty, from a tin in the kitchen cupboard and placed them on a dented steel quarter plate. She kept four cups of tea on the table. They waited for Sumathi's father to join them. The tea grew cold. Ravindran was uncomfortable after the long journey. He wanted to use the toilet. But he felt awkward about asking where it was. The clock in the small front room ticked extra loudly in the silence that made them feel unwelcome. At last Sumathi's father came in from his prayers, the sandalwood paste gleaming on his forehead, a freshly starched veshti over his shoulders.

'So Sumathi,' he said sarcastically, 'You forgot to send us, your old parents, your marriage invitation card?'
He sat at the table and looked at the tea.
'Take away this slop water, woman!' he shouted at his wife.
Parvatiamma got up quietly, took away the cups, reheated the tea and brought it back. They drank the bitter brew in silence. Ravindran munched the biscuits stoically.
'We're not rich estate people like you,' Sumathi's father told Ravindran, 'Just poor government service people.'
Ravindran looked at the Godrej refrigerator, the ceiling fan that whirred above, and the TV in the small front room. The kitchen was not blackened with a brick hearth. It had light green tiles and a gleaming steel gas stove. There were none of these creature comforts in their old farmstead at Munkuzhi. But Ravindran was silent.

'Is my superior estate owning son-in-law too proud to talk to his father-in-law?' Sumathi's father asked with a sneer. Parvatiamma looked unhappy.

'They have only come for the first time to see us,' she murmured almost inaudibly.

Sumathi hastened to smooth over the tension. 'He's tired. We've just travelled a long way . . .' she said.

They got up and took their bags to the dark inner room. It was a doleful dinner that they had later that night. There was no conversation. A silence hung in the air. Sumathi wished her two younger brothers had been at home. They were jolly and talkative. But they were both away in the northern sector. Sumathi and Ravindran ate the rice with a dish of spinach and curd curry that Sumathi's mother had made. They helped to wash the dishes and Sumathi's mother retired to her bed.

Ravindran switched off the bedroom light and stretched out his limbs, grateful for the hard wooden bed in the spare room. It had been a tiring, bumpy, journey from Mankuzhi, and he was almost asleep, when he heard a snuffling in the dark.

'Sumathi!' he exclaimed, instantly alert, 'What's the matter?' But there was no answer. He placed his hand on her face. It was wet with tears. 'What's it Kunjumoll, little one?' he asked.

'Your father was so loving,' said Sumathi tearfully, 'Maybe he wasn't educated. But father was always so stern with us and kept us all petrified. We had to walk around on tiptoe when he was looking at his post-office papers at home. They were only the accounts of stamps and inlands and envelopes. But if we laughed and father made a mistake in checking the account he'd shout at us. We couldn't even go by his room. He never hugged us. We had such an unhappy childhood. And, and . . . he was so unkind to you today.' Here Sumathi fell into sobbing afresh.

'Never mind, Sumathi,' Ravindran said stroking her face. 'Different people have different ways. Just go to sleep. Now you have my father too. So be comforted.' He put his arm around her.

They were just dozing off when a sudden shriek rent the air. It was from Sumathi's parents' room. Ravindran ran to the room and found Sumathi's mother sprawled on the floor. His father-in-law stood menacingly with a hand raised over Parvatiamma. There were deep red welts on her face and she was sobbing, tears streaming down her cheeks. Ravindran took two steps forward and twisted Soman Kurup's arm behind his back. 'You can't hit her ever again,' he said in measured tones. He turned to Sumathi's mother. 'Mother, you sleep in our room, I'll sleep on the sitting room sofa,' he suggested.

The next morning as they drank their coffee in the kitchen, Ravindran announced that mother was coming back with them to Calcutta, since she needed a change from her life in Kerala. They were leaving immediately. Soman Kurup looked up angrily from his glass of coffee. 'And who are you to decide these things?' he asked Ravindran in a loud voice. He looked at his wife. But Parvatiamma had a new look in her eyes and suddenly Sumathi's father was unsure of himself.

'You're – you're – not leaving me Parvathiamma, after all these years?' he asked. His voice was low and not aggressive. Parvathiamma looked at her husband steadily.

'I've worked all my life to make you happy, cheta. But for these thirty-two long years, nothing I did was ever good enough for you. You never gave me a kind word, cheta. You beat me for every small thing. Even today when the children came to visit for the first time after Sumathi got married . . . I think I'll now go and stay with the children,' she said.

'Parvathiamma, you – you just can't –' began Soman. But she had already got up from the table, leaving him with his protests unstated. She quietly packed her belongings into a travel bag. As Soman Kurup sat at the dining table in a daze, Parvatiamma left the house with her daughter and son-in-law. There was a taxi waiting at the door. The driver opened the luggage hold and Ravindran put their bags into it. Sumathi and her mother got into the back seat and Ravindran sat up in front. The driver revved up the engine and the taxi was soon lost in the distance.

In the shed near the house, the black goat tied to its post bleated anxiously. It was milking time. Soman banged his fists on the table, hollering for the servant Lakshmi. But no one came.

༄ ༄ ༄

A HOUSE IN DARIUS BAUG

I noticed her as she stood on the narrow kerb, waiting for the school-bell to ring and the children to come out of their classes. She wore a light pink printed cotton dress with short sleeves and a short pink scarf on her head. She was obviously a Parsi, fair with light brown eyes. She must have been not more than twenty-five. When the children came out of school, my daughter Rashmi came tripping up to me. Just then Rashmi caught sight of a friend. 'Persis,' she cried out, as she saw her friend running up to the lady in the pink dress. But Persis did not see her. She hugged her mother and then they walked towards Colaba Causeway. Persis waved at us as she passed by.

I saw the young woman standing pensively by herself at the school gate, waiting to collect her daughter, on a number of occasions thereafter. Then one day, bored of standing by myself, I tried to strike up a conversation with her. 'I think our children are in the same class,' I said. 'My daughter's name is Rashmi. My name's Renuka. What's yours? ' A look of irritation crossed her face as though she resented my intrusion. 'My name's Nilufer,' she answered shortly and her silence was like a drawn blind that shut down her face. I walked back home with Rashmi feeling rebuffed and a little annoyed with myself.

One afternoon we had to wait for the children quite a while outside the school. Nilufer was also there. The Principal had decided to have a special party for the kindergarten. It was the last day of school before the Christmas break. The December air was cooler and not as stuffy as summer. A few birds twittered in the trees outside the school-gate. We stood in the shade of an old Gulmohor tree.

'Aren't you tired?' I asked Nilufer after a while. 'Come let's go and get a coke.'
'I don't want anything,' she answered primly.
'Ok, just come with me. I don't like the idea of sitting alone in that small Udipi,' I cajoled her. She accompanied me reluctantly to the café Udipi at the end of the road.

We sat down on red plastic chairs, at a corner table which had a marble top and I ordered two medhu wadas and two coffees.
'I don't eat wadas,' Nilufer said.
'Then get us one vegetable grilled sandwich and one medhu wada,' I told the waiter who stood by, his pad in hand and pen stuck in his ear. He looked impatient and slightly distracted. People from five other tables tried to get his attention simultaneously. 'Arre Boss, zara baat suno,' shouted a young man in jeans and a tight T-shirt, from the table next to us, waving at the waiter with both hands, while a middle aged man wearing dark glasses, sitting further away, made an annoying

noise through his pursed lips and wagged a beckoning imperious forefinger. The door into the kitchen swung constantly, as waiters went in and out, bearing trays of steaming food or returning the used plates. There was an inviting smell of sambaar, coconut chutney and frying medhu wadas in the air. The sizzling sound of dosa batter being poured over a hot tava and the crackling of mustard seeds, escaped from the kitchen. I was longing to eat a hot wada. But Nilufer made a gesture of refusal.

'It's my treat. Please,' I said. 'Today is payday.' I waved the waiter away.

'You work?' Nilufer asked wistfully, 'Where do you work?' I told her about my job as a cashier at the Bharat Bank.

'I would also like to work but I haven't studied beyond the twelfth,' she blurted out.

'Why don't you do a course in shorthand and typing?' I asked her.

'There's no money for that,' she said bitterly.

'You look very worried,' I said gently. 'What's the matter?'

'We live with my in-laws, in a one room kitchen flat, in Darius Baug colony,' she murmured, her voice hardly audible. 'The Parsi panchayat has rented the flat to my in-laws. Actually, there's no space for us. Our bed is kept on the balcony. There's a screen between my husband's parents' bed and ours. But I really cannot . . . with them so near. There's an open ground outside the balcony. The neighbourhood teenage rowdies always sit on the tree opposite our balcony at night and whistle and laugh at us. And so my husband Pirosh is always in a bad mood. We can't even afford to go to a hotel for a day. His pay as a clerk in Rustom Textiles is so low. But I'm so scared that he may be visiting Kamathipoora with all this AIDS around. He says he loves me. But you know with men . . . You can't count on that when they get the urge.'

'Why don't you try to get a housing loan and buy a flat in the suburbs? Nowadays there are so many banks giving away housing loans. You can get a flat in Mira Road for as little as two lacs,' I suggested.

Her eyes widened in horror. 'Mira Road!' she said as though I had mentioned Siberia. 'It's so far away and there's no fire temple there. None of our relatives are nearby. How could we live there?'

'But what is the alternative?' I asked.

'We have to wait for the old people to die,' she said in a resigned voice.

I thought it over. 'Why don't you just put a rattan screen on the balcony. It won't cost more than two hundred rupees.'

'But I don't have any money,' she said flatly.

'Let me help you,' I said feeling suddenly recklessly generous. I had been saving two thousand rupees for my birthday sari. 'I'll give you a loan of two thousand rupees and you can buy a screen for two hundred and register for a course in shorthand at Davar's for eighteen hundred. You can easily get a job after that.' I counted out the notes and she took them with a look of gratitude in her eyes.

I was transferred unexpectedly the following week to a branch in Dadar. I didn't see Nilufer the day I went to get Rashmi's school transfer certificate. Unfortunately,

I had not asked Nilufer for her address or telephone number. My husband Suresh, a software engineer, felt that I had been careless. 'Fine sort of banker you are!' he said sarcastically, 'You lent some woman money without even taking down her phone number!' I told him that I could always meet her at the school. But I knew that I would have to forget about the money. I admitted Rashmi to the convent school in Hindoo Colony in Dadar. I did make some effort to see Nilufer but she was not at the school-gate each time I was there. I did not get much leave thereafter since I had cleared my banking examination and had got promoted as an officer.

Some years later I was walking by Rashmi's old school to the Sahakari Bhandar to get some rain-wear for Rashmi. She was now in the eighth standard. I saw a slightly stout lady in dark glasses get down from a scooter. It was Nilufer.

'Nilufer,' I called. She turned around and looked at me blankly.

'Remember me?' I asked. 'It's Renuka. We used to wait here for our kids when they were in the kindergarten.'

Her face beamed in recognition.

'I bought that screen,' she said laughing, 'and I did that course. Now I'm the PA to the Principal here.' She paused. 'I must give you back your money,' she said, 'I kept saving for it as soon as I got my first pay and I've been keeping it in case I should meet you.' She searched around in her hand bag.

'How are your in-laws?' I asked her conversationally, as she peered into her handbag.

'They died last August,' she said expressionlessly, after a moment. Her face suddenly looked pale in the sunlight. I was concerned. 'Then where are you staying?' I asked.

'We got the flat allotted to us by the panchayat,' she said shortly, 'I think I've left your packet behind at home. Why don't you just come over with me and have a cup of tea? I can give you the money also.'

I looked at my watch. It was two o'clock.

'I can come if it doesn't take long,' I said.

I sat on the pillion seat and Nilufer took the scooter through the heavy traffic around the roundabout near the Regal theatre and into Colaba Causeway. The glittering shops were overcrowded with shoppers and the pavements filled with hawkers selling cheap Chinese electronic goods, folding umbrellas, readymade clothes, shoes, and costume jewellery. The hawkers outdid one another in shouting 'nice laddies watch maddum, nice laddies watch, bran new from Hongkong', 'Buy one get one free, buy one get one free' as they held up their wares to entice pedestrians who tried to squirm past. Cars and buses moved slowly on the narrow street. Drivers blew their car horns and stopped as a cow ambled across the road into the market near the Strand theatre. We inched slowly through the traffic.

Nilufer's house in Darius Baug colony was just next to the Sassoon Dock. We turned into the colony with its grand archway. There were ten buildings inside. Nilufer's flat was on the third floor of a building near the entrance to the colony. We went up the archaic lift which could carry only four passengers. It was shut by sliding grill doors which squeaked. We got out of the lift. Nilufer unlocked her front door and we stepped into a large bright room with a piano in a corner.

'Persis learns to play the piano,' she said, as my eye went to the piano. A beautiful porcelain vase with lovely red roses stood on it. The room was crammed with carved antique rosewood furniture. A dresser with drawers and a high four poster bed with mosquito curtains stood at one end. Near the piano there was a small writing table with a green felt top. A lovely John and Mary sofa covered with crimson tapestry and a carved chair occupied the centre space.
'We're a bit crowded here but we're happy,' Nilufer said. 'Do sit down, while I make the tea.'

I sat on a sturdy stool because the sofa looked fragile. I looked around idly. The top drawer of the dresser seemed to be stuffed with old magazines. A back issue of *Woman and Home* jutted out with its colourful masthead showing. I loved the knitting patterns in *Woman and Home*, though in the sultry Bombay weather we didn't need any woollens. I took out the magazine and flicked through the pages. It was an old July issue. There were recipes for luscious cakes in it. Something slipped out and fell down from the magazine. I picked it up. It was a chemist's receipt for a bottle of rat poison, dated the 10th August of the previous year. I was looking at it when Nilufer came into the room with the tea.

'What is that?'she asked sharply. I had not noticed before how large and menacing her teeth were.

'Just looking at some of your old magazines and this fell out of it,' I said showing her the receipt.

Her face turned ashen and her eyes were suddenly veiled.

'Ah yes,' she said, 'we have a lot of rat problem here.' Her voice sounded rasping. She crushed the paper into a ball and threw it into a plastic waste paper basket under the piano. She gave me the tea cup with hands that shook and then took a packet from the dresser.

'Here's your money,' she said in a dull voice. I drank the tea and took the packet of money from her. 'Thanks,' I said and got up to go.

'Count it please,' she said imperiously. I counted the money, feeling tense under her stern gaze and lost count twice. She made a sound of irritation and took it from me and counted out the notes carefully and gave them back to me. I mumbled something about being late and got up to leave. She saw me off at the door without a smile. I scrambled down the dark wooden staircase. As I came into the bright sunlight, I hailed a passing cab and sank into the seat in relief.

The next Saturday I was alone at home. It was a holiday. Suresh had gone to the dentist. The telephone rang. I picked it up.

'Hello,' someone said in a low, unfamiliar voice.

"Who is it?" I asked

'Is that Renuka?'

'Yes,' I answered puzzled.

'This is Nilufer, I want to talk to you urgently. Can we meet somewhere?'

'I'm afraid I'm rather busy,' I answered. I found my heart pounding.

'Please,' she begged, 'I have to talk to you.'

'What is it?' I asked reluctantly

'You know, it was I who killed them. I really had no other option. They were so healthy and Pirosh was getting to be so impatient. I could see him eye the young lovelies in our colony. I had to do something so that we could have a life together. Please, I want to tell you all about it. I will wait for you at the Sri Krishna Udipi at three o'clock.' She sounded as though she was in torment.

I debated whether I ought to go and decided against it. Nilufer was none of my business. An impulsive gesture of kindness on my part in lending her some money didn't make me responsible for her life. Besides Rashmi was due home any moment from her dancing class and she would expect her tea. She would wonder where I had gone.

Late that night the telephone rang again. It was Nilufer. 'Why didn't you come? I waited for you for two hours,' she said. 'Please see me tomorrow,' she sobbed, 'I will wait at the café at three. Please – Please.' Although I was reluctant, I agreed to be there. I made up a story for Suresh about meeting a school friend.

The next evening when I entered the dark refurbished café I found Nilufer sitting in a corner.

She ordered two teas and the waiter went away.

'I won't waste your time. I want to tell someone why I did it. It's been dreadful keeping this secret for so long. It wasn't my fault you know. I too have a right to a life of my own. That's why I did it. And no one suspected it since they were both so old. Death due to heart failure the doctor wrote on the medical certificate. But I paid him a handsome fee. Now I want to discuss another little problem. You know Persis is growing up, she is so big and she hears everything though there is a screen between our bed and hers. Pirosh is also getting to be so uncaring. He even forgot my last birthday. I really don't need him around. This job at the school is so convenient. It's enough for Persis and me to live on. Soon she'll finish college and she can become an air-hostess and make a lot of money. Already there are so many boys who want to take her out. But I am very firm. No going out with boys before you're eighteen, I told her. Now what do you think? No one will suspect if Pirosh has an illness, will they?' Her beady eyes gleamed with a cunning intelligence and her teeth seemed too close to my face. She stirred my cup for me. A piece of paper dropped from her lap on to the floor.

I let the tea cup fall from my fingers as I lifted it, spilling the tea on the table.
'Sorry!' I exclaimed, 'I'm so clumsy.' She had a fleeting look of disappointment in her eyes. As I looked at her steadily, she looked down at her hands.
'I don't think you should do anything wrong, we all have difficulties,' I said. 'Life is about coping. I really have to rush now, my husband is expecting me to go out with him. His boss has invited us to dinner.' I picked up my handbag and left the café hurriedly.

A month later, I was walking by the old school. I had to get some tea mugs from the Sahakari Bhandar. Ours were all chipped and were no longer respectable. I had come for a meeting to the city office of the bank. It was evening and the setting sun cast an orange glow in the sky. A red double decker BEST bus trundled by. Taxis and cars honked. I crossed the street as the pedestrian signal turned green. A beggar woman, sitting on the pavement near the signal, begged me for a coin. She wore a ragged sari and a torn blouse and she looked weak and tired. But she had a mobile phone in her hand under her sari pallu. I fished out a two rupee coin and put it into her palm.

As I walked past the gates of the school, someone called out to me. I looked up. It was Nilufer. She was going home on her bike. She was wearing black nylon pants and a red shirt with a print of black and yellow flowers on it. Her face looked puffy and red.

'How are you Nilufer?' I asked, feeling dry in the mouth.

'It's been of no use,' she said defeated. 'My husband died of gastroenteritis. The doctor said it was something that he ate. But Persis no longer loves me. She doesn't want to stay with me now. She has gone to live with her aunt Meher in the next building. Meher is childless and she stole my baby from me. My baby doesn't want to talk to me. She says my hands smell of rat poison. Now what did I do wrong? I did everything for her. Everything. Just to see that she has a comfortable life and now she doesn't want me. I don't want to antagonize that Meher either. Suppose she says that the body should be exhumed? There are such few vultures these days at the Towers. There's some kind of disease that's making the vultures die. The body may still be there.'

I looked at my watch and smiled a bright smile. 'I'll catch up with you later, Nilufer, I'm in a mad rush just now,' I said and walked away without looking at her. Her voice followed me, 'I will call you this evening.'

When the telephone rang late in the night I did not reach for it. Suresh picked up the receiver and answered the call. He gave me the telephone. 'Call for you from that woman called Nilufer,' he said.

'Hello Renuka!' Nilufer said, 'Hope I didn't disturb you. I just couldn't sleep. Now tell me what did I do wrong? Was it my fault? I only wanted my daughter to be happy. She was growing up and Pirosh was so insistent. Every day of the week . . . Just imagine – for a man of his age . . . He was so loud too. Though I begged him not to make a noise. And he never cared for me. I wanted my daughter to grow up innocent. I want to get her back from that Meher. Could you just get Meher to your place one evening for tea? Just a friendly chat all of us together. No one will suspect. It is very easy I realize. The doctors just don't know or care . . . Now just one evening all of us together. She won't come if I call her,' she wheedled.

I telephoned Meher and talked to her about Nilufer. Meher got Nilufer examined by a psychiatrist. Dr. Gandhi came to Nilufer's house and saw her. He advised that Nilufer be immediately admitted to a mental home. He arranged for her to be treated at the mental hospital in Poona.

Nilufer was silent through the four hour journey in the ambulance. She did not even look me or Meher in the seat next to her and she ignored the three white coated attendants who accompanied us. She just sat smiling to herself and humming in an undertone.

When we reached the Yerawada mental hospital at Poona, the doctor in charge lead Nilufer to her room. Meher stayed behind at the registration counter to complete the admission formalities. The hospital room was large and the walls were painted white. Dr. Machinder Patil said in an unnecessarily loud voice, 'Nilufer behn, this is your room, allotted to you. Keep it clean.' It was a stark room, with only an iron cot and a cupboard in it. There was a window with strong black iron bars. It was closed. Light filtered in through the frosted glass window panes. Nilufer peered around the room. She looked up at the closed window and she cackled aloud in glee, and clapped her hands. 'Aah Pirosh!' she murmured, 'See we can live here now peacefully. There are no cunning mohalla boys sitting on the tree outside and watching us kiss. A second honeymoon for us now my darling . . .' she said in a coaxing, tender voice.

'Nilufer!' exclaimed Meher who had just come in then. Nilufer looked up at her. A look of recognition and then of anger crossed her face.
'Where is Persis?' she asked, 'What have you done to my baby?'
'Nilufer, Persis is fine,' Meher said softly, 'She didn't come as she has an exam tomorrow. You must stay here.

When you are better, Persis will come back to take you home and stay with you.'

Nilufer's lips puckered and she broke into tears. 'All for nothing, all for nothing, all for nothing,' she sobbed, 'Wanted to be like everyone else. Have a home of my own. But no home. Pirosh wanted to sleep with me every night, even if Persis was in the next bed. How can a fourteen year old be innocent if she hears these things? Didn't bother that he was undressing me so near the child. Now you have me here. But can you get back my child's lost innocence?' She lay whimpering, crouched in a foetal position on the bed, her hands across her chest. The doctor gave her a tranquiliser and she sank into a stupor.

I looked at Meher. Her eyes were sad. 'She was so full of happiness when she married Pirosh,' she said, 'It's that hunt for a home that twisted her mind.' The doctor hurried us out of the room. He said that Nilufer needed a lot of rest and urgent medication. She would also have to be steeled to face the criminal cases that had been made against her . . .

A year later Meher telephoned to inform me that Nilufer had died. She had met with a cardiac arrest in court, as the Public Prosecutor described how she had killed three of her family members and planned to kill yet another. When I asked after Persis, Meher said that she had won a Tata scholarship to study Psychology in the US and that she had already left for Stanford University earlier in September.

Persis called me one evening a few years later. She had come to India on a short visit, she said. She had graduated as a clinical psychologist from Stanford. She would be joining a psychiatric clinic in New York when she returned to the US. She invited me to the memorial meeting that she had organised the next day for her mother, in their building in Darius Baug colony. It was Nilufer's death anniversary.

I reached the memorial meeting a little late. Persis came forward to greet me with outstretched arms, as I entered the building. She had grown tall and slender. She looked attractive in a grey and mauve striped dress, with a thin mauve belt around the waist. There was a framed photograph of Nilufer placed on a small table at the front end of the lobby, near the lifts. It was an old photograph, taken when Nilufer was a beautiful young woman, her wavy hair in a side parting, a single strand of pearls adorning her neck. An incense holder held burning incense sticks near the photograph. A small gathering of about fifty residents from the colony stood around. Some of the men wore their prayer caps and the older women, had their heads covered in scarves. Nilufer's friends from the school that she had worked in had also come and stood a little apart by themselves.

Meher welcomed all those present. She thanked us all for coming to the meeting and expressed her happiness at seeing so many of Nilufer's old friends and well wishers after such a long interval. Meher's old white Labrador padded up just then and sniffed at the guests before settling down quietly in front of Nilufer's photograph, resting his head on his paws, his tail thumping a soft tattoo on the floor. Meher said that Persis had been through so much of unhappiness and it was the support that she received from all of us that helped her pull through the darkest days of her life. She patted Persis who stood beside her gravely.

Persis then spoke in a soft clear voice, full of dignity and poise. She said that Nilufer had worked so hard to bring her up and give her a good education. But her mother had been a victim of circumstances. Life's vicissitudes had proved too much for her. Persis bowed her head in a moment of silent prayer and placed a garland of white Jasmine flowers over the photograph. We each took a rose from the tray on a side table, and placed it near Nilufer's picture and bowed in obeisance with folded hands. We wished Persis and shook hands with her before we left.

After the meeting, Persis, Meher and I drove down to the Tea centre at Churchgate for lunch. Only a few diners from the nearby offices sat in the restaurant with their laptops on the tables, discussing their business plans animatedly. Pictures of old tea urns and a sahib smoking a hookah adorned the walls of the restaurant. There were curtains of green matting on the long French windows, which gave the room a restful club like atmosphere. We ordered a light continental meal of poached fish in lemon sauce, on a bed of steamed rice.

Nilufer's daughter had matured and did not blame her mother any longer. 'Mama was very unhappy. She did not get help in time,' Persis said quietly, making patterns on the checked yellow table cloth with her fork. 'I am going to help as many young women as I can. Face up to their problems and not wreck themselves.'

Meher squeezed her hand. 'I know you'll be alright Persis,' she said softly, 'You're a survivor. You'll succeed.'

We got up to leave and Persis strode ahead of us, her shoulder bag swinging. I watched her walk down the street confidently with Meher. As I stood at the bus stop, she turned back once to wave a final good bye before she got into a black and yellow taxi with Meher.

ॐ ॐ ॐ

A BUCKET OF HOT WATER

Rashid was a merchant seaman from Kozhikode. He had small, sharp eyes, a strong nose, firm lips and a lean and strong physique. He was short and stood five feet five inches in his socks. His face was bronze and leathery, from years of exposure to wind and salty air. Wandering among the seaports of the world, he had not had the time to get married. Firstly there had been the marriage of his nine sisters to arrange. His father Kunnjalli had been a prosperous merchant selling dry fruits in Kozhikode. But somehow the business did not flourish as he grew older. Kunnjalli had had three wives and three offspring each, from his second and third wife. There were four children from the first marriage, of whom Rashid was the eldest. The rest of the children were all girls. Rashid's mother had died early when he was a boy of ten. His father died of a heart attack, when Rashid was twenty-four and his two step mothers died soon thereafter.

Rashid arranged for the marriages of his three sisters and six half sisters with the men he met on his sea travels. They were doctors, engineers, accountants and sailors, working in the Gulf and in foreign parts, lonely and yearning for the delicious home cooked food made by doting mothers and the artless chatter of their sisters. They found the Arabic language distasteful and guttural, infelicitous in intonation and incapable of rendering the swooning ghazals of Hindustan. In their off duty hours, they listened to music from Akashvani and cassettes of Talat Aziz and Pankaj Udaas and dreamt about the malpuas, phirni and mutton biryani served by their mothers when they broke the fast every evening during Roza. The men he met were engaged by Rashid's candour and his good humour. They soon got friendly and when Rashid slipped into the conversation, the good characters and cooking abilities of Saida or Noori, careful to be casual as he discussed a letter or a photograph of Shabnam wearing the shocking pink salwar kameez he had given her for Id, his friends needed little persuasion to marry the girls, without haggling over the dowry. All of the grooms (Allah be thanked) had turned out to be good husbands and looked after his sisters well.

At last he was free to marry. The go-between Mumtaz-bi had promised that the girl though not so young, was a skilled housewife and pretty too. 'Not one of your new fangled stylish girls, but pretty in a modest, traditional way,' she had told Rashid. The girl's elder sister, Saira was a nurse from Mallapuram and worked in Kuwait. Saira was unmarried, said Mumtaz-bi. But she was anxious for her younger sister to be settled in life.

Mumtaz-bi handed Rashid a photograph of Fatima. She was twenty-four, and had passed the twelfth standard. She had long black curly hair and a middling fair complexion. Fatima's parents had died when she was a child, in a road accident when the bus they were travelling in was rammed by a drunken lorry driver. It was her uncle and his wife who had brought up Fatima and her sister. But the uncle too died when Fatima was twenty. Fortunately Saira had trained to become a nurse and had got a job. Saira did not marry. Few men wanted to marry a working woman, especially one who was a nurse, working in close contact with male doctors. They felt that nurses were disreputable. Saira with her independence and her air of self-confidence made most men wary.

All the neighbours in their village Puthottam in Mallapuram felt sorry for Saira. Poor unmarried spinster, working like a slave to support her younger sister, no life of her own, they said in sneering tones. Saira was determined that Fatima would be married and not remain a spinster, for men to cast their evil eyes on. Her sister would lead an honourable life, she decided. But Fatima was unwilling to marry Rashid. She had taken one look at the photograph held out by Saira and had averted her face and broken into sniffles. 'I don't want to marry this villain,' she had cried. She wanted to marry a young man, tall and good looking and talking English in a smart *Boambey* accent like the famous film star with the deep baritone, *Amidhabh Bajjan*. She was afraid of this raffish looking stranger, with the small, sharp eyes and the ugly scar over his right eye. She was also sceptical about how many girls he had been intimate with. A sailor it was said had a wife in every port.

But Saira was adamant. 'Already it's too late for your marriage, Fatima,' she said. 'Another year or two and it will be difficult to find a groom for you. We are orphan children without parents to guard our interests. We have no father or elder brother. It is lucky for us that Mumtaz-bi found this young man with such small demands. Marriageable men are scarce. They're all married by the time they are twenty-six. If you get any older you'd have to be content to be the second wife of an old man. Better to be the first. With any luck, if you please your husband, you could be the only wife. He will keep you in comfort and look after your children with care.'

After many days of listening to Saira talk again and again about the difficulty of finding a groom, especially for a girl without male relatives, the necessity of having a man's protection and the love she could lavish on her own children, Fatima agreed reluctantly to the marriage. The Nikaa was settled with a mehr of ten thousand rupees. In addition the groom agreed to give Fatima a pair of gold kadas weighing twenty grams each.

The marriage was in the hot month of May when Rashid was in Cochin after a long spell of sailing in the Pacific. The Kazi came with the elders and the witnesses and Rashid and his Uncle, to the hotel New Mermaid. They waited in the outer area of the suite that Saira and Fatima occupied. A curtain which hung across the room separated them from Fatima and her sister who sat in the inner area, which had a broad double bed and a writing table.

'Fatima, daughter of Muhammad Gulam Akbar and Ayeshabi, are you willing to wed Rashid, son of Kunnjalli Sulleiman and Sultanabi, for a mehr of ten thousand rupees?' Three times the Kazi intoned the question and each time Fatima replied, 'Yes, I agree,' in a low voice. The Kazi repeated the same question three times to Rashid, whether he was willing to marry Fatima and pay her a mehr of ten thousand rupees. Rashid replied that he was willing. They both signed in the Kazi's register.

They went down for the wedding feast in a hall in the hotel. The wedding lunch was delicious, with a rich and spicy chicken biryani, garnished with almonds and cashew nuts, and mutton stew in a gravy of coconut milk, seasoned with onions, garlic and green chillies. Round slightly crisp flat breads – barotas – made of fine wheat flour, were served in little cane baskets, lined with silver foil. There was also a dessert of mango ice cream. The hundred guests who attended the marriage were mostly relatives of the couple and a few seafaring friends of Rashid. They ate the food with much noisy conversation and laughter, while children ran around the hall playing tag.

Rashid and Fatima left for Bombay soon after the marriage feast. Rashid had arranged for them to stay for the few days of their visit, in the house of an acquaintance, Alexander, in Borivali. Rashid hoped to show his bride the dazzling world of Bombay, its colourful by lanes and theatres, its park with the Old Woman's Shoe on a hill and its planetarium where the stars swam before your eyes.

They came by the night Air India flight, which was cheaper. It was the first time that Fatima had travelled by air. The sight of the aircraft on the tarmac, the flight announcements and the constant flow of people in smart clothes, talking in English terrified her. She felt ill at ease, a country wench. She was clumsy and missed a step and nearly tripped as she climbed up the steps of the aeroplane. But Rashid grabbed her arm just in time. The seat belt looked too puzzling. She did not know how to secure it. She looked at Rashid, who came to her rescue, buckling her down with a laugh. It was late well past mid-night, when they reached Bombay. They stood in line for a paid taxi and again waited outside in the queue for a cab. A Sikh taxi driver drew up when their turn came. He asked them to enter his vehicle, with a surly look. Fatima stepped into the cab fearfully, afraid that some evil would befall her in the strange place. The man with his long beard and turban appeared menacing to her. The driver also did not like Rashid with his small beard and rough countenance. He kept a watch over the couple, from his rear view mirror.

They reached Borivali soon. Alexander's wife, Nina, had kept a hot dinner ready for them, in casseroles. Rashid had a wash and changed into a red checked lungi and shirt. Fatima also changed from her travel clothes into a housecoat. They all sat down to eat. But the delicious chicken curry and fried fish did not tempt Fatima. She was not hungry. She felt sick with foreboding. After dinner Rashid spent a few minutes talking desultorily with Alexander about his experiences in Saudi and Kuwait. He put a few playful questions to Monai, Alexander's six year old son, who was still awake, despite the lateness of the hour. Then Rashid politely excused himself.

'Yes yes, you have a long night ahead,' Alexander chuckled and winked.

Fatima had a bath in the bathroom attached to the bedroom, in the house. She sat quietly on the bed, reading the Koran, while Rashid had a bath. When she had finished reading, she sat on the edge of the bed. Rashid came and lay down by her side. He pulled her to himself, his strong hand gripping her arm roughly, without any pretence of tenderness. She broke into tears, pleading a headache. She begged to be left alone. Rashid moved away from her and they both slept on the narrow cot with their backs turned to each other. Fatima spent the night sobbing silently in the dark. The next morning she sat on the bed, huddled in a corner, still crying. Her eyes were red and her nose was swollen and puffed up. Rashid was distraught. Why was Fatima so unhappy? He asked her, 'Fatimabi why are you unhappy? Did I displease you?' But she cried all the more.

At last he called Nina. She came in with a cup of hot tea. 'Come drink this,' she coaxed. 'Why are you crying? Are you missing your family? You'll soon be busy with your own life!' When Fatima continued sobbing, Nina took her aside quietly into her own bedroom. At last Fatima answered. Her friend Mariam had married a college professor a few months earlier. On the first night of their marriage, he went into the kitchen and heated a tub of water for Miriam's bath. Rashid had not done this.

When Rashid heard the reason for the tears, he was dumbfounded. 'I have had no experience of women,' he told Nina apologetically. 'I do not know the ways of women. If she only cries and cries and does not say a word, how am I to understand her requirements? How is a man brought up rough and used to rough dealings among men, to understand that a little matter like hot water can be the cause of so many tears?'

That night Rashid placed a bucket of hot water for Fatima in the bath room. When she had had a bath after dinner Rashid insisted on his conjugal rights. Fatima submitted to the assault of the stern lips and the hard body which descended on her in cruel embrace. There was no escape for her. She shut her eyes tight and submitted to the fear and the pain. After it was over, she lay crouched in a corner of the bed. She listened to his breathing and watched him from the corner of her eyes. When she saw that he had fallen asleep, she slipped away noiselessly into the bath room and scrubbed herself thoroughly, as though she could scrub away the memory of the lust. But she could not wash the sheets. The next morning she washed out the blood stained bed sheet. There was still a faint pink shadow on it that made her feel ashamed.

She found that there was no respite for her. During the day Rashid took her to see the sights of Bombay and at night he took her shrinking, unwilling body. In time she schooled herself to submit to the demands of his body. She learnt that if she switched off her mind and pretended that she was elsewhere, the ten minutes did not have the agony of the first rough taking.

Rashid soon went on his journeys and left Fatima at his home *Dilkhush Manzil* in Kozhikode. She realised that she was lucky. For she did not have to submit to her husband's embrace every night, unlike the unfortunate Rubhaiya, her neighbour, whose husband demanded his rights every single night of the year. Rubhaiya had eight children and she was only twenty eight. Her husband also did not make enough money to feed the brood that he had fathered. He drove an auto-rickshaw and when he drank more than was good for him, he beat her on the pretext that she had smiled at their neighbour, the young and pleasant looking taxi driver, Omer. Fatima said her namaaz five times every day and thanked Allah for his kindness. She also lent Rubhaiya a few hundred rupees every month when the sound of Rubhaiya's hungry, crying, children became too tormenting to hear.

She was mistress of the large rambling house with its dishevelled garden of overgrown bushes, weeds and half broken pots filled with flowering shrubs. Bougainvillea grew luxuriantly, crimson and white, over the garden wall. Fatima clicked her tongue in disapproval, when she saw the untidy overgrowth. She got up early each morning and worked in the garden straightening out the mess. Soon it was a sight for sore eyes. The green lawn shimmered with soft, green grass. Rows of new, orange, earthen pots stood at the edges of the lawn, filled with seasonal flowering shrubs in an alluring array. Clusters of blue daisies, danced alongside yellow flocks. Gerberas, bluebells, lilies and roses, crowded in a vision of delight along the rough stone lined path that led from the gate to the doorstep of the house.

Rashid came on leave unexpectedly the following month. His ship had developed problems near the Indian Ocean and had to be docked at Cochin for repairs. As his taxi drew up at the gate of *Dilkhush Manzil,* it was nearly noon. His heart gave a leap of joy when he saw the lovely transformation of the garden that Fatima's green fingers had wrought. He came in at the front door which was left open, as Fatima had gone into the kitchen to get the gardening shears that she had forgotten. 'Fatima!' he called and Fatima stood still as she saw him looking at her quizzically, an amused smile on his lips. When she came up to him, he wiped the specks of dirt that streaked her face, with his handkerchief and hugged her.

Fatima was surprised that Rashid had bought her a set of gold jewellery from Bangkok. Beneath the hard face and the rough manners, she discovered, was a generous heart. After his short unlooked for holiday, Rashid had to go back soon on his seafaring duties. He phoned Fatima every few days and sent her parcels of saris and salwar kameezes through his friends and acquaintances. He also sent her tinned food – tuna fish and jam, cheese and chocolates. Fatima gave away some of the food to Rubhaiya's children. They enjoyed eating the jams and chocolates and chorused, 'Thangue aantie,' as they trouped out, clutching the presents of food.

A few months after Rashid had left, the door bell rang one morning at *Dilkhush Manzil.* Fatima opened it wondering who the early morning visitor was. She was surprised to see Rashid's youngest sister Noorie standing outside, her baby Saleem in her arms.

'Noorie!' Fatima exclaimed. Noorie looked tearful. She had a foam leather bag in one hand. Her face was haggard and her hair looked straggly and unkempt. Fatima hurried her inside. She took the baby from Noorie who looked as though she was ready to drop down with fatigue. They went into the big, warm kitchen with its open hearth and cheerful yellow checked curtains. Noorie sat on the bench in the kitchen, next to the wooden kitchen table. Fatima opened a tin of biscuits that stood on the kitchen shelf and gave Saleem a few biscuits to eat. She busied herself at the gas stove at the other end. She made two cups of tea and spread out a batter of rice and lentils on the hot frying pan, to make crisp dosas, as Noorie narrated her story.

Fatima poured out two cups of tea and laid out a plate of dosas and a tureen of creamy coconut chutney. Noorie sipped the sweet tea gratefully, but only picked at the food, as she fed Saleem. She said that her husband had got up in a bad mood the previous day at their home in Cochin. He had lost his job in the BPO where he worked, as the recession had lead to a downturn in the business. When the dosa she served him for breakfast turned a little scorched, as the baby began crying just when she had poured out the batter on the pan, her husband Jaffar lost his temper and slapped her. When she resisted him, he pushed her out of the house and told her to go back to her brother's house. He threw a bag of her clothes after her with a few hundred rupees. Here Noorie broke into sobs and buried her face in her hands.

Fatima put her arms around Noorie and consoled her. 'Don't cry Noorie, little sister,' she said, 'we'll find a way out to sort out things. Rashidekka's home will always be your home.' She took Noorie to the East room and looked after the baby while Noorie had a warm water bath. Fatima asked her to rest a while. Noorie needed no further invitation. She sank into the soft cotton mattress on the broad teakwood bed in the room and was soon fast asleep, cradling her baby in her arms.

Fatima busied herself making a hot meal for her sister-in-law. She cooked the fat red rice, grown on their own fields and made a spicy yellow fish curry with green mango and Avial in a gravy rich with coconut. When Noorie had rested, Fatima woke her up and persuaded her to have her lunch. Noorie sat down pensively to the meal. But as she fed little Saleem from her plate, the hot fragrant food made her forget her woes and she ate a hearty meal herself. Fatima pondered over what was to be done, as they sat eating lunch together. She telephoned Rashid that night and informed him about what had happened to Noorie. When he heard about Jaffar's behaviour, Rashid was very angry. He told Fatima that he would be home soon and that he would teach the scoundrel a lesson then.

Over the next few days Noorie told Fatima in bits and pieces about how Jaffar tended to slap her for every small dissatisfaction in their domestic arrangements. After a few days of listening to Noorie, Fatima came to a conclusion. 'Noorie,' she said, 'a husband must respect his wife. God surely did not mean for men to have all the rights and women only the duties. There is no need to suffer so much violence, just to be in a marriage. If you don't like this man, I'll ask Rashid to arrange for a divorce. You can marry someone else.' Noorie thought over what Fatima said. 'Jaffar doesn't seem to like me,' she said slowly, thinking aloud, 'I've tried to please him, every way. I learnt to cook all his favourite dishes from his mother. But nothing I do seems to make him happy.' She mulled over the matter for a few days. One evening as they sat on the front verandah watching the birds fly home and the dipping sun turn the horizon a bright orange, Noorie told Fatima, 'Chechi, I don't think I want to go back to Jaffar.'

When Fatima phoned Rashid that evening and told him of Noorie's decision, he advised them to wait for some time. They would decide about what was to be done when he got back on his home leave the next month, he said. However events soon moved out of their hands.

Noorie's neighbour Manimala in Cochin telephoned her to inform her that she had found out that Jaffar's family were arranging for his marriage with another young woman, whose father was rich and owned a large business, exporting spices. The nikaa was to be in ten days. Fatima was livid at the news. She contacted her sister Saira who knew an advocate named Raghavan Nair. He had a flourishing practise in the Family Court. Raghavan Nair came to their house the very next day. He agreed to file a petition for divorce on Noorie's behalf, on grounds of cruelty. They also decided that Noorie would ask Jaffar for a compensation of thirty lacs of rupees and for the return of Noorie's wedding jewellery. Fatima consulted Rashid over the telephone.

Rashid was unhappy about how quickly things had changed for his sister. It was only three years earlier that they had celebrated Noorie's marriage with such pomp and splendour. He talked to Noorie and comforted her and agreed that she should go ahead with her divorce application. When Jaffar received the notice of divorce, he filed a rejoinder resisting the application, stating that his wife had deserted him, forcing him to consider a second marriage. However Raghavan Nair produced the crucial evidence of the neighbours who had seen Jaffar pushing Noorie out of the house. The case was adjourned at the request of Jaffar's advocate.

Rashid came on home leave two months later in November, to find that Fatima was very visibly pregnant. She was due to deliver their child in the last week of January. 'Why didn't you tell me Fatimabi all those times that you phoned me, that you are expecting our child?' he asked Fatima gently. But Fatima was silent. She smiled shyly at the husband, whom she had lived with for just two months. She turned her head away and busied herself with folding the laundry. Rashid looked at her, a thoughtful expression in his eyes, as he watched her busy herself with the housework. Though Rashid asked her to hire a maidservant, she did not heed him but did all the work herself. There were so many things to be done around the house. She enjoyed cooking the food, making every dish that Rashid liked and finding out new dishes from the *Femina* culinary pages. Noorie was a big help too.

Rashid was happy to be back home. In a few days he slipped back into the household routine as though he had never been away. He got up early and switched on the motor which pumped water from their well into the overhead tank. He sent the farm hands to the fields with their duties for the day and sometimes accompanied them. Fatima also had a list of things which she wanted to be done – the switch for the front porch light had fused and needed to be replaced, the front gate needed to be oiled as the hinges squeaked and the hen house needed to be repaired . . .

Rashid took Fatima to see Dr. Mehfusa Hossain at St. Agnes' hospital in the centre of town. Dr. Hossain had already seen her every month since July when Fatima had first gone to see her. Rashid was relieved that the doctor found Fatima in good health, the baby progressing well. But now Rashid worried whether he would be there to look after Fatima when it was time for her to deliver the baby.

They came home from the visit to the doctor to find Raghavan Nair waiting to see them. He looked sober. He said that one of the witnesses had turned hostile and was retracting the evidence given. But he was optimistic. He had obtained evidence about the second marriage and the letters that Jaffar had written to his new wife's father. Jaffar had hidden the fact of his first marriage from his second wife. He had also not obtained Noorie's consent to his taking a second wife.

The final hearing of Noorie's divorce petition took place the following month. Rashid went back to his ship. Fatima accompanied Noorie to the Family Court for the hearings. Raghavan Nair presented the evidence of the neighbours regarding Noorie's being forced out of her home and the fact that Noorie had not even been informed by Jaffar of his second marriage. They won the case. Noorie was granted an alimony of thirty lacs of rupees. The judge also ordered that an interest of twelve percent be paid by Jaffar if he delayed making the payment. Noorie was granted custody of her child. She was also to be given back all of her jewellery that Jaffar had retained.

Noorie and Fatima were elated at the verdict. They thanked Raghavan Nair and hurried to telephone Rashid and inform him about the victory. Jaffar was forced to make the payment of the money, which he did with bad grace, throwing the cheque and a handkerchief full of jewellery at Noorie in Fatima's verandah, as he stood at the steps demanding a receipt. Fatima was furious at his behaviour.

'Get out of my porch this instant you coward!' she shouted, 'You can behave this way only in a house where there are just two women.' Jaffar left them, mouthing imprecations. When Fatima told Raghavan Nair about what had happened, he immediately filed and obtained an injunction from the Family court, against Jaffar, which forbade him from entering their home. They were relieved when Jaffar disappeared from Noorie's life and did not bother them any more thereafter.

One evening Raghavan Nair came to see Fatima and Noorie. They had a cup of coffee, in the verandah. Raghavan told them that the house next door, *Zeenat Mahal*, a small cottage with two bed rooms, was up for sale. He thought that Noorie may want to have a house of her own. It would give her a feeling of independence. Noorie went to see the house with Fatima. She fell in love with the little house with its orange tiled roof and teak panelled walls. There were white rambler roses climbing up the front verandah and a garden of shaded trees, with a small square of green. It had its own well in the backyard, and a hen house. The owner had migrated to Dubai and was ready to sell the house for eight lacs of rupees. Fatima telephoned Rashid as soon as they got back from *Zeenat Mahal*. She told him that it would be a good idea to buy a house for Noorie since it would make her feel secure.

'Does Noorie like the house?' Rashid asked.

'Yes Rashidekka I do like it very much,' said Noorie.

'Then buy it, but see that Advocate Raghavan goes over the deed carefully,' said Rashid.

They were pleasantly surprised when the owner agreed to leave them the furniture in the house for a mere fifty thousand rupees more. After they had paid for *Zeenat Mahal,* twenty one and a half lacs of rupees were left over from the alimony money. Raghavan Nair advised them to keep it in fixed deposits in the State Bank of Cochin and Travancore in Noorie's name, which they promptly did.

Rashid said that they were not to wait till he came on home leave, for Noorie to move into the new house. They had a small house warming for Noorie, heating the milk till it boiled over its pot on the hearth. Saira who was home on leave and Raghavan Nair were there for the house warming. However, only four of

Rashid's sisters were able to come to *Zeenat Mahal,* their husbands and children in tow. Zohra and Sultana sent their children with Zohra's brother-in-law, since they were both busy. The two elder sisters Razia and Chandni also did not come as they were indisposed. Fatima made Kallappam with mutton stew for all of them to eat. Saira stayed a few days with Noorie to settle her in. Then she went to stay with Fatima in case she went into early labour.

Rashid came home in January one evening, as the sun was almost setting. He had prevailed on his company to give him emergency leave, as Fatima was due to deliver her baby. He paid off the taxi and strode into the house. Fatima came out from her bed room into the hall, walking slowly, her body heavy with her pregnancy. Rashid saw her and ran forward the last few steps to meet her and he held her close. 'Ready for the birthing sweet one?' he asked her, anxiety in his voice, as he gently touched her belly. Fatima's face glowed with happiness. She breathed a long sigh of relief. Almost on cue, early next morning, she started a small pain which ebbed and came on again more insistently. She woke up Rashid. 'I think we have to go to the hospital,' she said.

Rashid dressed rapidly and took their small Maruti 800 out of the garage. He drove her to St. Agnes' Hospital. He waited impatiently outside the delivery ward, after Fatima had been admitted. The duty sister in the ward sent him to the hospital drug store to buy the medicines and I V tubes and needles for Fatima. Rashid brought back the medicine. Sister told him that it would take a long while and that he should go home. But Rashid hung around the hospital reading the newspaper, half a ear cocked at the entrance of the delivery ward. After a little while Sister gave Fatima an enema. As the pains increased, sweat stood on her brow and she whimpered in pain. Doctor Mehfusa checked her every hour.

It was five in the evening when they wheeled her into the Labour room. In a little while the baby was born and Fatima lay back exhausted, with her eyes closed. When she heard the cry of her infant, she opened her eyes and lifted her head. The doctor showed her the baby. A look of quiet happiness flooded her face. She sank back on the pillow and closed her eyes. The attendant wheeled her out of the Labour room back into her room in the ward. Rashid looked worried as Fatima was wan and pale after her ordeal. But the nurse Sister Sujata smiled reassuringly at Rashid. 'Here's the baby,' she said, holding a small bundle wrapped in white linen, 'A fine healthy girl!' Rashid held the baby and looked with wonderment at the tiny pink fingers which closed into a determined fist and the small tendrils of hair curled around the wizened forehead. He smiled at Fatima. 'What should we call her Fatimabi?' he asked, pride in his voice. They decided to call the baby Shabana.

Rashid was there every morning at the hospital and only yielded place to Saira at night. There was room for one relative to sleep on the couch, near the patient's bed. On the fifth day when Dr. Mehfusa said that Rashid was free to take his wife home if he liked, Rashid almost danced to the registration counter to settle the bills and take Fatima and the child home.

They soon settled in at home with the new baby. Noorie visited them every day. She had knitted her niece a small red and white woollen smock, with booties to match. Saira gave Shabana five gold sovereigns. Raghavan Nair and his wife Geetika called with a present of a baby set, with a soft brush, comb, powder case and a towel with the picture of Goldilocks and the three bears embossed on it. They had coffee and banana fritters with their guests, who all agreed that the baby looked like Fatima.

Rashid had to go back after his month's leave was over. Saira had also to report for duty at her hospital in Oman. Noorie remained with Fatima, only visiting her own house in the morning to sweep it and keep things tidy. The baby grew stronger. They took it every month to St. Agnes' for the polio and BCG vaccines till the courses were completed. Rashid telephoned them from his mobile every other day to check on them and the baby.

One morning Fatima opened the newspapers to see that the Poor Claires' convent across the road, had advertised for applications for their D.Ed. teacher's training course. Fatima immediately thought of Noorie. She rang her up. 'Noorie, would you like to train to be a teacher?' she asked. Noorie was eager to join the course. They decided to visit the convent the next day. Sister Louise, the principal, was a bit doubtful whether Noorie would attend the course regularly since she had a small child. But Fatima pushed herself forward determinedly and said, 'Don't worry Sister, I'll take care of the child when Noorie is at class.' So Noorie went once more to college, swinging a backpack filled with her notebooks and pen and a tiffin box. She left her baby every morning with Fatima and took him home at four in the evening, on her way back from college. When Rashid heard about Noorie's enrolment at the course, he was proud and happy. 'Now whatever will you think of next Bivee?' he teased Fatima on the phone.

Fatima took the two babies for a walk every morning with the young servant girl Leena, whom she had hired to help her around the house. She pushed the pram with little Shabana in it and held on to Saleem's hand. It was January and the leaves of the Badam trees on their street were turning orange. The Coconut trees on the broad road swayed and sighed in the breeze. Shabana gurgled in delight as butterflies and dragon flies flew around them and Saleem tried to catch the creatures.

Sister Louisa met Fatima one morning as she walked the babies. Sister was on her way back from the market after buying groceries for the convent. The convent kitchen maid walked behind Sister at a suitable respectful distance. Sister Louisa cooed at the baby who looked solemnly back at her, at her black and white habit, her black layered veil. Sister put her hand into the pocket of her habit and took out a sweet and gave it to Saleem, who bashfully accepted it.

'We'll soon be having a vacancy in our primary section as the class teacher of the Third standard has resigned to join her husband. He's been transferred to Calcutta,' Sister Louisa told Fatima. 'If Noorie is interested she should apply for the post, since she'll complete her course in a month.' Fatima's eyes shone with excitement.

'Thank you Sister!' she exclaimed, 'I'll tell her to apply of course!'

Noorie was pleased to hear about the job opening at the Poor Claires' convent. She applied for the job and went to the interview. Since she had topped her class in the earlier semesters of her D.Ed. course, the interview panel members were happy to select her. They also knew that she was divorced and in need of a job.

After her first day at school, Noorie came home to a surprise tea party. Fatima had invited their neighbours and Sister Louisa also. She had baked a cake since she had been attending baking classes in the neighbourhood. The cake had chocolate icing with 'Congratulations Noorie!!' written on it in rather squiggly lettering. Rashid joined in the celebrations when they called him on the phone. He missed being present in person to share in the happiness. But he had to be content with talking to Fatima and Noorie and giving a flying kiss over the wire to little Shabana.

The following week, the weather swiftly turned hot and humid. It was no longer pleasantly cool. A few days later as Fatima walked back home from the bazaar she was caught in a sudden evening squall. She got a cold and a fever. The illness did not abate in the ensuing days and Fatima felt listless and sat at home. However, she did not mention it to Rashid when he called. But on Saturday morning she was worse and her breathing turned raspy. When Rashid phoned her that evening, she was barely able to speak to him. Fortunately his ship had just docked at Aden. He took the next available flight home and landed in Kozhikode the following day. He walked into the house, his face ashen and tense. He carried Fatima into the waiting taxi and took her to St Agnes'. The doctors told him that he had brought her just in time. Fatima had caught pneumonia.

Rashid never left Fatima's side. He sat by her bed, alert and watchful. Each day Rashid asked the doctor whether Fatima was recovering. But Dr.Jehangir Mehta only shook his head bleakly. Rashid's heart sank. He held Fatima's hand in his. 'Fatima bi,' he implored, 'Don't go away leaving me. Or else take me with you!' Two tears trickled down Fatima's cheeks. She gripped the hand which held hers and gasped, 'Don't ever leave me Rashid! I need you in my life.' She hovered between life and death, her body weak with the fever. At last on the tenth day, Fatima wrenched herself out of her illness. The doctor told Rashid that she had responded to the medicine. Fatima ate a little rice gruel and dal.

She improved slowly and was well enough to leave the hospital a week later. Rashid took her home. Rashid and Noorie nursed Fatima. But all too soon, his shipping company recalled him and Rashid was forced to get back to work. Rashid's uncle and aunt stayed with Fatima till she was quite well and then went back to their house in Cochin. Noorie visited her every evening after school and went home after they had dinner together.

In April, as the weather turned hotter, it was pickling time. Fatima and Noorie bought mangoes and lemons from the market. They washed out the big, off white ceramic pickle jars and set them out to dry in the backyard. They cut the salted mango and lime into pieces and lay them on a mat in the hot sun. Little Saleem helped to shoo away the crows that tried to peck at the pieces. When the fruit had dried sufficiently, they pickled it in vinegar and coconut oil, seasoned with green chilli, ginger and garlic. They stored the pickle in the ceramic jars. It was evening when they were finally done.

They were rolling up the mats in the compound, when an elderly gentleman came up to the gate of their compound. There was a young man with him. 'Are you ladies very busy?' the old man asked. He introduced himself as Abu Bekker, a retired overseer from the Public works department in the government. Abu Bekker lived near the Poomalai junction. His son was a cashier in the Bank of Cochin and Travancore. Fatima invited him in. The old man accepted a seat on the arm chair in the verandah. The young man sat in the wicker chair that Fatima offered him.

Abu Bekker said that he had come to propose a marriage for Noorie for his son Mohammed Abu who was accompanying him. Mohammed's first wife had died after a year of the marriage, of a fever. It was two years since she had died. Noorie looked abashed and went into the house, a shy smile on her lips. Fatima sized up the pair. She asked them how they came to hear of Noorie. Abu Bekker said, 'Oh! He has seen her come into the bank. Her account is in the bank that Mohammed works in.' Fatima was silent. Then she told them that she would have to consult her husband and elders and also ask about Noorie's own wishes in the matter.

Fatima telephoned Rashid about the proposal. 'How does he look?' asked Rashid. 'Oh, he looks tall and fair and has black eyes and straight, black hair,' she replied. Rashid sensed her unwillingness for the match. 'What is it Fatimabi?' he asked.

'I just feel that he has a black heart – that they came to see us because Mohammed has seen the money in her account in the bank. I think we should check up a bit more about how his first wife died.' Rashid thought for a minute. He told Fatima to make discreet enquiries about the family.

Fatima went to St. Agnes' hospital and told the staff at the enquiry counter that she wanted to meet the hospital Director Dr. Mathew Ellenjikaad. Dr. Mathew was busy in a meeting. Fatima had to wait for half an hour in the waiting area. When they asked her to go into Dr. Mathew's room, she went in with a beating heart. She took a deep breath and sat down in the chair that Dr. Mathew offered her. She told Mathew that she wanted to check whether Abu Bekker's daughter-in-law had been admitted to the hospital two years earlier with an illness. The Director said that it would not be possible to disclose such details to strangers. It would constitute a violation of the hospital's policy on the right to privacy of its patients. But when Fatima told him the reason for her enquiry, he changed his mind. He picked up the intercom and told the Records department to help Fatima. After she had waited for an hour, the clerk in charge of the Records department told her that Abu Bekkar's daughter-in-law Jamila had been brought in with third degree burns and had died in the hospital two and a half years ago. There had been a police case but Abu Bekker had managed to hush it up with his connections in the government. Fatima went home with a feeling of fear. What an escape for Noorie!

Fatima telephoned Rashid that evening and told him what she had found out about Mohammed. Rashid was furious. He said that they would certainly not go ahead with the marriage proposal. But when Fatima informed Noorie about the horrifying facts of how Mohammed's first wife had died, she was a little disbelieving. She had found Mohammed handsome and attractive. Tired of living alone, she was now keen to marry. Fatima telephoned Rashid. But he was on duty and did not pick up the line. Noorie was distant and withdrawn, as she left *Dilkhush Manzil* that evening. Fatima was sorry that Noorie did not trust her judgement. She looked despondently at Noorie's retreating figure as she closed the garden gate. Her sister-in-law walked homeward without turning back to wave good bye.

Sister Louisa saw that Noorie looked unhappy when she met her the next day in the common room at tea break. When Sister asked her what was bothering her, Noorie told her about Mohammed's visit to their house and what Fatima had told her about the death of his first wife. Sister Louisa drew in her breath, shocked at the story. 'I think that I know about this case,' she said slowly, 'Nusreen who had resigned as class teacher of the third standard had once been very upset about her cousin's death. She had told me that her cousin's husband had been a banker named Mohammed. I'll get Nusreen's telephone number and give it to you. And you can speak to Nusreen yourself and find out what had happened . . .'

The following Sunday Noorie dialled Nusreen's residential number in Calcutta. She was full of misgivings, afraid that Nusreen would resent her curiosity about the circumstances of Jamila's death. But she was relieved to find Nusreen sympathetic. When Nusreen learnt that Noorie now had her old job as Class teacher of the Third standard at the Poor Claires convent and that she had received a proposal of marriage from Mohammed, Nusreen was quite candid about Mohammed's behaviour. She told Noorie that Mohammed had indeed been her brother-in-law. He had married her cousin Jamila over three years ago. But he had bothered Jamila for money. Jamila's father was a poor tailor and was unable to meet Mohammed's incessant demands. There were constant quarrels between the couple. One evening Mohammed set Jamila on fire and contrived to make it look like a cooking stove accident. Though Jamila's family had pursued the matter, Mohammed was able to bribe the police and close the case. It was filed as an accidental death in the police records since there were no witnesses. Noorie felt a shiver of fear go down her spine, as she listened to Nusreen's account of how Mohammed had killed Jamila.

Noorie put down the telephone on its stand with shaking fingers and almost ran to *Dilkhush Manzil*. Fatima hurried to open the front door hearing the frantic ringing of the doorbell and was surprised to see

119

Noorie standing outside. Noorie flopped down on a chair in the kitchen and told Fatima in a shaky voice, that Mohammed had indeed murdered his wife Jamila. Fatima was silent for a few minutes.

'Forget this monster, Noorie,' she said, 'We'll get you a much better groom than him.' However Noorie said that she never ever wanted to marry again. She would devote herself to her child.

'But chechi,' she said, 'We need to see that this man doesn't get away with his crime. How can we see that he's put behind the bars?' Fatima said that they would find a way out. Nooire went home looking sombre.

A few days later, Sister Edna from the Poor Clares' convent came to visit Fatima. Sister sat on the cane chair in the broad verandah of the house and drank a cup of tea with her. Saleem played in the yard, driving his toy car. Sister said that Saleem was growing so fast, he would soon have to go to nursery school. Shabana was also growing well. She crawled up to Sister Edna with a naughty look in her eyes. Sister Edna picked her up and Shabana yanked the shining silver cross on the chain on Sister's neck, making her squeal and laugh. Then Sister turned to Fatima and asked her whether she was interested in doing community work. She explained that they were setting up groups for poor women to help them save money for a rainy day, teaching them to make cane baskets, embroider bed sheets and table cloths and make cakes and savouries that they could sell for a profit. Fatima's eyes brightened. She immediately thought of poor Rubhaiya, who would certainly like to be able to earn an income of her own.

Fatima went to the convent the next day and started her training on being a facilitator for women's self help groups. She received a stipend of Eight Hundred rupees for her labours. She visited the poorer areas of her locality with Rubhaiya and they found eleven other women who were willing to join the group. Sister told them to pick a name for their group. The women sat at a meeting around the table in Fatima's large cheerful kitchen. They discussed a suitable name for their group. Fatima made them tea and handed around savoury murukku that she had just made that morning. One of the older women Heena, suggested the name "Ujwalam" and they all agreed that they liked it. Rubhaiya said that it conveyed their hopes for a bright future. So they went to the nearby Travancore and Cochin bank and opened an account for their new group. The women elected Heena as Chairperson and Rubhaiya as Secretary of their group.

Each of the members saved ten rupees every month. They put it into their bank account after every month's meeting. Fatima gave them lessons on writing their ledger books. Rubhaiya wrote the minutes of each meeting, painfully in her scrawny hand, as she had only studied up to the fifth standard. Fatima taught the women how to thread the needle and stitch fine even stitches. Soon they were embroidering their first order of altar cloths for the convent chapel. They also embroidered saris, pillow covers and other ornamental pieces.

Fatima organised the first sale of their products in an empty lot near the market, in the second week of December, just before Christmas. The stall was thronged with housewives who delighted at the fine embroidery and the bargain prices. The sale was a resounding success. Ujwalam was soon over flooded with orders for embroidered saris and dress material.

Noorie also helped with the embroidery. She was quite adept with the needle and in getting designs downloaded from the internet. Shohaib Ali, a quiet computer engineer who taught the children computer science at school, helped Noorie. He also encouraged her to enrol for a computer language course at NIIT. Shohaib came every evening to *Dilkhush Manzil* and together they selected the best embroidery designs for the self help group women. They also designed a website for the group, showcasing their various products. Shohaib found overseas buyers for the women's products on the internet and helped to register the trade name for their products. He ran around various government offices with the paperwork for exporting the articles. Heena and Rubhaiya went with him, to explain the nature of their work to dour government officials, who sat with glazed eyes behind their desks piled high with files. At last they had all the export registrations and permits in place and were able to send their exquisitely embroidered stoles and bags to discerning foreign buyers.

Fatima urged Shohaib to stay for dinner at weekends and the delicious smell of Fatima's biryani made him stay without much persuasion. Shohaib was a bachelor whose parents lived in Cochin and he had to make do with a tiffin service. He also made himself a morning cup of coffee. So he was very happy eating the delicious home cooked food made by Fatima. Noorie also helped in the cooking sometimes, making a sweet saemiya payasam or adda pradhaman, when she had finished correcting her students' homework.

At the next meeting of the Ujwalam women's group, the discussion turned to about how some women often had to suffer violence in their homes.

'So what can we do about it?' Fatima asked the women.

'Nothing, women are made for suffering,' said Rehana who was only twenty-four. Her husband drank too much and beat her every week. She often came to the group meetings with a bruised arm or a black eye.

'But there are laws in favour of women. Especially against harassment for dowry,' said Fatima.

'Why don't we complain to the police?' asked Heena.

'Who will listen to a woman? We'll get beaten all the more and even be thrown out of the house if we raise our voices,' said Nagina fearfully.

'I'm ready to file a complaint. If we go in a group, the police will be bound to listen to us,' said Rubhaiya stoutly. Fatima brought up the case of Jamila. All the women present had heard about Jamila's tragic death. The neighbours had seen her being beaten by her husband and had heard the quarrels in the house about money. The Ujwalam group discussed the matter and decided that they would use the statements of the neighbourhood women to petition the court to reopen Jamila's case. Fatima suggested that advocate Raghavan Nair could help them file a petition.

Raghavan Nair was surprised to see the group of women, in their trademark light blue saries, the next morning in his office. When he heard them, he readily agreed to file the review petition free of cost. The women decided to publicise the issue of the incomplete police enquiry into Jamila's death. They marched through the streets of Kozhikode, with placards in their hands chanting, 'We demand justice for Jamila.' The local press covered the story of the protests of the women's group and photographs of the group members appeared in the papers. When the petition was filed and the judge ordered that the case be reopened, the women were jubilant. It was their first taste of victory in raising a voice against injustice to women.

One evening Noorie sat at the kitchen table in *Dilkhush Manzil* correcting her students' continuous assessment papers. She got up when she heard the door bell ring and went to open the door. She was pleased to see Shohaib standing outside. His face was full of quiet elation. He smiled at her and held her hand as he asked her where Fatima was and he walked right into the kitchen. He said that he had something special to say to Fatima. She looked at him in surprise and put down the ladle with which she had been stirring the chicken broth that she was cooking. When Fatima and Noorie had both sat down at the kitchen table with him, Shohaib told them that he had got a teaching job at an engineering college in Bangalore and that he would be leaving the next week. Noorie was stunned. She got up quickly from the table, her lips quivering. 'Nooire! Don't go!' Shohaib almost shouted after her. He got up from his chair. Noorie stopped at the kitchen door.

Shohaib turned to Fatima and said that he was now confident that he would be able to support a family and though Noorie's brother was away, he wanted to propose a marriage with Noorie, if they had no objection. He said that he would look after Noorie's son as though he were his own.

Fatima took one look at Noorie's shining face and said with a smile, 'Shohaib I'm sure Noorie's brother will agree, if she herself is willing for this marriage. We'll call Rashid tonight. But first have a cup of tea with us!' Fatima's watchful eye had detected the growing attachment between Shohaib and Noorie. Fatima made Shohaib's favourite snack of spicy egg burji and parathas, while Noorie made the tea. Shohaib helped to lay out the quarter plates and spoons on the table and put three tea cups on the table. They sat around the table, drinking hot ginger tea and eating the parathas. Fatima opened a tin of sweet and slightly salty nan khatayis.

'Why should we wait for the night, let's call Ekka now itself!' said Shohaib. He wasn't able to endure the waiting. He rang up Rashid from his mobile. When Shohaib put forth his proposal for Noorie, Rashid was not surprised. Fatima had told him earlier that month, that she saw that Shohaib had grown fond of Noorie.
'Shohaib, you know that Noorie was married once before and that she has a small son. Can you care for them both?' Rashid asked Shohaib.
'Ekka I love Noorie very much and I want to marry her. And Saleem will be a son to me, don't worry about that at all,' Shohaib assured Rashid. Fatima moved into the

verandah and spoke in an undertone to Rashid. She said Sister Louisa had told her a long time earlier that Shohaib was a nice boy without any bad habits. His parents lived in Cochin and had a business selling tea and coffee.

'But does Noorie like him Fatimabi?' Rashid asked.

Fatima handed over the mobile phone to Noorie.

'Do you want to marry this Shohaib mollu? Do you think he will care for you?' Rashid asked his sister.

'Rashidekka, Shohaib is very kind to Saleem. He will look after both of us. I don't mind this marriage,' said Noorie demurely.

Rashid came on leave the following November. Noorie and Shohaib were married at a quiet ceremony. Rashid invited all his neighbours and well wishers for lunch under a shamiana in their courtyard. They had delicious chicken tandoori, white mutton stew with bun pav and barotas and sweet saemiya payasam. Noorie, looking ecstatic in her red ghagara choli, left for Bangalore with her husband and her son.

Rashid was bemused to find that his wife had become a celebrity of sorts in their locality. He was surprised at her business sense. As streams of women from Ujwalam and other women's groups and shopkeepers from the bigger shops in search of new designs for saris, came to see Fatima, *Dilkhush Manzil* resembled a business centre. There were incessant meetings, with women talking together all at once and being called to order from time to time by Fatima. Rashid helped to serve them tea with a happy, indulgent smile.

One morning, a few weeks after he had come home, an imp of mischief took hold of Rashid. He heated a basin of hot water and placed it ceremoniously in the bath room just before Fatima stepped into the bath room for her bath, while she scolded him. They had now installed a geyser in the bathroom and there was no need to waste the gas fire to heat the bath water, she said. However, she basked in the comfort of a warm oil massage that Rashid gave her. He kneaded her body, and gently pressed the base of her aching neck and worked down to the soles of her tired feet and ankles, releasing the tension in her muscles. She rose from the hot water bath, sated and half drowsy. She lay on the bed in luxurious languor as Rashid kissed her tired eyelids and her lips. His fingers traced the bones on her back and neck. He paused to look at a mole he had not noticed on her right shoulder. She touched the scar on his eyebrow and kissed it. They looked at each other steadily and then Fatima wound her arms around him. They lay entwined, coupling in wild abandon. It was well past lunch time when Fatima opened their bed room door to Shabana who had tired of her ayah's company and knocked on the door, wanting to be entertained.

Badruddin Uncle came to see Rashid with the accounts of the dry fruit business. The business was slowly dying. Rashid felt that the failing dry fruit business could do with some of Fatima's enthusiasm. He told his uncle that Fatima could help them with the business. Badruddin was a little reluctant to take a woman into a man's world. But when he saw that the bankers of the Travancore and Cochin bank recognised Fatima, and admired her business sense – they were even willing to advance her a loan of rupees three lacs for the business, his reluctance was won over.

The dry fruit business slowly turned into a profitable venture. The women's self help groups also became part of the business activity, by buying the nuts in the whole sale market, cleaning, roasting and packing them neatly into packets of hundred grams and five hundred grams and selling them to the store. The wily trader, who had sold rotting nuts at a high price to Badruddin Uncle, was dispensed with. Fatima was very vigilant that no unfair advantage was taken of her women's groups. As she saw the women develop into expert retailers of dry fruit, she converted her own business into a whole sale business and left the retail work to the women's groups. She helped them set up their own sale outlet as well. The women called their enterprise 'Ujwalam Women's Pure and Unadulterated Food Products Store'. Housewives from all of Kozhikode thronged the store which had whole and ground spices, lentils and rice all packed in plastic packets, printed with the Ujwalam logo of two women pounding spices.

In a few years the family dry fruits business grew into a multi city chain enterprise. Rashid was persuaded to give up his sea travels and help Fatima and Badruddin Uncle. Rashid left his job with the shipping company and came home for good. He was filled with pride as he saw his wife haggle over prices with bearded merchants, beating them at their own business. Fatima was busy with the business all day. She sat in the store and dealt with the customers and she also handled the bank work and the accounts. Rashid helped her manage it. He did the purchases, travelling to the large market centres for dry fruits. He also bought all the household provisions that were needed every month and attended to the children's studies, helping them with their homework.

One rainy June morning as Rashid travelled with Badruddin uncle to the large dry fruit market in Cochin, Badruddin remarked how Fatima was getting to be so unwomanly in her enthusiasm in working in the family business. Rashid was silent for a moment as he thought of how he could disagree with his uncle without being unfilial and offending his feelings. Then he quietly reminded Badruddin of how long ago Khadijah Begum, the Prophet's wife was also a very successful business woman in Arabia. Badruddin did not raise the subject thereafter again.

Soon it was time to send little Shabana to nursery school. Fatima bought her a colourful raincoat with a print of red and blue Donald ducks and a little shoulder bag. Shabana could hardly wait for the day when she was to don her rainwear and take the bag with its Tiffin box of biscuits and two nut chocolates. It was with a sore heart that Fatima dropped her daughter to the nursery. But Shabana just skipped into the cheerful play school with its rocking horses and toy cars.

The heavy rains in the monsoon were followed by the October heat. Fatima had another baby – a boy. They called him Rahim. Rashid was firm this time around. He did not allow Fatima to make herself weary cooking the food. He hired the gardener's wife Saroja, to cook their food instead. Saroja proved to be an excellent cook and a good learner too. Fatima taught her to make a light vegetable pullao as well as custards and jellies. Rashid enjoyed pottering around in the kitchen and also kept an eye on Saroja's cooking, relaying Fatima's directions from the bedroom where she sat nursing her baby.

Rashid was an early riser and often made himself a cup of strong tea. He boiled a special brew with elichi and ginger and poured it into the steel flask on the kitchen table. When Fatima arose, they sat sipping the hot tea together in the bedroom verandah, enjoying the stillness and the slight chill of the dawn, watching the sun rise gently over the eastern horizon. Fatima was contented, filled with a sense of happiness and fulfilment. It was so wonderful to be Rashid's beloved!

ॐ ॐ ॐ

CERTA BONUM CERTAMEN

One morning I met Meghna Lahiri at the local stationery shop where I had stopped to buy a few pens and some note paper. Meghna had been two years senior to me at school. She had completed her twelfth standard and she was looking for a job as her mother couldn't afford to educate her any further. Mrs Sadhana Lahiri was known to us as a respectable lady, although she lived in a tin shed near the railway quarters. It had a swaying tin door and Mrs.Lahiri was always fearful that some ruffian might come in and rape her beautiful daughter.

Meghna looked happy to see me at the shop counter. As I turned to go back home from the shop, she persuaded me to go home with her. I was bored since it was the summer vacation and I had nothing much to do. So I went secretly without informing Amma about it. Instead I telephoned Amma and told her that that I was going to my friend Neeru's for the day. Neeru also lived in the railway quarters like us, a few buildings away. Her father worked as a Guard in the Railways and Amma didn't mind my visiting her occasionally.

Mrs. Lahiri's husband had been the General Manager of Coal and Calcites Ltd in Bhopal. It was his drinking that had lead to his downfall. He was dismissed for being drunk at work and from then on he had found a smaller job each time, till at last he was unemployed and roamed the streets begging for a few rupees from his acquaintances for a drink. He left his wife and children in his married sister's home in Vishakapatnam. One day he came into the house and shut the door of the bedroom. When they opened it, they found him dead, a bottle of cyanide in his lifeless hand. Mr. Lahiri's sister asked her sister-in-law to leave her house two months after the funeral.

Meghna's mother now earned a living stitching clothes on her sewing machine and doing sari falls for women who were too busy to stitch the narrow bands of cotton material to the hemline of their saris. She also did tiffins for bachelors who wanted meals delivered to their homes and offices. Mrs.Lahiri's brother had helped her hire the small tin shack. They rented it from the local slum lord. Mehgna's elder sister was lucky. She got a job as an airhostess with Gulf Air when she was eighteen. She met a Filipino passenger on a flight one day and they got friendly. She married him after a few months. Mrs Lahiri said that her elder daughter, Mayuri, often wrote to them and sent them snapshots of her baby boy. She also mailed them a hundred dollars every now and then. However she always complained about how expensive life in the Philippines was and how cramped the house they lived in. Mrs. Lahiri told us that it was difficult for her elder daughter to take them to live with her in Manila.

I entered the small, one roomed shed which was Meghna's home. The floor was made of rough concrete. There was only a hole for a window. A small wooden table stood at one end. A pressure stove and a few steel utensils and three melamine plates and two cups were kept on it. Meghna asked me to sit on the iron hospital cot which was placed along one side of the hut. It had a thin mattress on it. I sat on it gingerly, in case it wasn't strong enough. There were two steel trunks under the cot. The walls of the shed were bare save for a picture of the Goddess Kali, with her ferocious face, tongue hanging out blood-streaked as she sat astride a tiger. There was also a yellowing calendar with 'Biswajeet Traders – sellers of tastee spices' printed on it and the numbers of the dates in large red letters.

Meghna busied herself with the preparations for our lunch. She poured out three glasses of water and wiped the plates and placed them on the table. Mrs. Lahiri had cooked chicken curry for the bachelors and she gave Meghna and me a generous helping with hot rice. It was delicious, though we ate off the slightly cracked, melamine plates. After the meal, we washed our hands outside, pouring the water into the open drain that had a stench. The *maavalis* hung around in the street outside the shed, picking their teeth, biding their time till an opportunity to make a killing presented itself. They gave Meghna an appraising stare, so we quickly went back inside. Meghna had cascading black hair that draped her shoulders and she had lovely almond-shaped eyes and a small shapely nose. Her expression was that of an impish child.

I said thank you to Mrs.Lahiri and went back home feeling subdued. I sat on the chair before my writing desk in my room and felt a little shiver go down, as I imagined Meghna and her mother sleeping every night with one eye open, alert about every sound in the street. I thought that I was so lucky to have such a nice home to live in, with a bathroom and a toilet. I even had a separate bed all to myself to sleep in. Both Amma and Papa looked after me so well. I didn't have to worry whether ruffians would push down the door and enter my home.

We lived safely in a government colony. Our house was in the railway quarters, near the railway tracks at Wadala in Bombay. You could hear the trains all day and night till the last train at one just after mid-night. They started again at four in the morning. In fact Father always said that he never could sleep without hearing the rhythmic rumble of a train going by. The house shook a little with each passing train. It was over seventy years old and made of solid stone. There were four large rooms, including the kitchen, in which we also ate our food. The front room was for visitors. It had a pretty dresser with an intricately carved design of flowers. It was here that Amma kept her few bits of crockery and two china statues of an English shepherdess and her swain. She had got the statues and the dresser from old Mr. Donald who had retired from the Railways as an Assistant General Manager. He had given away all his furniture and most of his belongings when he went back home to Scotland.

Amma came in from the kitchen and saw me sitting dolefully in my room. 'What's the matter Ranjini? What are you moping about?' she asked

I confessed that I had been visiting Meghna. 'They live such an insecure life in that shed, Amma,' I said, 'how can we help Mrs. Lahiri and Meghna to live in a better place?' Amma said that we would try and find out some way to help them.

Amma was kinder than ever to Mrs Lahiri when she visited us and welcomed her with a cup of tea each time. Whenever Mrs. Lahiri came home, she showed us the letters and the photographs of her elder daughter and her grandson, living in a real house and not in a shed like them. She also showed us the photographs of her home when they had been well off, before her husband had lost his job. They were her passport to respectability and a lifestyle now lost to them. Mrs. Lahiri looked sad as she discussed how dangerous it was living in her little hut. She was always afraid that the municipality would demolish it someday in a rare fit of efficiency. Then where would she go with her daughter, she said, tears welling up in her eyes. Amma bustled about and changed the topic whenever Mrs. Lahiri got gloomy. She poured out a fresh cup of tea for her and offered her a jam roll and cream crackers. The cream crackers always cheered up Mrs. Lahiri. She liked their crisp, slightly salty taste.

Amma was very religious. She often went for the novenas to the Mahim Church named after St. Michael, to pray for my brother Ronny's health and well being. He was studying in the third year of his engineering degree at IIT Powai. I was doing my B.Sc. although I had wanted to study Medicine. But Papa and Amma said that they couldn't afford it together with the expenses of Ronny's education. Ronny's college bills were very high and a strain on the family income. Papa was a railway engine driver. My marriage was sure to cost them at least two Lacs of rupees in a dowry. Amma had already bought my diamond nose-ring and kept it in the safe. She had also bought two *Kanjivarom saris*, heavy with gold embroidery. There would be many more that we needed to buy, but she bought them at the Kala Niketan annual stock clearance sales, as and when she saved a little money. A Tamil wedding was expensive because of the number of gold ornaments and the *Kanjivaroms* that were mandatory in a bride's trousseau. It was better, Papa said, that I did my B.Ed. and became a schoolteacher and that Ronny studied engineering.

I was quietly reading a novel one afternoon – Jane Austin's *Pride and Prejudice* – when the doorbell rang. I opened it. Mrs. Lahiri stood outside. She looked a little embarrassed to see me. She had a parcel in her hands. I asked her to come in and sit down. She sat on the edge of our Rexene covered, red sofa. She looked distinctly uncomfortable. When Amma came into the room, Mrs. Lahiri was silent. Sensing her discomfort, Amma signalled me to go into the bedroom. I went inside. I heard Mrs. Lahiri open her parcel.

'These crystal cellars are the last thing I have from my bungalow in Calcutta,' she told Mama with a sigh, 'we had bearers with white gloves who served at our table. And we always had either fish or meat. My husband was such a stickler for good food. Now Meghna has an interview with Swiss Air. She needs to get a new pant suit for the interview and a handbag and slippers.' I could no longer restrain myself. I just had to see what it was that Mrs Lahiri had brought. I peeped through the curtains and saw a pair of beautiful, crystal, salt cellars that gleamed with rainbow lights, on the front room table. Mrs Lahiri twisted her sari pallu nervously.

'I need five thousand rupees,' she said after a short silence. Then as Amma did not say anything, she went on eager to fill in the uncomfortable gap.

'I wouldn't part with this except that my Meghna needs a chance in life. Its genuine Belgian crystal and worth a fortune. But I don't want to go to pawn shops. Please can you take it and give me the money?' she whispered.

Amma had wanted the crystal salt cellars as soon as she saw them. However she now looked a little unwilling and embarrassed to buy something that Sadhana Lahiri had so obviously treasured. But Mrs. Lahiri had seen the first unguarded expression of delight in Amma's eyes and she pressed her to take it. At last Amma went to the steel cupboard in the bedroom, where she had hoarded six thousand rupees, just in case we needed the money in an emergency. She counted out five thousand rupees, in soiled rupee notes, that had been put away in tens and twenties, from the housekeeping money. Mrs. Lahiri took the money and went away immediately. She was too shy to wait for tea as usual. Mrs Lahiri did not visit us for a long time thereafter. I was puzzled not to see Meghna around either. Amma kept the crystal set on her dresser and dusted the pieces every day herself. The maid who came to do the sweeping was not allowed to touch the dresser.

About a year later, I was at home. It was the summer vacation, in the hot month of May. I sat near the window of my bedroom. The Gulmohor tree in the compound was resplendent with its flaming red flowers. There was a knock on the front door. I opened the door and found Mrs. Lahiri standing outside. She wore a new, printed silk sari in blue, with the abstract prints, that were in fashion just then. She had a small, black, leather handbag in her hand. I asked her in and called Amma. Mrs. Lahiri looked radiant.

'Meghna got selected for the job with Swiss Air,' she said with a happy smile. 'They've also given her a flat to stay at Andheri and we've taken a loan to buy our own flat in Lokhandwala complex.'

We were glad for her. I went into the kitchen and made three cups of tea, milky and sugary, in celebration and brought it with Mrs. Lahiri's favourite Cream Cracker biscuits. We settled down to tea. A little later Mrs. Lahiri's eyes went to the dresser. She looked apologetic. She fidgeted with her bag and coughed.

'I wonder if you'd mind giving me back my salt cellars,' she said quickly in a low voice, 'I've brought the money. You know it's my only memory of days gone by. My husband bought them when he was visiting Belgium on a trade visit . . .' Her voice trailed off.

Amma immediately got up. She took the salt cellars from the dresser and gave it to Mrs. Lahiri who returned her the five thousand rupees, in crisp, new Five Hundred rupee notes.

'Ranjini could you get a plastic bag from the kitchen?' Amma asked me. I went into the kitchen and took out a large, plastic Kala Niketan shopping bag from the kitchen cupboard and gave it to Mrs. Lahiri. She put the salt cellars in the bag and got up to go.

'I'll never forget your kindness to us,' she said pausing at the door, 'We now have a chance to live decently. Meghna has a boyfriend. He's a purser, a Punjabi. They hope to get married soon. A nice boy would never have looked at my Meghna, when we lived in that tin shed,' she said, wiping her eyes with a small cambric handkerchief. Amma smiled and said, 'God Bless,' as Mrs Lahiri left. She gently shut the door and then she went to the balcony to have a last glimpse of Mrs. Lahiri, who turned and smiled and waved as she walked down to the bus stop. Amma waved back. There were tears in her eyes and her face was bright with joy.

I sat down in my room to digest the news about Meghna. Living in that tin shed, she had dreamt about reaching the stars and now she lived her dream! It must be so marvellous to spread your wings and fly and see the world, be in Paris one week and in Germany the next. Then I thought about my own ambition. To be a doctor. A gynaecologist. To operate on women. To save lives. I had wanted to be a doctor so badly. If Meghna could fight her circumstances from that tin shed, why couldn't I? I brooded over it day and night. Somehow I must find a way out, I decided.

One morning I saw the advertisement in the newspaper, for the entrance test for St.James' Medical College, at Bangalore. I was overjoyed! I applied for it secretly, without telling my parents and did the examination. I waited impatiently for the results. Two months passed by and at last the results came in. I logged on to the college website with a beating heart and keyed in my roll number. It was included in the list of successful candidates! Elated I ran out of my room. I just had to tell someone! But then I stopped and walked back dejectedly. I was afraid to tell Papa and Amma.

When Amma came in to ask me whether I wanted to help her make the *Avail* for lunch, she saw me hastily switch the site on my computer. 'What are you looking at Ranji?' she asked me, a little sharply. Guiltily I told her about my medical entrance examination results. Amma looked happy, but then her face clouded over. 'How can we get the money for the fees baby?' she asked. I was silent. Amma left the room. I sat before my computer sadly. I went to the college website once again. The picture of the campus popped up tantalizingly. The lawns. The proud students with their stethoscopes around their necks. The class rooms and the laboratories. I was so unhappy that I would lose this opportunity which had seemed so near and was now so far away.

Then I saw the icon – *Scholarships and Assistance*! The site indicated that there were free-ships for excellent students who scored over eighty percent. There were also loans available at 4% interest for students who could not afford the fees. I ran to the kitchen excitedly and told Amma that the college website said that there were low interest loans for students who could not afford the fees. I begged Amma to let me take a loan and that she would never regret the decision. She said that we could discuss it in the evening with Papa. I could hardly wait for Papa to be home.

That evening Papa was late home. As he sat eating his dinner, we broached the topic with him. I told him that Meghna had achieved her dream and I too wanted to become a doctor and chase my dreams.

'What about your marriage Ranji?' Papa asked looking worried.

'Oh Papa! I'll take care of my own marriage!' I said, 'Kalpana Chawla has been to outer space. I can certainly become a successful doctor!' I looked at Papa earnestly, willing him to agree to send me to study medicine.

He was quiet as he thought about it. My heart thumped wildly. At last he said, 'If you are so keen on it, we'll take a loan and send you to study medicine Ranji.' He had a twinkle in his eye. 'It's a very prestigious institution and it would make us very happy when you become a doctor.' I hugged Papa and told him that he was the best Papa in the world.

Papa and Amma decided to come with me to Bangalore and see me settled into the women's hostel. Papa booked our second class train tickets. I packed my suitcase and took my photo frames of our little family together, taken when Ronny had come home for his vacation last December. I was so excited on the trip I could hardly keep still in the train. It was an overnight journey and we reached Bangalore in the morning by seven. I had a bath in the bathroom in the Second Class ladies waiting room. After Papa and Amma had also bathed and dressed, we had a breakfast of Uthappams and filter coffee at the railway station dining room. We left for the medical college in a taxi.

I was excited as we entered the broad gates of St.James' Medical College. The gates had the college coat of arms of two elephants with their tusks entwined and a spreading Frangipani tree with its star like flowers in the centre, with the college motto in Latin at the bottom of the figures: *Certa Bonum Certamen*. Papa said, 'You know what that means Ranji? To fight the good fight. It's taken from the first letter of St Paul to Timothy. We expect you to live up to this motto Ranji!' I vowed to myself that I would study so hard, Papa and Amma would only have reason to be proud of me.

I was admitted into the medical college, after I had paid my fees. I was also given a room in the Indus Ladies hostel. My room was small and compact, with a bed, a table and a chair in it. It had a small bathroom and toilet attached to it. I unpacked my clothes and hung them in the cupboard and put away my things into the drawers. Papa, Amma and I had lunch together in the nearby college cafe. Then we looked around the college. The grounds were huge, with broad, tree lined avenues. There were pathways to the various departments, each in its own building. We boarded the special bus to take first time visitors around the campus.

Then I remembered that I needed a tube of toothpaste. I had forgotten to pack it. We went into a local provision shop and I bought some toothpaste, a ceramic coffee mug, a melamine plate and two steel spoons. We had coffee at the Madras Coffee House next to the provision store. Then it was time for Papa and Amma to leave by the evening train back to Bombay. I waved at them from my hostel balcony and I was a little sad. But mostly I was excited at the new life that now unfolded before me. I ate my dinner at the hostel mess with the two girls who there in the dining hall and went back to my room. Only a few girls had joined. The others were expected to come the next day. As I lay on the narrow hostel bed with its snow white sheets, I saw from the open window next to my bed, the clear velvet sky, with the stars shining so brightly outside. I thanked God. I was so lucky to have Amma and Papa. I would study well and become a famous doctor and they would be as proud of me as they were of Ronny – no – even more! *'Certa Bonum Certamen,'* I recited, as I fell asleep.

ॐ ॐ ॐ

THE ELIGIBLE BACHELOR

Teresa felt the labour pains coming on as she sat cutting the vegetables in the kitchen, at ten in the morning. In the next room, Rachna the eleven-year-old waif who stayed with them and helped with small chores, sat minding one-year-old Laila as she lay in her cradle kicking and waving her rattle. Teresa got up slowly and walked into the other room.

'Rachna I have to go to the doctor. If saab comes tell him I have gone to the Tambole hospital,' she told the little maid, 'And give the baby her milk when she is hungry and starts crying. See that you wash your hands before you touch the bottle.'

Teresa did not take a bus. She did not have the money for the fare. The hospital was two bus-stops away from their chawl in Ulhasnagar. She walked slowly, fearful that the baby might be born any moment. Suppose she delivered the baby on the street? What a shame for Teresa of the ancient Plamoodil family of Kavuukadu! What would her father have said if he were alive? At last she reached the hospital. She sat in the waiting room patiently till the nurse addressed her.

'I am getting my labour pains. My husband will be coming soon from work,' she said in a low voice.

Fortunately the nurse recognized her from her previous visit for her Tetanus injection. She hurried her into the labour ward. It was the general ward for poor women. But now that they were safely in the hospital, the baby took its own time. The woman in the next bed moaned every half hour as the pains came on. Teresa merely clutched the dirty bed-sheet they had spread on her white, iron, hospital cot. The floor was made of grey stone and there was a strong smell of urine and blood smothered by disinfectant. From the labour room there was the scream of a woman in acute pain followed by a resounding slap. It was the heavy ox-faced nurse Tara, who told the woman to quit yelling, that her baby would not be born without a little pain. There was a lovely bougainvillea plant with magenta blossoms clambering up the window near Teresa's cot. She fixed her eyes on the flowers and tried to block out every other thought. But invariably her thoughts went back to the infant at home. Would Rachna be able to manage? She was just a child herself. Would Joseph come in time?

It was seven in the evening when Joseph reached the hospital. He burst into the labour ward in his usual jolly manner. It was his five-year stint in the army as a non-commissioned officer, with British commanding officers, that had given him this hearty manner.

'Still at it?' he asked cheerfully in a loud, booming voice, 'I know we won't get there for another few hours,' he added breezily, with a knowing look, as though Teresa was on some kind of a joy ride. Teresa nodded, unable to speak for the pain. He patted her head kindly and left the room. The tearing pains increased and beads of perspiration stood on her brow. But she was determined not to scream like the poor woman in the next bed.

The doctor came in to check on the patients. He was a greying, middle-aged man with a rumpled shirt under his yellowing white coat. He had a tired looking face. He looked at the chart and the nurse's notes. He examined Teresa.

'Yes, in another hour or so,' he told the nurse.

'Where is your husband?' he asked Teresa.

'He's outside,' she said softly. Teresa lay back exhausted. The other women's husbands were waiting at their bedsides or if there were women folk accompanying them, they were banished unwillingly outside. Yet they hung on, peeping in at the door, anxiously eavesdropping into every word that the doctor uttered.

The assistant nurse, Reenu, was sent to look for Teresa's husband. She looked up and down the corridor. But she found no anxious, pale-faced husband waiting. There was a small group of three men playing cards at the far end. Joseph slapped his friend on the back, as he laid out his cards.

'Good trick there, but my cards are better,' he guffawed. The nurse looked disapprovingly at the group,

'Has anybody seen the husband of Teresa?' she asked. Joseph was engrossed in dealing out the cards and looking at his hand. He did not hear her. Reenu came back.

'There's no one there,' she told the doctor.

They looked at Teresa coldly, all sympathy effaced, wondering whether she was an unwed mother. There was a gold chain around her neck with the Syrian Christian *tali* – a small gold leaf the size of a cooked grain of rice. It was the marriage chain that had been tied around her neck at the wedding ceremony in church by her husband, strung on with seven silken threads from the bridal sari. However the hospital staff did not know this. In fact the *tali* was so tiny that they did not see it. She also had a gold band on her finger. But there was no black-beaded mangalsutra that married Marati women wore. Who would pay her bills? 'Where's your husband?' they asked her roughly and more urgently, 'What's his name?' 'Joseph,' answered Teresa in a whimper of a voice, 'He works in Dongerkhadi in a chemical factory. Maybe he was asked to go back.'

The ward boy went back to the corridor bawling out, 'Joseph, husband of Teresa to report to the doctor.' Thambi shook Joseph. 'Achaya they're looking for you, some good news eh?' he winked. Joseph got up and said lazily, 'Yes? What's the matter? I am Joseph, husband of Teresa.' 'You're wanted by the doctor,' shouted the ward boy. 'Alright alright, I'm coming.' Joseph got up reluctantly. The other fathers to be, pacing up and down the corridor nervously, looked at him in amazement, as he walked by. 'Your wife's in labour and you're playing cards with your friends?' they asked him incredulously. Joseph gave them a slow wink.

'The trick is not to get anxious,' he said 'my mother delivered ten children like peas popping out from a pod. It takes some time for the first few. Women get used to it.'
He ambled off to see the doctor. Teresa had been shifted to the Labour room. The doctor looked grave.
'You wife looks anaemic,' he said. 'You will have to be very careful about her diet. I hope everything goes well for her.'

Joseph looked a little irritated. More expenses? He had just about managed to borrow a thousand rupees from his friend Sitaram for the hospital expenses, to be paid back on payday.
'She will need medicines, injections too,' the doctor said. Joseph shrugged his shoulders.
'I'm sure she'll manage. She's strong,' he said. Teresa would be able to look after herself. After all she was four years older than him. But she still looked so young. Joseph remembered how he had been smitten by her beauty at the village church fair in their village of Kavuukadu in Kerala where they had met. He was on home leave from the army. Teresa was fair and had soft, wavy hair, which she wore in a small bun at the nape of her neck. She was of middle height and slim. He was twenty-four. She was twenty-eight. She was still unmarried and at home, when they first met. She had wanted to become a nun and had joined as an aspirant in the Adoration convent in Kavuukadu. Her father had sold a field which grew cardamom and pepper, to pay the portion to the convent that the better off families sent with their daughters who joined the nunnery. But Teresa had been unwell at the convent with joint pains and a constant headache. The nuns did not want a

sick postulant on their hands. After two years, they regretfully told her that they did not think that she was wanted in the Lord's vineyard. When she returned home in some disgrace, her brother's wives made it quite clear that she was an unwelcome addition to the family's expenses.

Teresa took up typewriting and shorthand. After Joseph had met her at the church fair, he began meeting her secretly in the nearby town where she went for her typewriting classes. Later she got a job in Bombay. Joseph then took to visiting her there. They married when he left the army and got the job of a store keeper in a chemical factory. Teresa moved from her room in the YWCA, to the little two roomed tenement in Ulhasnagar, where Joseph got rooms cheap enough for them to stay. The first baby had been lucky for them since he got a promotion at work, the day she was born. Now the second one was on its way . . .

The baby was born a few minutes after Joseph left the doctor. It was another girl. Joseph was called back by Tara the nurse, to look at the baby. He looked disappointed. Teresa lay on the bed with her eyes closed, the little bundle beside her. It was a brown baby too, brown like him. Not fair like its mother. Unlucky for girls to be dark, he thought. He gave Teresa a peck on her cheek and went out.

'A girl,' he told his friends, 'let's go and get a drink.'
They went to a nearby bar and ordered a few rounds of drinks with khababs. Joseph took out the money from

his pocket and paid for the food with a flourish. It was good to feel the crisp notes in his pocket.

The next morning, he was back at the hospital.

'I say old girl,' he told Teresa, 'we're a little short of money, so if you feel ok and the doctor doesn't object why don't we just go home? It's the second baby, so it's not as bad as the first is it? It will save the rooming charges.'

Teresa got up weakly from the bed. She had just fed the baby.

'Alright Joseph,' she said.

She was worried about the child at home. They asked for the doctor's permission to leave. The doctor told them a little doubtfully that they could leave if they wanted to. But in fact he was relieved that they were leaving, since he wasn't sure that they would pay their hospital bills. Teresa said that she had a one-year-old baby at home.

'Then you should have waited a little before having another,' the doctor told Joseph curtly. But Joseph chuckled and winked at the doctor as he left the consulting room.

Joseph picked up the small shoulder-bag which held Teresa's tooth-brush and house-coat and handed it to her. She held the baby on the other shoulder. He did not want to carry the baby. Not quite the thing for a young man whom most strangers with marriageable daughters took to be an eligible bachelor and invited home readily enough. He had often laughed over such incidents with Teresa.

'The fellow was a supplier at the factory and he invited me home after work. The man and his wife just couldn't believe that I was a married man with a child!' he had chuckled, 'I just ate the ethaka boli and drank the tea that his wife gave me. Then they had asked me where I lived. When I said that I had to go home, my wife would be wondering why I was getting late, they looked so disappointed!' Now, he thought ruefully, there were *two* children, not just one.

They left the hospital together. His friends reached them home in a taxi. As they left Joseph called out, 'Remember cards tonight at eight at Nambisan's place.' It was too dull for a young man of twenty-six to be cooped up with a fretful woman and two crying infants. One deserved a little fun sometimes. Besides Teresa would understand. She was thirty years old after all. She was really quite capable of taking care of things herself. Now if she had been one of those weak, clinging vines, it would have been difficult. As soon as the children were a little older and could be put into a crèche, she could get a job in an office as a typist and their finances would improve. He strolled out of the house whistling and walked up to the corner pan shop for a packet of cigarettes. He was dying for a smoke.

ॐ ॐ ॐ

VOLUME II

A STRING OF WILD JASMINE

Samuel had just finished his bath. It was a hot Saturday afternoon in Delhi and he was thirsty. He saw the bottle of red Burgundy wine on the dining table. Sushil the pahadi servant boy had placed it there, with a napkin folded neatly on a quarter plate beside it. Samuel reached out for the wine and drank it straight from the bottle in one gulp, just as Rani entered the room. She looked at him contemptuously and took out a little crystal wine glass from the sideboard and half filled it. 'Don't drink it like that – like a drunkard,' she said in a low hiss, 'you only pour out a little wine and then you sip it slowly.'

'OK Memsahib.' Samuel replied in mocking tones and sat down to his lunch. *My head is bleddy but unbowed* he recited silently, remembering a scrap of poetry that floated into his mind, from his English language text book at college in Cochin. He had been a student of English Literature at Maharaja's College and later a teacher of English to uncomprehending village school boys in a Muslim school in Mallapuram.

Samuel was a short man. He was brown complexioned and his hairline was just beginning to recede. As he was a senior civil servant – he was a Joint Secretary in the Ministry of Forests, he was allotted a two bedroom apartment, in the prestigious Pandara Road officers' apartments. Samuel had married Rani as soon as he had left the civil service academy at Mussoorie, more out of economic compulsions than from a desire for connubial bliss. In this he was quite unlike the other men in the academy, who seemed to be intent on urgently abandoning their bachelor status in order to savour the joys of matrimony. Samuel had sold his IAS tag to the highest bidder, to Rani's father – Mathan Moolathottam Modalali – the landlord. The enormous dowry that Rani had brought with her, helped to buy his parents some of the creature comforts that they had done without all their lives.

❦ ❦ ❦

Samuel lived with his parents in a one-roomed, laterite stone cottage, in the village of Neerakattu in Alleppey. It had a small kitchen attached and a narrow front verandah. The house had only a cot for Samuel's father and a writing table and a chair at which Samuel studied for the civil service examination. The latrine was outside the house and was screened by the palm leaf matting around it. There was no running water in the latrine, instead, a brass *kindi* with its long spout was used to carry water.

"That Mathan Modalali is very keen on an IAS son-in-law,' Vavachan the village marriage broker said, as he sat down on the only cane chair in the verandah in Samuel's house. Hearing Vavachan speak, Samuel's mother came out of the house to see who it was who had come to see her husband. Her white mundu was messy with ash from the kitchen fire. When she saw that it was the marriage broker, she went back in and got him a cup of black coffee. They did not have any milk in the house. Samuel's father lay reclining on the long armed easy chair, with its striped, handloom cloth seat. His eyes were closed, with an air of tiredness. But Samuel's mother stood in the doorway to the inner room, leaning forward eagerly, her eyes gleaming and her attention rapt on every word that Vavachan let fall. Samuel sat negligently on the verandah ledge, contemplating the bright green paddy fields, hardly attending to what Vavachan said.

'Mathan Modalali has given me an ultimatum – I have to produce a list of eligible IAS boys for Rani within a week,' Vavachan said, laughing nervously. Mathan had summoned him, he said. He had reported to the landlord and stood quaking before him, his dog-eared, and worn out diary of names and addresses of eligible bachelors, almost slipping out from under his armpit. Mathan abused his neighbour Devasi, so puffed up with pride ever since his only son had cleared the Income Tax service examination.

But Vavachan was distraught. How could he, a small time village marriage broker, produce a suitable IAS boy, when the list of successful candidates did not have a Syrian Christian in it? And then there was the additional caveat that Mathan had stipulated – the boy had to be from an 'ancient' family – landowners of unblemished lineage. Not any poor, landless peasant's son. The Moolathottam family owned a thousand acres of rubber estates in Pallai. Rani was the only child of her parents, an heiress. Moolathottam also owned a chain of Jewellery shops known as 'Moolathottam Gems and Jewellery'.

Vavachan sipped the hot coffee and glanced at Samuel's mother. She seemed to be the only person interested in hearing about his encounter with Mathan Modalali. 'Kochamma,' said Vavachan, addressing Samuel's mother respectfully. Samuel's mother straightened up. Though she was poor, she was now the mother of an IAS officer who would soon startle the village out of its slumber, when he arrived with a flourish in his government car, with a flashing, red beacon. 'Mathan saar wants to get Rani married to an IAS officer. He thinks he can force Devasi to bend and write *Khsha* in the dust with his nose,' the marriage broker said, with a short disdainful laugh at Mathan's foolhardy ambitions. But he looked around hastily to see that no one else had heard him laugh.

In the end Mathan had agreed to the marriage broker's proposal for the alliance with Samuel. Rani was getting older and it was not likely that the next year's IAS examination would yield any better candidates for Rani's imperious hand in marriage. After all, only poor Malayali boys were studious and sat for the IAS examination. Most of the rich estate types were wastrels who rode around on bikes, wearing goggles and blue jeans and ogling girls who were on their way to college. The Kottayam *Ichayaans* usually spent two or three years in every class, graduated with a pass class at twenty-five and then gave up studying altogether. They preferred to sit in the verandah, with their glasses of toddy and fried fish, swapping largely untrue stories about the number of girls they had successfully enticed.

❦ ❦ ❦

Rani had graduated in Home Science at the Women's Christian College in Madras. She was slim and fair and an inch taller than Samuel. She always grumbled about Samuel's lack of a good height, which prevented her from wearing her four inch stilettos to the office parties that Samuel occasionally took her to. She knew both Chinese and Continental styles of cooking, in addition to the finer aspects of setting a table in style – how to make a duck for the table centrepiece from a green gourd, a carrot and a few cabbage leaves; how to bead purses; embroider saris and pillow cases in fine hand embroidery and do ikebana flower arrangements. Her homemade gooseberry wine was famous in Pallai. She played the piano and the veena and was an exponent of Bharatnatyam, having trained under the famous Guru Thamparam Krishnamoorthy. In the initial years of their life together, she had insisted on making Samuel miserable with bland continental food for his dinner, until he hinted to his mother-in-law, during their annual visit to Kerala, that he preferred homely *nadan* fare.

Rani looked down on him because his family was poor. They only had half an acre of coconut groves, which yielded thirty thousand coconuts every year. But the yields dwindled, as the trees aged and were not nourished with manure.

'Good manure these days is the price of gold,' Samuel's father grumbled petulantly, as he watched the trees slowly dying.

After he married Rani, Samuel took a bank loan and with a little help from his father-in-law, he built and furnished a bungalow with two bed rooms in Neerakattu for his parents. Rani often referred to it as, 'The house my father built for your parents.' Each time he smarted at the reference. But he could only be silent in the face of these barbs. He made up for it by being a tyrant at the office.

Rani dressed in the latest styles and she bought herself new salwar kameezes and saris every two weeks. Samuel continued with his spare and abstemious ways. He had just four pairs of trousers and five shirts. He wore each pair of clothes for two days and then washed and ironed them himself. Nobody was as surprised as he was, when he got the letter in the brown government envelope that informed him that he had cleared the IAS examination. There had been excitement in his class room and the headmaster had given invited him to his room and ordered a special cup of tea and called him 'sir'. 'Don't forget us sir when you grace your important chair,' he had said, already humble and bent, in an ingratiating half bow with folded hands.

Rani asked nothing of him and when she had borne him two sons, she put them both in her old public school at Lovedale. 'So that they turn out to have at least a little more starch in them than you,' she told him sarcastically.

She always complained that Samuel never took her out anywhere because he was afraid of spending money. It was true. Rani had expensive tastes. Once, early in their marriage, when he took her out to dinner, she insisted on eating only at the Oberoi and then she ordered an expensive grilled Lobster dish, with fried rice and two side dishes. She chose the most expensive dessert on the menu and ate it as though she had been starving. It was lucky for him that he had his credit card with him so that he could pay up the whopping bill of Two thousand rupees. It put him back by six months in cigarettes and evenings at the club, playing rummy with his friends. Smoking was his only vice. It relieved him of the tension from Rani's constant, high decibel tongue-lashing. He fled from it every evening to play cards with his friends.

♪ ♪ ♪

Samuel was agreeably surprised one morning to see that the Department of Personnel had sent him a lovely young girl as his Under Secretary. Preeti walked into his room, her transfer order in hand. The fragrance of jasmine flowers wafted into the room from the flowers entwined in her hair. She was neatly dressed in a sky blue chanderi cotton sari with a design of tiny dark blue paisleys. 'I've just joined today sir,' she said gravely. Samuel gave her an outline of her responsibilities and a few tasks for the day. He was again surprised when she reported to him at the end of the day, all the jobs but one done and the reason why she would only be able to complete the undone task the next day.

He discovered in time that she was a Hindu Punjabi and that she was a post graduate in Nuclear Physics. She had joined the Central Secretariat service as a section officer and had come on her first promotion to the Ministry of Forests. She always wore starched, cotton saris and a string of white Jasmine coiled into her hair. He was pleased to find that she was not silly but knowledgeable and efficient. He did not have to spend hours correcting her drafts painstakingly as he had to do with the other officers'. He just told her what he wanted and she had it all done and ready for his signature. She soon made herself indispensable. On the days she was absent, the office seemed out of gear and everyone knew that they were bound to have a rough time, as Samuel Saab would then be in a bad temper. Nobody else seemed to know where anything was kept.

There was a special presentation coming up that month. It was on the initiatives taken by the Ministry to stop the depletion of forest cover in the country. The UN envoy would be in attendance and the World Wild Life Fund authorities were also invited. They were considering a special project for the Ministry. Preeti devised a perfect presentation on her computer. Samuel only had to make one or two small corrections. She did all the work and then retired quietly into the background. He made the presentation and received fulsome praise from the Secretary himself. The Secretary Misra, did not know that it was the new Under Secretary in the Ministry, Preeti who had worked on the project. Samuel was thankful that he was lucky enough to have an assistant who did not want to reap the rich harvest of applause for herself and wangle an out-of-turn promotion or at least a nomination for a trip to Washington or London. It had taken all of his ingenuity to see that he was not dislodged by the Joint Secretary (Wild Life) from the trip to Johannesburg for the crucial meeting on Forest Wealth convened by the UN.

Samuel came home in high spirits, filled with the success of the presentation. Preeti had skilfully inserted a photograph of Misra inspecting forests in Karnataka, into the presentation . . . Misra had looked at him with approval, surprised that Samuel was such a computer buff. 'You must come with me for the meeting next month in Washington,' he had told Samuel.

Samuel strode into the house jauntily, for once feeling that he owned the place. There was a formal dinner party that evening at the Oberoi hotel in honour of the foreign delegates. Sushil, came in silently and placed a glass of water on the bedside table, as Samuel sat on the bed pulling off his socks. He was in the shower when Rani came in from her afternoon tea meeting with her friends. 'There's a party today at the Oberoi,' he shouted through the door.
'Why do you tell me these things at the last minute? Couldn't you have phoned?' she complained.
'I tried to phone you, but you weren't at home,' he answered. His voice was muffled through the sound of the water splashing.

Rani stomped off. When he came out of the bathroom towelling his hair, she sat in a huff at the writing table.
'I haven't a thing to wear,' she said crossly. 'I wish you'd told me a few days ago. I could have got a sari from the emporiums.'
'But you just got a new sari last week,' he remonstrated.

'Oh that – I wore it to Seema's house for her Ladies *Sangeet* Party for her niece. The marriage is next Friday,' she replied.

'None of that crowd will be there for this party,' he said trying to mollify her. He did not want to spoil his good mood with a quarrel.

Rani wore the new Orissa silk sari that she had worn in Kerala two months earlier, secure in the belief that no one at the evening's party would have seen her in it. It was a black silk with red and white motifs and a lovely woven border of white and red elephants. It had cost fifteen thousand rupees. He had been caustic then. Some poor family could have lived off that amount for at least ten months, he had remarked in an undertone. Rani had bristled.

'I've not ever come to you asking for any money from your sarkari pay package,' she had retorted sharply, 'and you've never bought me a thing other than that pitiful *mantrakodi* which you bought from the dowry money my father gave you.' Thankfully she did not now remember his remark and they reached the hotel without further quarrels, just in time before the more senior officers and the important guests arrived.

Preeti was already at the hotel seeing to the arrangements with the hotel staff. She looked at Samuel from a distance and nodded slightly to indicate that things were under control. She looked charming in a pale mauve Kashmiri silk, with an embroidered black border and the white jasmine in her hair. She had put kohl in her eyes and stuck a crimson, red, readymade bindi in the middle of her forehead. But he was relieved that she had the good sense not to linger around him in Rani's presence. Rani (like the Secretary Forests) wasn't quite aware about Preeti's role in the efficient management of the Ministry.

At dinner Samuel was privileged to be in the select circle of the Secretary, the Additional Secretary and the UN official. Then they seemed to want to go into a huddle by themselves. Samuel found himself in a corner with nobody around. He had finished his food and he held out his empty plate for his wife to pick up like a dutiful Indian wife. But Rani looked away and then wandered off to talk to Mr. Heathcliff from the World Wildlife Fund. She told him that she was quite good at photography and that she had a bunch of rare photographs which might interest him. Mr. Heathcliff smiled down at her from his great height and thought, 'there's a beautiful woman wasted on a wimp.'

Samuel suddenly became aware of his own outstretched hand, holding out the plate and he felt foolish. He took the plate to the tub for used plates in the corner of the room. Preeti had been watching him and she felt the snub delivered by Rani, as though it was a snub directed at herself. She hurried forward and took the plate from Samuel and deposited it in the tub. Then she disappeared back into the crowd.

ॐ ॐ ॐ

The next week Samuel had to tour the Gir forest. He asked Preeti to accompany him. It would save him the trouble of taking notes he said and they could write out the report much faster when they came back. So they formed an Inspection Party of two and a tour plan was drawn up for their visit.

Their train from Delhi arrived late in the afternoon at the Junagadh railway station, which sprang into life when the train came in. Vendors selling tea and samosas advertised their wares in a loud cacophony. Muscular coolies jumped into the train and snatched the luggage from the passengers before they could decide whether or not they wanted a porter. After a short stop for a bath and a cup of tea at the Junagadh resthouse, Samuel and Preeti took the dusty one hour drive by car to the dak bungalow at Sasan Gir.

The dak bungalow was a grey stone structure with a roof of brick red tiles, perched on a little hillock in the middle of the jungle. A stream ran in front of it. Grey stone steps lead up to the veranda which went around the bungalow. It had a half wall of white lattice grills. Bougainvillea and white rambler roses, climbed up the grills. There were trees and unruly bushes all around, as the forest almost crowded in. The heady fragrance of the Champa flower hung in the air. The mali had tried to keep a neat front lawn and an orderly bed of gerberas, petunias and daisies.

Samuel climbed the mossy stone steps of the dak bungalow, followed by Preeti. They entered the wood panelled lounge which had a high ceiling of polished teak wood. On one side of the walls the panelling unevenly displayed varnished wood samples of the many trees in the jungle with typed paper labels on them – bamboo, teak, ber, gulmohor, banyan, peepul, mango. The rooms were cool and restful.

The Chief Conservator, Richard D'Sousa, was there to meet them at the dak bungalow, with two of his staff. He gave them both a bouquet of fresh flowers and a neat folder of notes about the Gir forest. As it was already seven in the evening, he left them, promising to return early the next morning.

They had a simple meal of dal, mashed potatoes, rotis and a little rice. They were too tired to talk during the meal in the small dining room. Samuel fell asleep as soon as he lay on the bed, with its curtain of white mosquito netting gone brown with grime. He had been exhausted by the rattling train journey, especially as he had got a narrow side berth, instead of the more comfortable berths in the main area of the air-conditioned coach.

The next morning the bearer laid out the breakfast table in the veranda. The air was balmy. A koel called in the bushes and there was the cheerful twittering of myriad birds. A cool breeze rustled in the trees. The morning sky was clear and blue, unlike the smoggy Delhi air. It had rained the night before and there was a hint of wetness in the air.

Preeti was already seated at the breakfast table when he came in. She was dressed simply and tastefully in a pista green, cotton Lucknowi sari. It had cost only five hundred rupees at the Hastkala sale at Khadi Bhandar. Samuel looked at her appreciatively and smiled indulgently, as she looked at him with soft eyes, like a dog waiting to be patted. As he sat down, he asked her conversationally whether she had had a good night. She said, 'Yes sir,' and and buttered him a piece of toast which she held out to him. He took it from her hand gratefully.

She carefully poured out his tea for him, with a pursed under lip as she concentrated on not spilling any tea into the saucer. Samuel eyed her with an amused look. She knew that he liked his tea with only one cube of sugar. She put in a cube and stirred it before handing it over to him. She then made a cup of tea for herself. She buttered him some more toast. While he normally ate only two dry toasts with an egg – under Rani's stern gaze, he now ate four buttered toasts.

'I've overeaten,' he said in mock dismay and they went out giggling, like a pair of school children. He opened the car door for her to get in with a courtly air and said 'After you,' with a little self conscious bow. He stood tall beside Preeti's five feet two inches. Of course it helped that he had artificially raised heels in his shoes, which made him an inch taller than his height of five feet and six inches.

They set out for the inspection tour of the forest and D'Sousa pointed out with pride the newly forested patches of Teak and Ber. He said that they had tried a novel scheme with success. 'The Madaris have been most cooperative, Sir,' he said, puffing out his chest, as he launched on the story of his successful efforts at conservation. Unfortunately for Richard D'Sousa, just then Samuel's sharp eye detected a clearing in the woods and he resolutely went further to investigate it. The junior forest officials looked evasive and tried to stall him, with suggestions that the way was too long and tortuous. Samuel was quietly insistent and walked ahead and found an area of freshly cut wood. It was with a feeling of grim satisfaction that he ordered the suspension of the officials in charge of the area.

The foresters were subdued for the rest of the inspection. But the sighting of a herd of fleeing, spotted deer excited Samuel. The forest had suddenly turned noisy with monkeys chattering, the grunting of wild pigs and frantic birds calls that rent the air. The reason for the commotion became apparent soon enough when near at hand, they traced a lion's pug marks. But though they followed the track some considerable distance, the lion eluded them.

They returned to the bungalow exhausted and hungry. They had only had a picnic lunch of sorts in the forest, sitting in the jeep. The Assistant Forester had brought them a few squashed vegetable sandwiches and a thermos of tea. They had planned on returning to the dak bungalow for lunch. But it well past lunch time when they came back after the futile attempts to track the Gir Lion.

They sank gratefully into the easy chairs in the long veranda. The bearer brought in the tea in a tray, with a porcelain pot in a pretty red checked tea cosy and pots of milk and sugar. It was pleasantly cool. Bees hummed busily and birds winged their way home. After tea, D'Sousa excused himself from further attendance as he and his assistant were required to attend the meeting convened by the Chief Minister the next day at Gandhinagar. The district officials also sought permission to leave, since they were staying at another rest house fifteen kilometres away. They promised to return the next morning at nine.

As they sat sipping their tea, admiring the brilliant setting sun, Samuel suggested that they should sit in his room and finish off the report together. That way they would save time, instead of waiting till they got to Delhi. Preeti agreed. They would not forget any important details when the matter was fresh in their heads, she said.

Preeti excused herself prettily and went into her room. She switched on the big, old-fashioned geyser in the bathroom. The huge bathroom, with a separate dressing room, was as large as the bedroom in the tiny, two-roomed flat, in which she lived in Karol Baug in New Delhi. She washed her long black hair and had a refreshing shower in the warm water. She dried her hair with the frayed, Turkish bath towel, which hung on the bathroom rack. Then she wrapped the towel around her head and sat down to pluck her eyebrows at the dressing-table. It was a large, solid, teak wood table.

A few minutes later, she looked at her watch and drew in her breath in consternation. It was already seven forty-five. It wouldn't do to be late. Samuel Sir was such a stickler for punctuality. She dressed quickly, slipping into a simple off-white, khadi salwar kameez and parted her hair in the middle since it was still damp. She put on a pair of simple, two-strapped, leather sandals and knocked at Samuel's door.

'Come in,' he said. He sat in the armchair, looking fresh from his bath, in a white Jubba and dothi – his normal home wear. He had a string of wild white Jasmine in his hands, which he had asked the mali to weave. 'Here's some Jasmine for my Jasmine,' he said playfully. A smile of delight lit up Preeti's face and she wound the string of flowers into her hair. They ordered a tray of tea and sat cosily writing down facts and figures.

'The main problem in forest areas is – the local population,' Samuel said. 'What should be the proper policy of government towards tribal people in forests?'

He looked at the copy of the old note drafted by the Under Secretary, who had been Preeti's predecessor. "Gir is an area infested by pastoral tribal people known as Madharis," it began. Samuel frowned. An unfortunate beginning. As though the tribal population were some sort of vermin. It would make a very bad impression on the World Wild Life chaps, who felt that tribal populations needed to be protected and their lifestyles secured, just as much as those of tigers and antelopes. Some of the programmes on TV by the National Geographic even had special episodes on the daily lifestyles of tribal communities, just as they did features on rare animals and birds.

Though the aboriginals in Gir felt that the forest belonged to them, the foresters felt that they were intruders who helped to deplete the forest. They often argued that the aboriginals colluded with poachers who made them hack the teak trees for a small compensation. But the forest officials conveniently forgot that it was they who looked the other way, when poachers entered the forest with their vehicles and sophisticated saws. There had been a forest ranger whose brother had been a prosperous timber merchant . . . The police had also booked a case against the brother of an MLA who had a large saw mill just outside the forest reserves. A merchant had been caught red-handed shooting black buck in the forests in Karnataka but by the time the case came up for hearing, he had become a Member of Parliament and he said that he had been framed in the matter by a jealous rival. A hapless villager by the same name of Veeralingam Ramanappa was forced to record a confessional statement which proved his guilt beyond all doubt and he was jailed . . .

Samuel pursed his lips and highlighted in yellow the figure of forest depletion in the Gir area. The figure looked suspiciously small. The Under Secretary had taken the figure from the report of the Chief Conservator. Some forester had tried to cover up the extent of poaching and how slack he had been and the Chief Conservator had merely put his signature to the report. No verification. The problem was essentially one of sloth. If you thought all your job entailed was to camp in the forest, feasting on the rabbit meat and khababs of wild fowl and the bottle of scotch the local warden brought you with an oily smile . . .

His train of thought was suddenly brought to a halt by the sound of sobbing. Preeti was crying. Samuel was concerned. It turned out that she was worried about her old mother who was sick and alone at home. Preeti's father had died when she was twenty-three. Only Preeti's younger brother, Amulya, who was studying for his degree in Arts, was now at home with his mother. Samuel comforted her and suddenly he found her in his arms. He always swore, upon his dead mother's head, that he had never intended to seduce her . . .

ॐ ॐ ॐ

In New Delhi he continued seeing Preeti in motels. When they were together he called her "My little Jasmine". He always stopped at the flower vendor near the Mahalakshmi temple at the corner of Nityanand Avenue and bought a string of Jasmine flowers wrapped in *palas* leaves, bound with twine. In the motel room, he undid the parcel and wound the flowers into Jasmine's hair. He buried his face into her luxuriant tresses, sniffing the fragrance of her young body. He could never understand how he had earned this incredible happiness. It made him a gentle lover. Her trusting innocence aroused every protective instinct in him. He often left small notes for her, addressed to "J". Sometimes she stayed on for extra "work" in the office, when all the staff had left and Samuel told the impatient peons that Preeti would lock up the doors and hand over the keys of the office to the chowkidar.

It was a perfect arrangement . . . Until Preeti dropped the bombshell one morning. Her family had arranged her marriage with a boy from her own community, she said. He was a computer engineer and he worked in

Chandigarh. Samuel was jerked out of his complacency. 'Preeti! How *could* you?' he asked her in agonised accents. But she said in a calm voice, 'I like you sir, but I have to think of my future.' He had expected a torrent of heartbroken sobs. When he imagined the scene of their final parting, he had always thought of her as clinging to him, while he had to comfort her with false promises of meeting her soon. Her stoic acceptance of their imminent separation, made him suddenly feel that life without her – a life in which she would live happily as someone else's wife, an unbearable thought.

Samuel was forced to make a choice. He thought quickly. He chose Preeti. He filed for divorce. He sold the bungalow constructed for his parents in Alleppy and gave the money to Rani as alimony. He got his father to live with him in his quarters at Pandara Road. And he married Preeti at a simple function at the local marriage registrar's office, attended only by a few of his close colleagues.

꽁 꽁 꽁

After the divorce, Rani continued to live in Delhi. She opened her own boutique of exclusive saris and salwar kameezes and called it *Rani's*. As she had often told Samuel, the only reason that she lived with him was because she couldn't abide Pallai. It had nothing more than the Ammachis in mundus and gold bordered *kavanis* held in place by a gilt brooch at the shoulder of their T shirt like, hip length V-neck blouses. They gossiped in the church compound, discussing their stomach ailments. Pallai was a place where no one had even heard of Ritu Mankaad's special durries.

Rani held her famous coffee parties with unabashed elan, despite Samuel's absence in her life. Senior civil servants, musicians, failed politicians and persons with literary aspirations, thronged her court. She was allotted a bungalow on Baba Khadak Singh Marg by a special dispensation, since a senior Malayali minister Poonamkavil Radhakrishnan had recommended her case to the Prime Minister. At one of her parties, a friend brought along Rudraswami Gurumurthy, a foreign service officer who was looking for a trophy wife after his divorce from his first wife. Rani married Gurumurthy.

Mathan was forced to accept the situation. He was surprised that his daughter had preferred to live in Paris with an "unbeliever" and had so willingly given up Samuel. But since she seemed happier with her second choice, he did not make any serious objection to her marriage to Gurumurthy. In any case, he realised, his objections had no effect at all on Rani. She did exactly as she pleased. Devasi came to visit Mathan every other Sunday. They sat drinking whiskey together in the verandah, a plate of fried beef on the side table between them. Devasi was forced to acknowledge defeat. Although her IAS husband had abandoned Rani, her new husband, though not a Kottayam *Ichayan*, was the hot shot Indian ambassador to France. His photograph appeared in the Malayalam papers with accounts of the progress of Indo-French cooperation in building a new housing complex in Cochin, using French pre-fabrication technology. The accounts invariably ended with a small reference to Gurumurthy's Malayali wife Rani, the daughter of Mathan Moolathottam from Pallai. When Rani and Gurumurthy had visited Pallai on one of their rare visits, they gifted Devasi a fake Pierre Cardin wristwatch made in Bangkok. Devasi was very proud of his "expensive" foreign watch "made in Paris" as its label proclaimed and he never failed to check the time on it several times, as he spoke to his neighbours after Sunday mass, about the importance of the French connection for India.

ॐ ॐ ॐ

THE COMPLICATED LIFE OF MRS. CLARAMMA THOMMEN

Mrs. Claramma Thommen came to see me one day in my office at the Urban Development Authority of Greater Raniganj where I was the Project Director. When the peon brought in her chit, announcing that she was "an NGO working for the uplift of people", I told him to send her in right away. I was in a hurry to turn Raniganj overnight from the smelly, open drained, small market town that it was, into a modern metro and I wanted to involve as many of the local residents as possible, since I felt that the dull eyed, silver haired Chief Engineer and the wily looking Administrative Manager in the Development Authority, had only lame excuses to offer for the huge list of undone tasks in the township.

Mrs. Thommen entered my office with a clack of her high heeled sandals. She wore a dark blue, Orissa ikkat sari, with a pretty design of woven black peacocks on her sari pallu. She had short hair, with a side parting and she had stuck a red plastic bindi in the middle of her forehead. Her large fleshy nose set in her round face, had a little, gold nose stud in it. She had small, black eyes which darted all around my office like a sharp, intelligent animal taking in its surroundings. When she began speaking, I noticed that she spoke through her nose, with a strong Malayali accent.

She said that she wanted to work for the uplift of street children. She had made a lot of money exporting grass mats and wooden handicrafts to the US. She now felt impelled to give something back to society. She had been to the retreat at Pota and during the sermons by Father Simon, she had felt Christ's call. She had been too selfish and self centred till then. Her first project was to take the street children of Gunjanghat – the little satellite town of the metropolis of Raniganj, for a day's picnic to the nearby picturesque hill station of Sambapur. At the end of the day, the happy children were to be addressed by the local Member of the Legislature and be given a bag of provisions each – rice, lentils, sugar, milk powder and tea leaves. They were to wear T-shirts printed with a picture of three monkeys covering their eyes, ears and lips, with the words 'See no evil, Hear no evil, Speak no evil' written on them.

'When I heard about your generous nature, I simply had to come and see you,' Mrs. Thommen gushed.

She told me the story of her life, how she narrowly escaped death just because of a wrong prescription by her gynaecologist. She had to spend six lacs of rupees in Escorts hospital after consuming a pill worth two rupees. She then told me about her social work project and requested me to lend her one of our staff buses, to transport the children to Sambapur, which was sixty kilometres away. She also wanted the Development Authority to contribute to the cost of the pandal needed to protect the children from the hot April sun as they awaited the MLA's arrival. 'I could put up a banner which reads *with best wishes from Greater Raniganj Development Authority,*' she assured me. 'The public would then know that the Development Authority also cared for street children.'

We requested the local MLA Mr. Haribau Thakkar to be present at the grand function for street children in Sambapur. The cards were printed and we were in readiness for the event. Life was dull in the small town of Raniganj. The function for street children provided us with a little respite from the monotony of our lives. But four days before the event, Mrs. Thommen came to see me. She was in tears.

'Madam,' she said, 'Everybody has let me down. The businessman who had promised to contribute the T-shirts has now backed out and the trader, who promised to give the provisions for the children, is also away for the whole of the week. The hotelier who had agreed to pay for the snacks for the children is now saying he has to be paid five thousand rupees beforehand and that he cannot do it free.' I was a little taken aback.

I rang for my Social Service Officer, the efficient Miss Molly Braganza. Molly came in briskly and when she saw Mrs. Thommen, she sniffed. It was clear that she did not like her. But Molly soon contacted several charitable trusts in Raniganj and persuaded them to contribute to the cost of the snacks, provisions and the T-shirts.

On the day of the function we reached Sambapur a little in advance. I was embarrassed to see that Mrs. Thommen had put up a banner, which read: "Hearty Welcome to Ms. Remini Iyer, Munificent Project Director, GRDA." 'You should have put up a banner welcoming the MLA,' I told Mrs.Thommen feeling a little foolish, 'Please take that banner down before anyone else sees it.' They hastily took down the banner before the MLA arrived. Mrs. Thommen's Public Relations Officer bawled at the unruly children. The MLA came and made a speech about the importance of children. They were the hope of the future, he said.

The function was a grand success and made it to the banner headlines in the *Raniganj Daily Mail* – a paper which was published only every week, despite its title. There was a photograph of the Honourable Haribau Thakkar making his speech with his Gandhi cap slightly askew, since he had been buffeted by the crowd of children and their parents who had taken advantage of the opportunity of the meeting to present him with petitions about the leaking roofs of the township houses in Raniganj, the bad drainage, the lack of water and the need for a shopping complex. They also complained about the truancy of the local government school teacher who was absent for the most part of the week. They expressed their unhappiness that the government dispensary did not stock any medicines other than family planning tablets, condoms and loops. The Medical Officer in charge merely gave them distilled water injections for every ailment, they said agitatedly. What would happen to them and their childrens, if this state of affairs persisted, they demanded. The MLA looked visibly moved by their plight and wiped the perspiration from his forehead with a large checked handkerchief. He had obtained a stay from the Health Minister to the transfer of his wife's brother's son-in-law's brother to Raniganj as Chief Medical Officer. Raniganj lacked several basic amenities, it would be impossible for his family to live there his kinsman had said while pleading for the posting to be stayed. He had with great difficulty just secured admission for his two children to the prestigious St. John's convent school in Rokada. So now there was no one posted at Raniganj as CMO.

The MLA took all the letters of complaint and dissatisfaction and promised to look into them and handed over the letters to me, asking for a detailed report on each and every item. 'Especially explain me why there is no any medical service in Raniganj, which is justifiably so, making the people's condition so pitiable and objectionable,' he said, making a strenuous effort to speak in English, since he had been informed that I was a south Indian officer, who was not fluent in Hindi.

The next Saturday was a holiday and I was sitting in bed looking at the snapshots Mother had sent from home. My twenty year old brother Subramaniyam posed smirking beside his brand new Hero Honda. I smiled at a picture of our cat Smoochy with her new batch of six kittens. Just then the telephone rang. It was Claramma Thomman. She was sobbing. Her Public Relations Officer Miss Ritoo had made her threatening phone calls, she said. Claramma had not paid her the entire amount that she had promised for event management, since she had not organised the benefactors properly. They had all dropped off at the last moment and she reminded me that it was I who had helped her out then. The PRO had only come on the day of the function and yelled into the mike. Claramma had paid her five thousand rupees, instead of the ten thousand rupees that she had promised her. Now Miss Ritoo was threatening to have her beaten up by goondas if she didn't pay her the entire amount. 'Why don't you just file a complaint with the police?' I asked. Claramma was silent for a moment. 'I'm going to issue Miss Ritoo a lawyer's notice for damages for breach of contract,' she mumbled. 'Do that. It's the right thing to do,' I told her and put down the receiver.

Claramma called me again in the evening the next day. 'Please, Please, Miss Iyer, please call up the Police Commissioner,' she told me, her voice trembling with fear. 'There's a Police Inspector outside my door and Miss Ritoo is with him. My son has gone out and they will beat him up if he returns just now. Please help me,' she pleaded.

I did not fancy telephoning the Police Commissioner, asking him to send back the Police Inspector who was at Mrs. Thommen's door. But I told Claramma to open her front door and that I would talk to the Inspector. It turned out that he was only a constable and not an Inspector. Miss Ritoo had complained to him and induced him to accompany her to Mrs. Thommen's house.

'You can't harass people in their homes,' I reasoned with the constable, 'Unless you have a warrant you can't arrest her or compel her to go to the police station.' The constable was suitably chastened and left her house. There was no news from Mrs. Thommen after that.

A month later, I was sitting by my bedroom window. It was a clear sunny day in May. The Gulmohor tree, on the street outside was laden with flaming red flowers. In my lap was a letter from my friend Kaushik, who was the District Magistrate of Porbandabad. Claramma was all smiles as she walked into my living room through the open front door. She had brought me a little present she said and unwrapped a pretty piece of English china – a small gold and brown hedgehog. But it was expensive. I remembered that the British Airways in-flight duty free shop on the London – Bombay flight had priced it at forty pounds. 'It's very nice, but I'm sorry I can't keep this,' I told her regretfully. Claramma looked disappointed. Then she told me all about her latest project. It was – "Save the Street-child". She wanted to have a mobile school for street children. I was interested in the proposal and we discussed several possibilities for funding the project. Then Claramma told me that she was shifting her residence from her present one. The landlord had threatened to throw out her belongings if she didn't vacate the flat in the next two days.

'But what does he have against you?' I remonstrated.

'Nothing,' she sniffed. 'He has just come to know that I am a single woman living with my only son here and so he feels that he can take advantage of me,' she said.

'But you're paying your rent on time?' I asked.

'Yes of course. He's got six months advance rent with him,' she said.

Claramma shifted in a hurry to another house. It was a crumbling, small cottage by a park and she had to get it repaired. When she got it ready, she invited me home for a cup of tea.

'How's the house?' I asked her, as I sat in her tiny sitting room. The sofa barely had space between it and the wooden teapoy. A glass cupboard stood squeezed in a corner, filled with books.

She exchanged a significant glance with her son Nathan, a small nondescript looking boy-man with a drooping moustache and shoulder length, mousy hair, tied with a ribbon.

'It's O.K. umm. But . . . yesterday we found a horrible, black, snake on the front door step,' she said. 'We're so scared especially when the lights go out. The power supply is so undependable here. I'm scared to wake up in the night and go to the bathroom, in case I find a snake crawling up the door. You see the park is such a jungle and it's so near the edge of town – it's practically a forest out there. There's a nest of snakes in the park.'

Claramma spent the next few weeks getting her house made snake proof. She closed all the openings in the bungalow and fixed wire meshing near the drainpipes in the bathroom. She also bricked up the low French windows and made them smaller, with frames that fitted into the ledges snugly. She had the compound cemented all around and cut away the under growth and the wild bushes in her garden.

I went on training to Delhi and was back only after a month. As I entered the hall and flopped down on the sofa, tired after the two-hour flight, the telephone rang. It was Claramma. She told me that her new landlady, an East Indian Christian, had come to the house and had surveyed the repairs that she had got done. The landlady had never bothered to replace even a broken window pane and now that the house looked cute and livable, she felt that she could easily get a higher rent from another tenant. So she had stood on the pavement abusing Mrs. Thommen and accusing her of spoiling her house. Hearing the commotion the whole neighbourhood came out of their houses. The landlady had demanded the immediate payment of her rent.

'But didn't you pay her?' I asked.

'Of course I did. But she wants advance money. Five thousand rupees. My father will be sending me the money next month. He has gone on tour to our factory units in Karnataka,' she said.

There was an uncomfortable silence. Did she expect me to tell her that I would lend her five thousand rupees? She also said that her landlady had taken away the gas cylinder, which she had earlier promised that Mrs. Thommen could use. Now Claramma had nothing to cook her food with.

'I wish someone would lend me a microwave just for a few days,' she said. I remembered her exclaiming over the new microwave that I had purchased when she had visited me the last time. There was another awkward pause. Claramma waited expectantly.

'Buy a kerosene stove till you get your own connection,' I told her shortly. Claramma rang off after a pause and a sad sigh. I put the phone back on its stand feeling ungenerous and unfeeling.

My old school friend Mrs. Ram rang up shortly thereafter to ask me whether there was anyone who would adopt her two-year-old boxer. It was too sad, she said. It wasn't cheerful. It moped around the house and it made you morose just to look at it. I thought of Mrs. Thommen and her son. I could make it up to them for being mean about not lending them my micro-wave. When I spoke to Mrs. Thommen about the dog, she jumped at the idea. She collected it from Mrs. Ram the very next day. The boxer just trotted up to her son as soon as it saw Nathan and went home with him.

The following week I went to see how the dog was getting on in its new home. As I was petting Batty, Claramma told me that she had been to a picnic with Mrs. Ram and her friends.
'Which Mrs. Ram?' I inquired.
'You know your friend who gave me Batty,' she answered. Mrs. Ram though divorced was a friendly soul, she said.

I asked Claramma cautiously about her own husband.
'Oh we don't get along,' she declared in a matter of fact voice. She said that her father had been a high court judge. He hailed from Cochin. Her mother was a famous poetess. They had met and fallen in love. But her mother had got seriously sick when Claramma was only fifteen. The doctors had given up hope. So her mother had wanted her to be married before she died. Her mother had been a Jacobite. They could not

find a good Jacobite boy willing to marry her. So they settled on a poor Latin Christian boy from Cochin. His grandfather had been a low caste fisherman before he had converted to Christianity. But Lucas was good at his studies and Mrs. Thommen married her seventeen year old groom when she was sixteen. Thereafter Mrs. Thommen's father sent Lucas to London to study Medicine.

When he came back to India, Lucas had acquired distinctly *propah* manners. He insisted on eating only rice and ice-cream. Indian food was too greasy and spicy and did not agree with him, he said. He only ate with a fork and a knife and he insisted on being given a finger bowl after every meal. He made fun of Claramma when she scooped up the rice from her plate with her fingers. But when he went to Cochin to his own broken down family thatched roof hut, he ate *kappa puzhuka* and fish curry with the fiery, red gravy with relish. He also ate everything that he professed to abhor and licked his fingers as well, Claramma told me scornfully. He had numerous relatives and their monetary demands were endless. He always gave them his money. He also sold Claramma's jewellery and property and gave away the money to his impoverished relatives.

They had had a child when Claramma was seventeen. But Claramma had not wanted to be burdened with his upbringing. Her mother who had fortunately lived on for four years more, devoted herself to caring for the child. After her mother's death, Claramma put the child in a boarding school. Thus he had grown up deprived of his parents' love and he had a peculiar frightened look all the time. Claramma had reclaimed him as her son after he had completed his course of studies and graduated as a doctor and now she would not let him out of her sight.

Claramma herself suffered a severe shock when her mother died. She felt that she was alone in the world and that there was no one she could rely on. She clung to her father, going with him everywhere. Sometimes she got up at night and checked whether her father was alive and breathing in his bedroom. Her father had taken over the management of her factories after his retirement from court. She had now come to Raniganj because her psychiatrist had told her that she must try living independently from her father. Otherwise she would suffer another shock when *he* died. Her father was already seventy, she said. Claramma's account of her misfortunes, did not somehow strike a chord of sympathy in me. I was a little sceptic – how could one person have accumulated so many miseries in life? I hastily left her house saying that I had to look into some papers that I had got from the office.

It was about this time that I realised that I needed a good maid around the house to manage things for me. With my demanding work at the Development authority I just wasn't able to manage my home and I often had only an omelette and bread for dinner. Mrs. Thommen told me that she had just the right person for me. Her father no longer needed their very competent servant Rukmi at home. Rukmi would be able to look after me very well, she promised. She would see that Rukmi set out for Raniganj that very week. When I

rang Claramma two weeks later and inquired about
Rukmi, she told me that her father had just set out
for their factory at Madras. He would be travelling by
train from there to the outlet at Bangalore and then
take a train to Delhi. He would soon be in Raniganj,
she said, with Rukmi. The next time she rang me up to
say that her father was held up in Madras with a fever
and that he would resume his tour when he was better.
Thereafter he had got all right but he had to rush to
Coimbatore to their factory there, as some workers had
filed a petition in the Labour Court, asking for higher
wages. I felt a bit awkward about calling her up after
that. There was always a long story regarding another
unexpected delay in her father's arrival.

For many months thereafter I did not hear from
Claramma. Then one day Mrs. Ram rang me up.
'That Mrs. Thommen you introduced me to is a fine
cheat,' she said curtly. I was a little taken aback.
'But you only gave away your dog to her,' I said, 'what
did she do?'
'Well she wormed her way into my friendship alright.
And she borrowed small sums from me. Then one day
she said her landlady was harassing her and she begged
me to let her have ten thousand rupees to pay her and
that she would pay it back when her father came from
Madras. She then borrowed another fifteen thousand,
saying that her father was seriously sick and couldn't
reach anyone for help so she had to send it to him. Now
she refuses to talk to me and doesn't even answer the
phone.'

A month later Claramma came to see me at home in the evening. It was getting to be dark and the road outside was empty of traffic. Claramma wore a crumpled cotton sari. She looked tired and worn out as she sat in the shadows of my sitting room. A long sliver of evening sunlight from a small chink in the curtains rested on her forehead like a spotlight. She was sweaty and the eye-black she had put on her eyebrows had streaked, making her look like a witch. 'I need a thousand rupees urgently,' she sobbed, 'I have to save my son's life. He is dangerously ill and his blood count has gone so low. I have to buy platelets. My father has not yet got back and the court has frozen my bank accounts. My PRO has gone to court about her dues. She just walked into my office and stole my digital signature and computerized receipts and she misappropriated donations in my name from many companies. Now the companies are asking me back for their money since the project has not yet come up. They don't believe in me when I tell them that a cyber crime was committed by a cunning ex-employee. The police also do not know how to handle this cyber crime. And now my son is dying and there is no one I can turn to for help,' she said, tears streaming down her haggard face. I wordlessly took out a thousand rupees that was all I had to last me till the month end and gave it to her.

Claramma came again to see me six months later, one morning in December. She looked lean and defeated.
'My father died in Coimbatore,' she said, looking sick with worry, 'and I have to rush down for the funeral. I don't have a single rupee with me. I can give you this gold chain, till I return you your money. Can you please

give me five thousand rupees?' I had just got my salary. I went to the steel almirah and took out five thousand rupees, which was kept for the month's groceries. Claramma took the money eagerly and left hurriedly.

Mrs. Thommen did not return me the money even after many months had gone by. A servant answered my telephone calls. Claramma did not return my calls. Later an answering machine responded to my attempts to contact her. In the end I took the chain she had given me, to a jeweller in the Sonar Baug quarter of the bazaar to be tested. The jeweller rubbed the chain on the touchstone and looked at me as though I were a cheat. 'This is just imitation jewellery Behen ji,' he said testily and flung it at me contemptuously.

I took the chain feeling embarrassed and walked thoughtfully down the road. Was Claramma a cheat or was she just very unfortunate? Did she deliberately lie to me? As I turned to cross the road to my car, an approaching police van slowed down. A hand waved at me from the grilled windows of the van. I heard a familiar voice say, 'Remini Iyer please stop.' It was Claramma Thommen. She was weeping and her eyes were red. She said that she was being arrested in the false cheating case filed by the companies that had funded the van for the mobile school. She handed me a letter and requested me to contact her advocate Anthony D'Mello who had an office at Rijwaan Gulley. As the police van sped away, I read Claramma's letter.

Dear Remini,
I am sorry that I could not give you back your money despite my best intentions. I lost both my father as well as my son and now I am alone in the world. I wanted to do some good works in this world before I pass away, as we all pass this way only once. But somehow all my plans have got derailed. I will return you your money as soon as I get out of this court matter. Only please do me a favour. Poor Batty is alone at the house. Please take him home and look after him for me. Also please give my lawyer Rs 1000 as his fees. Otherwise he will not make my bail application. I will certainly pay you back when I am out. Please help me as you are my only friend in the world.

Affectionately,
Claramma

I read the letter over once again. I saw her face in my mind's eye, her eyes red with crying and the eye black streaked over her eyelids. I went to Claramma's house. I found the door key under the flower pot near the door step where she always kept it. A loud woof greeted me and Batty jumped at me as I opened the front door. The afternoon paper was deposited on the step and the headlines caught my attention. I picked up the paper. "High court Judge warns against con woman claiming to be his daughter," said the head lines. The report went on to read – "Former High Court Judge Kurian J Kurian warned the public that a woman who posed as his daughter and claiming to be a businesswoman had duped many gullible women of their money and their valuables. She usually struck up a friendship with single women and then borrowed money for various domestic emergencies from them and vanished. She had an accomplice – a young man who pretended to be her son, or her brother . . ."

I took Batty home with me and gave the dog a meal of bread and milk. Then I rang up advocate D'Mello and requested him to file a bail application for Ms Claramma Thommen. I asked him to send his clerk to collect his fees from my house. 'All right,' said Anthony D'Mello and promised to visit Claramma in the police lockup at Chinchwad police station. After a short pause he asked me how I was connected to Mrs. Thommen. I did not speak for a few minutes as I considered my reply. Then I told him that I was her only friend and that she had no one else in the world.

ॐ ॐ ॐ

NOTES FROM THE MARGIN

Shiva Shambo from the Sindustan Administrative Sterling Services (known as the SASS) had just been posted by the DOP (the Department of Personnel), as Deputy Secretary at the Sindustan Science Commission in New Ashokapur. The Commission's pooled staff car for Deputy Secretaries dropped him off at the nineteen storey glass and steel office of the Commission at Parliament Street. Shiva got out of the car briskly and walked into the building. He rode the elevator to the nineteenth floor and paused outside the door of the Additional Secretary, Pissapati Parmahans Chaturvedi, known in the secretariat as 'Old Pisspot'. Pissapati's vinegar and hot tar tongue did not exactly endear him to the secretariat staff. The lady PA Ms Subbhalakshmee, who wore an outsized red Usha Uthoop bindi, looked up enquiringly at him.

'Shiva Shambo, SASS, Southrashtra cadre. I'm the new DS,' Shiva said briefly, 'Can I see the boss?' He took out a pocket comb and combed his hair swiftly and gave it a final pat, before restoring the comb to his pocket, while the PA informed the Additional Secretary that the new DS wanted an audience with him. Ms Subbhalakshmee told him that he was allowed entry into the Presence. Shiva took a deep breath, knocked on the door and entered. Pisspot looked up with a slight frown on his face as he saw Shiva come in. Being cautious by nature, Shiva folded his hands in greeting (some bosses resented the familiarity of a handshake). 'I am Shiva Shambo, your new Deputy Secretary Sir,' he said, waiting for the customary polite phrases of welcome to his new posting. But there were none. Instead, Pisspot waved him to a slightly uncomfortable wooden chair – one of the three in front of him, made of cheap mango wood, varnished a vivid orange. He looked at Shiva Shambo with a look of slight distaste and asked Shiva where he had been last posted.

'I was Collector of Sitapur sir, a drought affected district in Southrashtra.'

'OK, OK,' Pisspot said in a tone of irritation. 'But unlike in Southrashtra, we mean business here in this Commission,' he said sternly. He proceeded to enlighten Shiva Shambo on the nature of his duties, the first of which was to cut down the scientists to size. Shiva nodded his head intelligently, rather like a wooden mandarin doll with a spring neck. He said nothing, in case it made an unfavourable impression. He wanted more than anything else to secure the good opinion of his boss and an 'outstanding' in his confidential report at the end of every year, so that he would get his empanelment as Joint Secretary. With careful management, he could even get a Commerce Ministry posting. But he did not know how difficult a task this was to be.

At the end of his initiation Shiva walked out of Pisspot's office shakily. He asked a passing peon about the location of the gents. Feeling considerably relieved as he left the men's toilet, he looked out for the office of the Deputy Secretary Research Projects. After two false detours he reached his office on the fourth floor. Three Section officers stood at the entrance of the door to the Deputy Secretary's office, craning their necks forward in eager anticipation.

'Welcome Saar,' said Srinivasan the senior most Section Officer, thrusting a bouquet at Shiva's stomach and piercing his tender belly with the thorn of a rose. Shiva recoiled with a howl of pain and glared at his assailant. Srinivasan was surprised at the reaction of the new Deputy Secretary to his gesture of welcome on behalf of the Science Commission. But being a well trained civil servant, he ignored the unconventional behavior of his new boss. He apologized smoothly for the absence of P.K.Mody, the Under Secretary who had gone to the Supreme Court for an important Public Interest Litigation that a vigilant citizen had filed against the Commission, regarding the allotment of a tender for bicycles for peons. As Joshi, the second Section Officer, explained, the vendor had actually provided tricycles instead of bicycles and this had been distributed to those of the employees of the Commission who had children under the age of five, instead of the peons. Hence the vigilant citizen (an uncle of a disgruntled peon) had filed a PIL in the matter.

'Alright, alright,' said Shiva cutting short the discussion, about bicycles and tricycles. He felt insecure and depressed that he had landed in an office that had peons who were aggressive enough to file public interest litigations against the hand of the government that fed, clothed and shod them, though it must be admitted

– only in khadi and cheap leather from the public sector leather development corporation.

Shiva entered the room gloomily and sat down cautiously on his swivel chair. Chairs, he knew, from his previous experience in Southrashtra, could be treacherous. You could slip off them, if you didn't sit firmly. He saw that his subordinates were still standing. 'Siddown,' he said, with a look of annoyance and they flopped down together. But they sat on the edge of their chairs to indicate that although they were seated, they still treated him with deference. As he was looking at the sheaf of notes in a file marked "IMPORTANT – CON NOTES FOR NEW DS" about the subjects he was to handle, a small troop of minions came in, bearing trays of stationery: Two glass paperweights (there were already six on his table) a ruler, a stapler, a paper punch. Several reams of the best quality, light green, legal noting paper were also brought into his room and ceremoniously laid down. He had to sign for these receipts, which he did with a trembling, indignant hand.

Shiva dismissed his staff and embarked on writing his first paper for the Commission's meeting: 'The high level of wastage of stationery in scientific establishments around the country'. He correlated this with telling data on the shortage of funds for drinking water and schools which could have been provided to thirsty, illiterate citizens, if the Commission had ceased to be so profligate with stationery. Why should every officer have his own stapler, he concluded with a flourish, can't we at least limit it to one in each section?

But the Chairman of the Commission, Dr.Y.Z.Z. Codeshwarappa (known as The Old Codger) saw the note and merely deleted it from the agenda.

'Humph! Another nasty bug in the rug, sent by the DOP to plague me in the Secretariat,' he said sourly to himself.

The Old Codger had bushy white eyebrows and should-length silvery hair. He disliked the members of the Sindustan Administrative Sterling Service singly and collectively. 'The SASSes are asses,' he was heard to say acerbically. (His thought processes were not known to be original.) He had an early morning coffee meeting every day at which he asked every bureaucrat present at the meeting from Additional Secretary right down to the Under Secretary, disconcerting and irrelevant questions about the distance from the earth to the moon and who discovered that e was equal to mc squared. If they managed to acquit themselves creditably on these opening teasers, he went on to grill them on more slippery ground – what did e, m and c stand for in the equation, did a black hole have any force of gravity, what was a quark, and what was the theory of everything – much in the manner of a popular matinee idol turned TV quiz master, whose baritone voice ruled the idiot box. Clearly a tactic aimed at demolishing the natural savoir-faire of the SASS and the propensity of its bureaucrats to raise objections to proposals for expenditure on scientific projects, on the files that they handled. The bureaucrats had to prepare for each morning's meeting, feverishly reading up general knowledge hand books and the Competition *Combat* magazine which they had left off reading once they had made it to the SASS.

The Old Codger picked his nose at important meetings with the Prime Minister. He had a habit of examining these excavations profoundly, before giving a reply to the question posed by the PM, as to when the long awaited *Stink Bum* would be ready. PMO officials felt that it was because he did not know the reply to the question raised by the honourable Prime Minister that the Old Codger spent so much time contemplating the result of his nasal explorations.

The PM was heard to say cantankerously that he wanted to drop a *Stink Bum* on his mincing competitor, Moochad Panwala, in Humptidumptistan across the border. 'That should lay him low at least for a week,' he said. It had rankled with him that the foe had been so popular during his state visit to New Ashokapur. 'Just call me MP,' the enemy had said to those who had wangled invites to his delightful evening soirees. MP had stood upright, at the parties, resplendent in white (as against the PM's dull black) and later chameleon-like, he changed into khakhis. His ferociously charming, three cornered grin extended all the way up to his ears and nose. In the background, the band played *Mera Moocha hai Afghani, Pathloon hai Sindustani, Par Dil hai Humptidumptistani* – my mustaches are Afghani, my pants are Sindustani but my heart belongs to Humptidumptistan. His epaulettes, his swagger stick and his suave heel clicking, compared ill with the portly PM's ungainly duck walk up the steps of the dais set up for the press briefing.

The press swarmed around the preening pretender to the throne of Humptidumptistan in adoring droves, while the PM was left to sulk in a corner, after he was asked a question about 'crass barder tarrorism', by a turbaned reporter from *The Fatiala Times*, to which the PM replied, 'Hum sochthe hai, I think . . .' followed by a fifteen minute pause, which some of the more astute members of the press took advantage of to snatch forty winks, since the trail had been so punishing.

Stung by the disloyalty of the press (which had hailed the imposter from Humptidumptistan as being one of their own, since he had gone to school in their own backyard in Cyberabad, before he had crossed the border in search of his fortune) the PM issued a fiat for the immediate launch of the *Stink Bum*. He summoned Pisspot and the Old Codger, as well as Dr. Rory Ramachandran Raghupati Rao (R 4 as he was known in CIA dossiers) from Potarpotta, who was the Scientific Director in charge of the SLUG project – the official name of the *Stink Bum*. (The project was also known informally among R4's competitors within the Commission, as the **S**cientifically **L**ousy **U**seless **G**izmo.) But Pisspot and the Old Codger had never agreed on any matter of scientific policy or administrative inconvenience. Now they disagreed about the possible date for the launch of the *Stink Bum*.

The Old Codger felt a considerable pride in the SLUG project, which Pisspot felt was beyond all reason, based as it was on pilfered imagination. The Old Codger also believed that the young in the scientific community needed to be pampered and cosseted, in order to shield them from the shock of the discovery that nothing worth discovering was possible in the laboratories in which they slaved. To Pisspot, the scientists were vastly overrated, underworked, ****s who needed to be kicked out by their trouser seats.

'Do much good if the numbers were cut down to one fourth,' he fumed. 'All those blathering demands for bigger houses, five star hospitals and tours abroad would then disappear.'

The scientists, in the meanwhile laboured endlessly, jumping through intellectual hoops, in a game of follow-my-leader which lasted their entire careers. Some of them discovered too late (when they were consigned to the 'dummy track' group of non achievers and had to report to their laboratories wearing dunce caps) that they had followed the wrong leader, who had been beaten to the post of Chairman by the machinations of a more sophisticated rival.

A week in the secretariat led Shiva to concur with his boss' views on the issue of profligacy in the scientific establishment, the only excuse for which was – the stock of xxx *Stink Bums* (still under trial for stinkiness) stored in the Old Codger's garage. The Old Codger always locked his garage door personally, looking craftily over his shoulder, in order to ensure that no one was peeking, since though there were only one and half *Stink Bums* in the garage, he had sent a report to the PMO that there were ten. On the Smelliness Scale of one to ten, the SB also scored only 4, though the scientists claimed that it was 9. Even a small *Bum* they said was enough for every skunk in the vicinity to run a hundred miles and retire humbled and defeated. It was at this stage of bureaucratic and scientific waffling that Shiva had entered the research establishment as the Deputy Secretary R&D or – for those unfamiliar with bureaucratic jargon – Research and Disappointment.

In Shiva's previous posting as the Collector of Sitapur in the state government, there had been a proper respect and a commendable level of miserliness with regard to stationery. Ball pens had to be requisitioned well in advance, along with supplications for envelopes, and the inferior quality note paper supplied by the Directorate of Printing and Stationery. The paper was so thin that noting on both sides of the paper resulted in a ghastly shadow on either side, like a conversation overheard – there but not quite there, often making the legitimate noting indecipherable. This was of course convenient during court cases when it was impossible to understand what had been recorded by the non-decision-maker.

The demands for stationery were scrutinised by the Director of Printing and Stationery and then the requests made were cut down to half, in the belief that all government officials were useless profligates with no eye for economy. Government employees were also expected to rally round and join the nation's thrift drive by turning out used envelopes and re-using them. The money thus painfully saved, was then used to fund the lavish changes in décor of ministerial bungalows and offices and the frequent travel to foreign climes of the people's representatives and senior officials in plum posts. The visits perpetrated 'in the larger national interest', were timed to coincide with New Ashokapur's inhospitable *loo* – not a smelly toilet, but ferocious, dry summer heat.

One morning, the scandalous file of the scantometers landed on Shiva's IN tray. Scantometers were a scientific device, used by scientists to detect a strange ray called *scant-ideaons*. Two scientists who sat on adjoining tables refused to share their equipment. They wanted a separate one each, though the machine cost twenty crores of rupees. Shiva sent his peon with an innocuous note to the scientists with a request for information on their annual demand for funds. He asked the peon to hang around the laboratory and check on what the scientists actually did with the machines.

The peon reported after a day's observation, that the scientists only dusted the machines and switched them on, so that they did not rust from disuse. They did not even take down any readings or printouts of recorded information. They didn't fiddle with the buttons to make new scientific discoveries. The screen was blank, a dull grey, peppered with dots – 'Cable c'nexun cut gaya TV Jaisa,' the peon observed. The scientists kept the machines on and went out in the Commission's shuttle bus to the city centre and came back with their shopping, after which they switched off the machines.

'In my view this is a serious misuse of government funds which could have been used to purchase us better uniforms and shoes. The Khadi cloth now supplied is rough and gives us itches under the armpit and the cheap leather shoes give way after the first month's journey on the Central line,' the peon's note concluded.

Pisspot read Shiva's note with a smile and sent it to on to the Old Codger who got angrier by the minute as he read the note. That non-scientists had the gall to comment on scientific activities, that too on information researched by a peon! But he was left with no alternative but to agree to Shiva's suggestion that the second scantometer be sent to the research station in Gamdipamdi, which had just asked for a new scantometer: They had actually registered one or two *scant-ideaons* that needed to be investigated.

Pisspot invited Shiva to lunch in his room, one afternoon. 'Come along by one,' he said while extending the invitation to Shiva, 'Your stand on that scantometer file was really commendable.' But actually it was because he needed Shiva's company and unqualified admiration, from time to time, in order to feel that he was really a boss. The scientific establishment had too many scientists who tended to treat bureaucrats as an unnecessary and unwanted appendage, some even described them as an un-evolved low species of animal life. Pisspot did not want to take Shiva out to lunch to the nearby China Dragon restaurant as it would easily set him back by a thousand rupees. (The stinginess he practiced in his official life, also spilled out into his personal life.) Instead, he ordered two "paper" masala dosas which the Commission's canteen was famous for. It made him feel generous, while only paying twenty rupees for the government subsidised dosas, which came with a generous dish of sambaar and a soup bowl full of coconut chutney.

Shiva did not look forward to having lunch with his boss. But he turned up punctually at One O'clock. Pisspot led him to the black, Rexene visitors' sofa in the room, instead of the hard wooden chairs in front of his table. In a little while, the canteen boy rapped on the door to the room and entered with the tray of dosas and set it down before them on the low teapoy.

Once they had settled down to the meal, Pisspot began discussing his favourite topic – his successful bureaucratic career till he had come to the Commission. 'When I was the Municipal Commissioner of Slowpal,' he said, 'I saw to it that the roads were swept every day and hosed down with water. You don't see that kind of action today,' he said, looking self satisfied.

'What about the area near the sweeper's quarters sir? I saw that it looked very dirty, when I visited Slowpal last August,' Shiva said foolishly, not knowing that he had slipped into dangerous waters.

'Of course the roads near the sweeper's huts were a ghastly mess, since they preferred to shit outside their own homes! If that was the way they liked it, who was I to prevent it?' Pisspot asked with a nasty glint in his eye that brooked no further comment. Sweepers, in his view were clearly less than human. He then switched over to the topic of his successful efforts at quelling rioting mobs at Quaidabad.

'First, we fired in the air. Six rounds. But they still stood around the encroachments that we had demolished, clutching their tin trunks and bed rolls, some of them poking around the debris for their belongings. Then we socked it to the bastards. We fired twelve rounds and every one of them hit the target. It was only then that they came to their senses and ran with their tails between their legs,' he said boastfully. The poor, like the sweepers, were another unjustifiable category in Pisspot's dictionary. Their existence, an abomination and a slur, on the fair name of the country. He was of the view that a political party's famous electoral slogan 'Garibi Hatao' ought to have been 'Garib Hatao' since the poor were so unnecessary in the general scheme of things.

Shiva's face was a carefully contorted mask conveying rapt attention and cloying admiration: After all he was getting a free dosa. His small civil service pay and his wife's constant grumbles about the other ladies' new saries and her wistful expression whenever they passed Sari Palace or Sari Bhandar, added to the woes of his life as Pisspot's assistant. The compulsory recitations he had to undergo on a hot summer's day often put him to sleep. After they had finished lunch and while they waited for the after lunch filter coffee, the dull drone of Pisspot's narration, made Shiva doze off. He woke with a start when the noise ceased. Pisspot had come to the dramatic end to his story.

'Were you sleeping?' Pisspot asked suspiciously and Shiva replied, 'No sir, just thinking very deeply about this deeply moving incident in your distinguished career. A deeply moving story you just narrated sir,' he said, while rubbing out the sleep from his tired eyes, which Pisspot fortunately mistook for tears.
'Don't take everything so emotionally,' Pisspot said patting him gently.

A few days later, Dr. Rory Ramachandran Raghupati Rao came to see Shiva. He was greatly agitated.

'I zimbly have to get the money for the Hush Husssh SLUG project,' he said. 'The Charman just sent me an express top secret message on the HOT line, about the PM's directive to launch the *Stink Bum* yimediately.' Shiva called for the SLUG file from his Section officer. As he ran his eye through the file he was mystified to find that no financial sanctions had ever been issued during the eight years of the project. There had been merely telegraphic orders of budgetary allocations issued after each meeting with the PM. There was an old, moth-eaten order on the file, indicating the size of the project. He made a rapid total of the annual releases in the allocations sent by telegram and found that it amounted to Two Thousand Crores of rupees, while the original amount projected for the proposal had been only One Thousand Crores. He examined the papers with a special microscope used in the department to look at secret projects and he made up his mind that the SLUG project would not take off unless he took drastic measures. Then the tug of war between Pisspot and Shiva began.

When Shiva sent his note underscoring the top secret nature and urgency of the project, together with the need to release funds immediately, Pisspot returned it with a laconic comment in the margin in pencil, 'page numbering not done.' Shiva examined the file. Indeed none of the two hundred odd pages of the file had been numbered in the last ten years. The Science secretariat was not known for its secretariat practices. Shiva called his Section officer and asked him to return the file with its pages duly numbered. When the file was submitted the next day, Pisspot kept it with him for a week and returned it with the remark, underlined for added emphasis that the papers were bottom up and not top down as he had ordered all files to be in the secretariat, after he had taken over as Additional Secretary.

'We from Ultapulta Pradesh we can teach you a thing or two about administration, you chaps from Southrashtra who fancy yourselves so much,' he had stated acidly, 'The level of file management is appalling. Kindly see that all files are top down, every file should read like a book with all the correspondence one after the other, the first one at the top and the last one at the bottom.'

There had been murmurs of rebellion from the clerical minions. 'Just such an SASS officer had come to the secretariat from the Funjab cadre five years ago and he had ordered all the files to be bottom up and we had spent months rearranging all the files and now this officer from Ultapulta Pradesh asks us to do them the other way,' they grumbled. Hence there had been no response to Pisspot's fiat from Shiva's sections in the secretariat. But a compromise had been worked out. Every new file was made 'top down'. Shiva kept quiet in the hope that Pisspot's bee in the bonnet would just fly away. Alas Pisspot seemed to want his way in respect of the SLUG file.

Shiva received a fax message from an anxious Rao from Pottarpota. 'Funds have been exhausted. Important Research held up! Our competitors are stealing a march over us!! Nation's security in peril!!!' Alarmed, Shiva sent him a fax asking him to come to NA for an urgent meeting. R 4 came by the next flight, his brown face sweating with the exertion of climbing the four floors, to Shiva's office since the lifts had stopped working and the technicians hadn't fixed them.

'Who are our competitors?' Shiva asked Rao in a hoarse, conspiratorial whisper, 'Humptidumptistan? Pikineesthan??'

'No,' Rao answered, 'Professor Sanshod Singh Gumbhir of Jalandha University. He's going to make a first class *Stink Bum* before us if we don't look out and we'll have yegg all over the face. The One and a half *Stink Bums* I delivered to the Charman need much more improvement to reach the 9 level of stinkiness. We have only reached till 4.' Shiva looked dazed. Jalanda was an obscure university was on the outskirts of New Ashokapur.

Shiva sent the SLUG file up to Pisspot once again, marking the fax communication from Rao for his boss' immediate attention, indicating point wise in his note in his neat hand, as he had been trained at SADOPS (Sindustan Academy for Delays, Obfuscation, Procrastination and Stonewalling) that: since the matter involved the nation's security, which was at peril, and the urgency due to their competitors stealing many marches (he thought one march did not sound alarming enough, though he naturally refrained from indicating who the competitors were), it was imperative that the funds be released immediately.

Pisspot returned the file with the remark that 'Although considerable funds have been released for this appropriately named project — which does not seem to be making any progress (when was the last review meeting held to find out how many SLUG/s had been made or how many Slug/s were working on the same?), I see no utilization certificates on the file, of previous releases made.'

On checking with his Under Secretary, P.K.Mody, Shiva was informed by Mody, 'Surr, of course since the project had been so hush husssh, the department had never insisted on any utilisation certificates, in case the communication of the same amounted to a violation of the Official Secrets Act.' When Shiva wanted him to actually put down this reason, he seemed ill at ease. 'One cannot actually put down some things in writing, sir,' he said apologetically. Shiva was obliged to return the file to the AS with the remark in the margin in pencil, that though it was difficult to actually put down some things in writing, it was understood that the non-filing of the utilisation certificates had something to do with the violation of the Official Secrets Act. Pisspot blew a fuse when he read the last missive. 'I WANT THOSE UTILISATION CERTIFICATES – OFFICIAL SECRETS ACT OR NO ACT' he bellowed in large print, spiking the paper with a sharp lead pencil and almost exhausting the space in the margin.

Rao invited Shiva to Pottarpotta see his laboratory. 'It will convince you more than yany utilization zertificate, tsar,' he said earnestly with his hands clasped in a gesture of supplication. Shiva left by the late afternoon flight to Ramnagar and thereafter took the two hour car ride to Pottarpotta. The terrain was dry and dusty and he was glad to enter the cool well appointed guest house for VIPs. He turned in early after an evening meal of rotis with lentils and fried potatoes. Rao met him and briefed him about the next day's itinerary: Shiva was to get up at five in the morning and bathe and wear freshly laundered clothes.

'Don't wear any clothes that have only been re-ironed after use, tsar,' Rao advised.

When they entered the laboratory building, the next morning Shiva was asked to leave his shoes and clothes outside in a bath room next to the laboratory and have another bath. Thereafter Rao (who wore only a mask and nothing much else himself) handed Shiva a large sterilised, plastic overall. 'Kindly wear only this tsar,' he said in a muffled voice. Shiva entered a chamber where he was airbrushed for any recalcitrant dust particles. At last gowned, masked, bare-foot and feeling vulnerable without his underwear and trousers, he entered the laboratory with Rao.

'The SLUG can be activated from the computer screen in front of you tsar,' said Rao, ' Just press the icon marked PING. But don't forget to hold your nose before you do it.' Shiva pressed the icon and as the room was filled with the malodour of the *Stink Bum,* a trigger of anxiety raced through his mind: he could feel a gas attack developing in his own stomach, bearing menacingly downwards. He had eaten too much of the delicious lentils and fried potatoes at dinner the night before. He squirmed and made a desperate attempt to withhold the gas, as it made its way out. But he failed. He broke wind with a great whoosh of smelly air and a minor explosion. 'Tsar! Tsar! Look at the Stinkometer!'

yelled Rao, 'We've reached seven! I told you! We're nearly there now! Just need some more funds.'

Shiva raised his hands and murmured, 'OK, OK,' a little diffidently, not sure of his own contribution to the success of the experiment and hurried out of the laboratory. He felt that he had had enough of the *Stink Bum* for the day. As he was leaving, Rao looked at him expectantly, in a bid to extract the promise that had been the object of the visit. Shiva mumbled an inaudible, not to be encashed assurance, that he would look into matters at an early date and get back to him as soon as was feasible, under the circumstances, if the situation otherwise permitted.

The conversation with Shiva set the alarm bells jangling in Rao's head. He put his staff to work and after working ceaselessly day and night for eight days, he got the utilization certificates and brought them himself to New Ashokapur. He went to see the Old Codger.

'I am an umble scientist, tsar,' he said, 'but even I draa the line at some things. We have never yever issued yutilization zertificates in this Commission and this Jonny-come-newly of a Pissingpot insists on them now for the SLUG. How on earth are we to launch the *Stink Bum* in time? Ask him to release the money or else –'

The old Codger called Pisspot for a conference. 'Release the money for the *Stink Bum* or else –' he said.

'Or else, what?' asked Pisspot guardedly.

'Oh well, your empanelment for Secretary is coming up next year I'm told,' said the Chairman, nonchalantly.

This altered Pisspot's view of the unimportance of the SLUG project. He called for Shiva and asked him to put up the file, 'Complete in all respects for an official sanction and release of funds.' This was so contrary to the department's then style of functioning that it shook the whole secretariat.

'What does he mean – complete in all respects?' the Section officer asked, honest doubt writ large all over his face. Could any file, at any stage be deemed complete *in all respects*, by Pisspot?

At last they took out a financial sanction referring to all the earlier expenditures, the excess expenditure, enlarging the scope of the project and sanctioning the release of additional funds of One Thousand Five Hundred Crores of rupees. The financial sanction ran into forty pages, in order to avoid missing any point that Pisspot may have considered essential. Pisspot signed the file, though he remarked in the margin of the noting sheet, 'Too short, some more details on project location could have been inserted.' Rao took the top secret order in a specially made see-through envelope which had laser guards that restricted access to any unauthorized snooper. However the Outward clerk, the Daftary and the peon while sealing the envelope had been attracted to the Top secret stamp and had sufficient leisure to read the contents of the order.

'The *Stink Bum* job hasn't yet been completed,' the Daftary Pandurang observed to the peon Shantaram, while picking his teeth in the peon's official lunch hour which was from 12.30 p.m. to 3.30p.m.

Shiva congratulated himself at having pleased the cantankerous scientific lobby, his imperious and difficult to please boss, as well as the sharp tongued Chairman. But Shiva's complacency did not last long. The Chief Minister of Ultapulta Pradesh, called Pisspot on the telephone as he was enjoying an after-lunch pan.

'What's all this nonsense about shifting your Central Zone head quarters from Mucknow to Khaskhot in the land of that lathi distributing poltroon, a land which has no laa and arder?' he asked in a loud, belligerent voice.

Pisspot pressed the buzzer of the bell attached to his table and summoned Shiva. 'What's all this nonsense about shifting the Central Zone head quarters from Mucknow to Khaskhot in the land of that lathi distributing poltroon, a land which has no laa – I mean, law and order?' he asked in a loud, belligerent voice.

'Oh! That!!' exclaimed Shiva and paused thoughtfully and then decided that a clean breast would only meet the purpose.

'Some years ago the Commission bought a thousand acres of land in Khaskot in order to save money that would have lapsed otherwise. The land was going cheap. The Commission saved the money. It was spent and did not lapse.'

'Really?' asked Pisspot looking interested, 'How much did it cost?'

'Only Rs. Ten Lacs an acre. We saved a hundred crore of rupees,' Shiva answered proudly. He had already forgotten his days as Collector and worries about money for drinking water and literacy. He had got into the spirit of things at the Commission. 'Then,' said Shiva, 'the department forgot all about it. Till the Accountant General reminded us and raised an audit query on *Unfruitful expenditure*. The Commission therefore decided to put the land to use and approved a large set of offices, bungalows for officers and staff quarters and also a large number of fruit trees – fruitful expenditure. These facilities were set up at a cost of Two Hundred and Fifty Crores of rupees. That set aside the audit query for a few years during the construction phase. The engineers managed to delay the construction and the project was not completed for ten years. However once it was complete, the AG's man was there again demanding why the houses and buildings were empty and why were we were paying a huge lease of Fifty Lacs of rupees every month for the offices in Mucknow. The Central Zone Director telephoned me last week and asked for permission to pay the staff transfer allowance when they shifted offices to the new offices built at Khaskot, in order to avoid the audit enquiry. He only asked us for a clarification whether double allowance was payable or single.'

'What's the difference?' demanded Pisspot.

'Double for shifting headquarters and single for ordinary transfer. I told them to pay single for the time being, till you returned from tour and then we would clarify.'

'Is that so? Then why was this fax issued by your Under Secretary permitting double allowance?' asked Pisspot angrily, waving the message under Shiva's nose.

Shiva looked dumbfounded 'But – but – I had only permitted single,' he gasped.

'You have shifted the head quarters without the authorisation of the Commission,' Pisspot snarled.

'But surely that was a foregone conclusion sir? The Commission could not have sanctioned the construction of the massive mausoleum at Khaskot with the intention of continuing with the offices at Mucknow?'

In the end, the dispute was taken to the Old Codger who read through the file and paused at the touristy description of the project on a flyer developed by the young Director of the Central Zone, Mansur Ali Khan, a Toon school man (from the famous school in the hills for *Babalog* in Tehratoon) who fancied his own writing style: "Khaskhot *the Right Choice!* A township nestling in the hills, an abundance of nature in its verdant atmosphere! Come commune with the gods at Khaskot!!"
'*Yeh hi hai right choice Baby! Ah Ha!!*' The Old Codger said in a high falsetto, mimicking the Cola ads on TV.

Pisspot was miffed that in the end it was decided that only a small branch office be retained at Mucknow. The Chief Minister of Ultapulta Pradesh turned into a raging bull. He rang up Pisspot everyday and threatened him with dire revenge. 'Useless Dunkey! Unable to protect own home state's interests!' his verbal poisoned darts sped over the telephone, making Pisspot reel in his swivel chair.

A few months later Shiva sent in his Confidential Roll form to the AS for his assessment. Pisspot looked at the self-congratulatory descriptions of the sanctions for projects issued against his will and thought of his soon to be missed plum postings on his return to UPP.

The Chief Minister had a long and nasty memory. Pisspot licked the nib of his pen. Then he finally wrote – "An over enthusiastic officer. Must learn to collect his thoughts and put up more effective proposals." He thought of adding "Always wooing the scientific establishment," but then decided against it. After all the Old Codger would be reviewing it.

The Old Codger saw the uncomplimentary remarks and remembered Shiva's note on profligacy in expenditure on stationery in scientific establishments and how his hand had been forced on the scantometer issue by Shiva. The scientists had been angry that he had not intervened in the matter. It had been seen by them as unwarranted bureaucratic interference on hallowed scientific turf. "I agree," he wrote below the AS' remarks and signed with a flourish.

When Shiva learnt of the fate of his Confidential Roll from Pisspot's personal assistant Ms Subbhalakshmee, he felt like the worm that thought that it needed to turn. He was bound to miss his empanelment as Joint Secretary. He decided that revenge was the only honourable course of action left. He took to extracting every note submitted by the Additional Secretary to the Chairman and adding in the margin, at the end of the last line of each note, "And I am sure you don't understand a line of this, you old blockhead." And . . . "Stop picking your nose in public, Pig's Snout." The Chairman was amazed by the notes and wrote back in the margin, "I understand you very well, you numbskull. You don't have to be so verbose and offensive. And see that the *Stink Bum* is launched this month you DELAY MASTER. The PM wants to see the SLUG."

Pisspot was surprised when the files were returned to him. How had his eye escaped the derogatory lines? Had he actually put his signature to those notes? Yet he had a faint sense of déjà vu. He remembered harbouring those very thoughts. No doubt it had been written by his PA who had skillfully read his thoughts during the dictation, or perhaps he had inadvertently voiced his thoughts aloud? He did not know what to make of the additions. The abusive postscripts to his notes continued to appear, challenging the sanity and the scientific acumen of the Chairman, with angry rejoinders from the Chairman, resulting in the Confidential Roll of the Additional Secretary being written as, "An immature officer, who has a bee in his bonnet about the 'Top Down' approach. Moreover he does not have his heart in the development of the scientific temper. Only given to displays of his own bad temper. Seems to have left his brains behind in Kashi Hind University, when he left it thirty years ago. An irresponsible sluggard who delayed the launch of the SLUG despite my constant injunctions. A Despicable, Disobedient, Dumbhead." The Chairman looked admiringly at his own work, its wonderful alliterative ending. He licked the envelope after putting the CR into it and posted it to the DOP himself so that Pisspot could not intercept it.

Thus Pisspot missed the bus to being empanelled as Secretary to Government. The DOP was alarmed at the prospect of elevating to the post of Secretary, an officer who had allegedly left his brains behind at Kashi Hind University thirty years ago. The selection panel also added a remark to the minutes of the proceedings, that it was a tribute to the Sindustan administration that the officer was able to perform in various assignments without his brains and also did so without doing any lasting damage to the organisations he had been entrusted with hitherto.

Pisspot retired regretfully to his farmhouse in Kailashnagar, in the outskirts of New Ashokapur, where his bossy wife Kamalnayana made him serve her breakfast in bed every morning and clean out the kitchen cupboards every weekend, while she stood over him and supervised his efforts with a critical eye and a severe tongue. And when she went off to play golf every Sunday at the Golf club with her ladies group, he had to follow her meekly, carrying her golf bag. This saved her the expense of hiring a caddy, an expense they could ill afford on his meager pension, she pointed out caustically, when he had ventured a murmur of protest. She didn't even allow him to use a golf cart. She said that walking was good for him because he had got too fat sitting on government files when he had been at the secretariat. His junior was empanelled (a man considerably his inferior in intellect, according to Pisspot) and posted as Secretary. And as for Shiva – he went back to the state government, content that he had done a job well, a worthy son of Southrashtra.

ॐ ॐ ॐ

PUSHPA

Rachel was Deputy Secretary (Legislation) in the Department of Labour. Her husband George worked in a stock broker's firm and they had two daughters aged ten and thirteen. Rachel was desperate for a cook since their maid old Cheeru, racked by arthritis had gone back to Kerala, to be with her family. Cheeru had tired of being cooped up in a Bombay flat. She longed to see the lush, green, paddy fields and the swaying, coconut palms of Kerala and eat *Chakka Puzhuka* – green jackfruit cooked with coconut and chicken curry and tapioca with pungent red hot, fish curry. Since she had saved up a little money, her brothers' wives would be polite to her at least till the money ran out. They would of course be borrowing the money from her till, 'Chetan gives me the money next month.'

Rachel registered her request for domestic help at the Nirmala Convent Desolate Women's Institute at Goregaon. The shelter for women in distress also had a domestic help placement agency. The nuns sent out the women who enrolled at the centre, to work with families known to the convent. Mother Concepta had been the Principal of the Primary school when Rachel was a student at the Nirmala Convent School in Goregaon. They gave her the registration form to fill up. Rachel filled in the details of her name, occupation, address and number of family members. Then she paused at the column, 'Weekly off on Sunday'. The small pamphlet given to her by the convent entitled "Guidelines for Families intending to use Nirmala Convent services for Domestic Helpers" said that they would appreciate it if the Helpers were treated as a part of the family and given a weekly off on Sunday to attend Holy Mass. Her pencil hovered over "No" and after some deliberation she ticked "Yes". The nuns might just reject her application if she had marked "No" under the weekly offs column, she thought. She would have to manage the Sunday cooking herself.

Later that month Mother Concepta telephoned Rachel from the institute and said that they had a girl looking for housework and that Rachel could take her home if she was still looking for a housemaid. Rachel went to the convent immediately, since she had only two days of leave left and she had to find a maid before that. As she sat in the car, she thought of the various maids who had entered their domestic service fleetingly, always promising to do wonders and then leaving a detritus of undone tasks. There had been Rani who had a constant cold and always sniffed, Sita who had dirty finger nails and chewed pan, Rosy who had lice in her hair and Sejala who had run away with the watchman . . . She sank back in the car seat, exhausted at the idea of dealing with a new house maid's tantrums.

Pushpa was in the kitchen when the sisters called for her. She had been earning her keep, stringing beans for the evening meal in the convent. She walked briskly into the parlour where Rachel sat in an arm chair. She sat on a chair opposite Rachel and calmly answered her questions. Rachel tried to assess her nature from the way Pushpa walked in and from the answers she gave. Pushpa told Rachel that she knew housework. She knew how to operate a mixer and a washing machine, even a vacuum cleaner. When Rachel told her that she did not have a vacuum cleaner Pushpa looked disappointed. She wore a bright orange sari that hurt the eye. One string of wormy hair hung over her forehead, in a ludicrous imitation of a famous film actress. That alone should have warned Rachel. But the urgent need to have someone at home with the children and cook the food, when she went to work made Rachel careless. She thought that the sallow, pimply face with its flat nose, wouldn't attract the attentions of the liftman or the milkman. There would be no boyfriend trouble.

Rachel made up her mind. She decided to hire Pushpa and informed the sister-in-charge of her decision. Sister permitted Pushpa to take her belongings and go with Rachel. She gave Pushpa a few parting words of advice about the importance of hard work. Pushpa nodded at Sister and stood uncertainly near the car door, clutching her plastic shopping bag, which had all of her belongings. Rachel opened the door and asked Pushpa to ride in the rear seat with her and not in the front seat with the driver.

On the way in the car, Pushpa told Rachel in a flat monotone that she was twenty-five. Her sister-in-law's brother had raped her when she was sixteen and she had a child by him. He had avenged himself on their family. Pushpa's brother had alcoholic rages and beat his wife Somi every day. Hence Somi's brother had raped Pushpa. He kept her confined in his house, without marrying her. At the birth of Pushpa's child, her mother got her secretly operated right after the child birth in the local government hospital. Pushpa was only seventeen, when her tubes were ligated. She could not escape her tormentor as he was the leader of a powerful gang of hoodlums in the town. When her attacker released her after three years, she was too old to go back to school. But her mother gave Pushpa the family house with the little patch of land on which it stood. Her rapist soon married a woman with money and fifty tolas of gold and he settled down to being a family man. He had four children by his legal wife.

Pushpa's own son was nine years old. She said that her ambition was to get a job in the Gulf, as a housemaid, like her elder sister and earn six thousand rupees a month. Rachel listened to the matter of fact voice telling her the story, with a sickening feeling welling up inside her.

'Pushpa don't ever tell anyone that you were raped and that you have a child by your rapist,' Rachel said at the end. 'If you go to anyone's house to work and tell them your story, the men in the house would exploit you.'

Rachel had to leave for a meeting in Jaipur two days thereafter. She was away for a week. When she got back, her mother informed her that Pushpa came to the drawing room in the mornings and sat reading the paper on the sofa there. Pushpa also hung around the drawing room in her spare time, looking out of the long French windows.

'You should have told George to tell her not to sit on the sofa, even if you didn't want to tell her anything yourself,' Rachel said. Her mother said that it should not be said that all the servants left their employment because she was rude to them. Rachel was annoyed at the prospect of having to talk to Pushpa herself. When she went into the kitchen for a glass of water, she told her, 'Pushpa don't read the paper sitting on the front room sofa. You can stay in the kitchen after your work is over. When you have any spare time, you can watch the TV in the children's room, if they aren't studying.' Pushpa nodded, looking crestfallen.

'I just thought I was part of the family here,' she muttered. Rachel went away feeling as though it was she who had been reproved.

The next day was a Sunday. When Rachel passed by the children's room in the afternoon, she noticed Pushpa lying on the floor on her stomach in front of the TV, her chin cupped in her hands, her legs in the air. She wore a nightie with a V neck and her generous cleavage was displayed prominently, in a pose often adopted by starlets in the evening tabloids under provocative titles – "Sweet Nothings" or "Naughty Tit Bits". Pushpa was eating a thick slice of the chocolate cake that had been kept on the dining room table for the children's tea. Pushpa had helped herself to the cake and was seeing a Malayalam movie. Rachel felt outraged. This was somehow inappropriate. But she couldn't bring herself to ask, 'Pushpa why are you eating the children's cake?' She went into the kitchen where she found some crushed orange rind on the kitchen table. 'What's this?' she asked Pushpa who came in just then to wash her hands and the specks of chocolate cream from her face. 'It's some orange rind. I want to get rid of the pimples on my face,' Pushpa replied sulkily.

Rachel found herself unequal to the situation. She felt that it would be undignified to reprimand Pushpa about eating the cake. Marie Antoinette had – she remembered vaguely and inconsequentially, said something about giving the poor cake to eat, it was better than bread. Besides the children may get a stomach ache eating the cake by themselves when it had been coveted by Pushpa. George always said that he got a stomach upset if they ate any payasaam without leaving some for the cook. Domestic Helpers also had a right to beautify themselves and have aspirations about being pimple free, she thought. Rachel's uncle Vakachen Velliappachan, was a communist leader from the CPM and often talked about workers' rights whenever he paid them a visit. So Rachel maintained a silence about the cake and the orange rind.

But soon there were other causes for disagreement. Rachel found that Pushpa didn't make the beds every morning. 'Pushpa come here,' she told her one morning. 'I want you to fold the bedclothes every morning, after the children have left for school.'
'OK,' Pushpa said sullenly. Rachel left the room. She came in a little later to find that Pushpa had spread out the bed sheets neatly – and left the coverlet in a high mound in the centre of the bed. Rachel was livid. She yelled out for Pushpa.
'Come here, you hussy! Is this the way you do the sheets in your house? And when you get your Gulf

job, do you think you will last a second in the house, if you leave the bedclothes this way?' Pushpa raised her eyebrows stylishly. She had been to the beauty parlour the previous evening and had got her eyebrows plucked in a thin arch.

'But you didn't say anything about the coverlet, chechi,' she answered, as she tucked the bed spread over the bed.

Pushpa asked Rachel for some of her old salwar kameezes. All of them were old and Rachel wasn't able to buy any new ones. There were so many expenses for the children's school and their music and drama classes and the groceries, that buying herself new clothes seemed an extravagance that could wait. Nevertheless she gave Pushpa some of her salwars. Pushpa certainly looked smarter than Rachel in those salwars. She was less dumpy than Rachel. She wore her hair now tied up stylishly in a topknot, at the top of her head. She also sat every evening in the kitchen balcony, filing her nails.

One morning, Rachel saw Pushpa rummaging through the cupboard shelves in the children's bedroom.
'Pushpa, what on earth are you doing?' she asked her.
'I'm sure I've seen a small mirror in one of the shelves or cupboards. I need a small mirror to look at my eyes,' she said.
'You've seen a small mirror in one of the cupboards!' Rachel exclaimed. 'Pushpa you've been searching through my cupboards and things in my absence!' She was very angry. 'You've no right to look into my things and take what you see,' she scolded. After that Rachel had the tiresome task of locking every cupboard and drawer. Since she was absentminded she often lost the

keys to the drawers, just when the children needed to put their crayons and felt pens into their bags and leave for school. So she had to give up locking up all the cupboards, except the bedroom almirah, in which she kept her gold necklace, her long *kash-mala* of flat small one pice shaped gold coins and ten gold bangles. She only wore two thin gold bangles and a small gold chain with her tiny marriage *thali* strung into it.

A few weeks later it was Diwali. Pushpa had not been working with Rachel even for a month. But she wanted an advance from her wages, to send her son to buy him Diwali clothes.

'But you said you were a Christian at the convent in Goregaon,' Rachel said.

'Yes but in Kerala every one celebrates Diwali. My mother is a Christian but my father is a Hindoo and all my uncles are Hindoos,' she replied.

Rachel gave her an advance of five hundred rupees, which Pushpa took to the post office to post. But she came back looking downcast.

'My cousin Manoj Kumar was there at the post office. He took the money from me, since he had lent me a thousand rupees when I came to Bombay. He wanted to marry me. But I had refused.'

'Manoj Kumar! What kind of a name is that? Is he a film actor? Why can't he have a normal name like Balachandran or Venugopalan?' Rachel asked sarcasm in her voice.

Thereafter Pushpa complained of a headache and she worked slowly. Her eyes looked tear-stained. When

Rachel asked her about it, she said that the thoughts of her son tormented her.

Rachel had a part time maid, Durgabai who did the sweeping. Rachel gave her a new sari for Diwali. Durga had worked with her for three years. Rachel was annoyed with Pushpa. Her constant visits to the beauty parlour and her frequent watching of Malayalam movies in the children's room, irked her. She was afraid that the suggestive scenes would affect her children. So she did not buy new clothes for Pushpa for Diwali. Pushpa looked disappointed when she saw Durgabai wearing her new green and red sari and asked Rachel once more for an old salwar kameez. Rachel told her that she could easily buy herself new kameezes which were cheaply available at Dadar TT or outside the church at Mahim on Wednesdays, when there were the novena services.

Pushpa left one afternoon in a taxi on a shopping spree, with her Diwali salary. She left behind a note on the kitchen table. It described in poetic Malayalam, the tall graceful buildings of Bombay, hanging with the coloured lights of Diwali. The whole world was bright and rejoicing except a lowly servant, Pushpa. Her life was without any colour. Did the people who ate the food that she cooked even think for a moment of the happiness of the person who had cooked the food, she asked. Rachel was bewildered when George read out the note to her, since she was a Bombay Malayali who didn't know how to read Malayalam. She was completely at sea with the complicated, round, curly letters of the Malayalam alphabet. 'But what does she want?' Rachel asked her husband. 'We don't celebrate Diwali.

229

And only yesterday when I had bought the children Fiest ice-creams, I had bought one for her also. And I remember that I had given her the three biggest sweets from the box of Diwali sweets you brought from the office.'

'She wants a hero in her life,' guffawed George.

Pushpa returned from her day's outing to Dadar TT with her arms laden. The next day she wore an orange outfit, with a shimmering lace chunni. She also wore bright orange lipstick and dressed her hair for an hour. She stuck a red bindi on her forehead and asked Rachel's mother for some talcum powder. Rachel's mother said in an embarrassed, inaudible voice that she didn't know where the powder was. Pushpa went to Rachel's room, since she knew that Rachel had already left for the office and took some powder from the dresser, in a piece of paper. She didn't notice George sitting in a chair in a corner reading the paper. She thought that he had already left for work. When she saw George, Pushpa stopped guiltily and said, 'I – I, was only taking a little powder,' and ran out of the room.

When George told Rachel about Pushpa's search for talcum powder on her dressing table, Rachel was irritated. But she didn't sack Pushpa. Who would cook the food and how would the children get to school on time? But Rachel took the precaution of locking up her Yardley (Red Roses) in the steel almirah. She took down the dog's talcum powder from the top of the cupboard and another spray that they used to prevent him from scratching the sofa legs. "Repel All. Crab apple Dog and Cat repellent. Spray on furniture and objects that you want your dog to avoid," the label on the tin said. Let Pushpa use this, Rachel thought with grim humour and left it on her dressing table.

Pushpa looked so smart in her new clothes that when Rachel opened the door to the shop boys she found that they looked over her shoulder at Pushpa and asked whether they could speak to madam. When Rachel sent Pushpa down to buy a few vegetables, she dressed elaborately, wearing eye liner, rouge and lipstick with her shimmering clothes that had zari work on them, as though she was going to dance at a navratri dandiya. She looked out of place in the elevator. The other women residents of the building, dressed casually in jeans and T shirts or cotton salvar kameezes, stared at her. They gossiped that Rachel had got a hooker as a paying guest in her house. 'How convenient for George,' they snickered, 'He just has to ask for room service.' Rachel stopped sending Pushpa out of the house for errands.

Rachel found that Pushpa never ate the food leftover after each meal but threw it away the next morning. Rachel told her not to waste the food, there were many poor people who starved for food in Bombay. Then Pushpa took care to heat up the leftovers and serve them to her employers, sometimes even carrying them on to the third day. But she herself only ate what she had made fresh for the day. She explained that at home she was never allowed to eat any leftovers. Her mother was careful in case she got sick eating stale food. Then one morning, as Rachel entered the kitchen to get her morning cup of tea, she found Pushpa polishing off half a dish of chicken curry, from the previous evening's dinner party.

'I'm eating *pazang kanji,* left over rice,' she explained, with her mouth full. Rachel pursed her lips.

'You should have served that chicken curry with chappatis, for breakfast,' she told Pushpa reproachfully.

'But you are always asking me to eat leftovers, chechi,' Pushpa replied in an aggrieved tone.

Pushpa had bought a book of Arabic and she sat poring over it every day, in her spare time. Her sister was in Muscat and had written to Pushpa that her employers knew someone who needed a house maid. As Pushpa watched the Malayalam movies on the Asia Net channel every day, she longed to be the heroine of her own life story. But there was no one prepared to play the hero. In one "bathing" scene, the heroine emerged coyly from the bathroom wrapped only in her bath towel, to find the hero "unexpectedly" waiting in the room. She was demure and shy and spoke with lowered eyelids. She stood near him in a seductive pose, her hand protectively over her breasts. But she made no move to dash back into the bathroom and put on her clothes. The next afternoon as George went into the kitchen to get a drink of water, Pushpa came out of the bathroom next to the kitchen, dressed only in her decidedly small, Kerala towel. 'I – I forgot to take my clothes to the bathroom,' she told George, simpering coyly at him, one hand over her breasts, as he beat a hasty retreat out of the kitchen.

When George reported the incident to Rachel, laughing uproariously as he described Pushpa in her thin, wet towel that revealed suggestively the contours of her body, Rachel was speechless. She got up in anger to rush into the kitchen and slap Pushpa and throw her out with her baggage into the passage. Just then her daughter Irene called from the bedroom. 'Mama, tell Pushpa to make me allu parathas for tea. I'm hungry.' Rachel paused and thought regretfully that she would have to wait to sack Pushpa till she got another maid. But she found everything that Pushpa did insufferable. Her manner of speaking to George in a soft, seductive, submissive, Malayalam film heroine voice irritated her the most. Why don't they make the women speak in normal tones, in these films, Rachel thought in exasperation. Now all the servants spoke as though they had laryngitis.

Soon it was Christmas time. Pushpa was expecting a present from her employers. But Rachel was merely biding her time, looking for another maid. On Christmas morning Pushpa went to visit one of her numerous "brothers" who always called to inquire after her, especially towards payday. It was in vain that Rachel warned her that these men were only after her money. She went with them in a taxi for the day and came home late in the night at twelve. Rachel warned her each time that she would never open the door to her again and that her house was not a hotel. But every month after her day's outing Pushpa came in after midnight. And despite her threats, Rachel opened the door to her. She had not yet found another servant. Rachel found herself tied to Pushpa, though she had begun to hate the sight of her pert, self-confident, pimply face. Despite her ungainly appearance, Pushpa had the poise of a beauty queen – it was surely the result of much love lavished on her by a doting mother.

Rachel had told Pushpa that there would be guests for Christmas lunch. The Secretary Labour Mr. Shamsuddin and his wife Selena were coming to visit them. Pushpa promised to get back in time to cook the lunch, after going to morning mass and visiting her brothers. Rachel waited for her. The clock in the sitting room seemed to be racing. At eleven Rachel waited no longer and entered the kitchen to find that Pushpa had left it messy with the previous day's vegetable peals on the work table. Muttering to herself in anger about Pushpa's laziness, Rachel took the duck out of the freezer to be defrosted and set about cleaning the kitchen table. She cut the onions, ginger and garlic and made a paste of the pieces, with coriander powder and red chilli powder. She had cooked the duck roast and the mutton curry and was frying the papads when Pushpa rang the doorbell. 'Just came in time for lunch?' Rachel asked her in sarcasm.

The door bell pealed again and the guests came in. Rachel greeted them with her hair wild and unkempt, her face full of perspiration and her gown streaked with saffron. She cast an appealing look at George and rushed into the bathroom, leaving him to entertain the guests. Pushpa followed her into the bedroom and began a long story through the bathroom door, about having had to wait to see her uncle who had sent her a message to meet him before she left. Rachel cut her short and asked her not to waste any more time telling her unbelievable stories but to serve the guests.

Despite her irritation with Pushpa, Rachel was a socialist at heart. She felt guilty that Vakachen Velliappachan would not have approved of the way she treated Pushpa. She was nagged by doubts about Pushpa's rights to entertain herself in the season of peace and joy. Just because she was a domestic worker, did she not have any rights to visit her near relations and celebrate the spirit of Christmas? Rachel fought a silent battle within herself about workers' rights and employers' legitimate claims. Her doubts got more acute when, as part of the annual work plan of the Labour department, she was asked to organise a workshop on "Legislation to secure the rights of Domestic workers and other workers in the unorganised sector". When the legislation was finally passed, they would certainly arrest her, she thought, for violation of all the various clauses which she had drafted herself. (Workers' right to a living wage, weekly offs, Provident Fund, right to an annual bonus, Human Rights, Right not to be exploited, Right to socialise with friends and relatives . . .)

The day after Christmas, Rachel's cousin Vincent came visiting with his wife. George opened a bottle of gin and they drank a few pegs together before lunch. Vincent's wife Mary also had a little of the gin, with soda and ice and a piece of lemon. Pushpa saw Mary *chechi* drinking the gin, as she served at table. After the visitors left, they all had an afternoon siesta. The weather was hot and sultry in Bombay although it was December. They left the bottle of gin on the kitchen table.

Pushpa was late in making the tea that evening. As she had not got up till five-thirty, Rachel went to wake her up. Pushpa staggered to the gas stove and blinked her eyes, as though the light was too strong. Then she came into the room swaying with the tea tray and bringing it down before Rachel, on the sitting room centre table, with a bow. She walked back to the kitchen staggering and holding on to the walls.

'I'm feeling too sleepy,' she muttered. 'I had such a lot of work last night.'

Rachel kept quiet, not knowing what to make of this display. She wants to try me and get me all worked up, Rachel thought. So she just ignored Pushpa's bizarre behaviour. But when she told George of Pushpa's strange antics, he jumped up and went into the kitchen. He saw that the bottle of gin was nearly empty. Pushpa had helped herself liberally to the alcohol.

A few days later when Rachel came home from work, Pushpa announced with a superior air, that her visa for Muscat had arrived and that she was leaving the next morning. She would be getting a salary of six thousand rupees, she said, with free food and living quarters and a weekly off on Sundays. 'Fine,' said Rachel, feeling guilty that she had not given Pushpa the weekly off every Sunday that she had promised the nuns at Goregaon. She had also not given Pushpa a room to herself. But their apartment had only two bedrooms. So Pushpa had slept in the kitchen.

Pushpa was a long time bathing the next morning. She dressed herself in her best, red salwar kameez and she put kohl in her eyes. Her lips were a brilliant red gash. Rachel gave Pushpa her wages for the month and Pushpa took her two large rexin travel bags with her and went down with them in the lift. Half an hour later she rang up from the ground floor security desk, on the internal telephone.

'Madam, there's a taxi strike,' she said, 'I can't get a taxi. It's only a short distance, to my uncle's house, can you please tell the driver to give me a lift?' Rachel was silent for a minute.

'Pushpa, there's a bus service, you can take the bus,' she said shortly.

'But I have to wait a long while and it's so crowded,' she argued, 'Please Madam. Just this once.'

'Take the bus, it won't kill you,' Rachel said, feeling somehow mean and small minded and put down the receiver.

Rachel found to her surprise that the roof did not cave in after Pushpa's departure. But a month later they still hadn't found a replacement for Pushpa. One morning, the driver Raman told Rachel as she gave him the car keys, 'Madam, yesterday I saw Pushpa wandering in the street. She was looking very dirty in her orange dress. Her hair was uncombed. She said that her visa had got cancelled at the last moment and that she has no place to sleep in. She has been sleeping on the footpath. None of her brothers have come forward to help her now. They call her a *vaishya*. She has no job . . . ' He left the question hanging in the air, whether they would like her back. Rachel stifled a gasp.

'Oh No! But we can't have her back Raman. She – she – was – very unsuitable . . .' Rachel tried to look sorry and suppressed the unworthy thought that Pushpa had only got what she richly deserved. 'May be you can give her this money, let her go back to her family in Kerala if she wants,' Rachel said lamely, feeling guilty that Pushpa was wandering homeless in the streets.

The next day Rachel was late for office and she dressed in a hurry, combing her hair in her usual, careless fashion. She reached for the talcum powder and dabbed it on her face absently and took the spray on the dresser and sprayed herself, when its malodour wafted to her nostrils. She looked down at the metal container. It was the crab-apple dog repellent and the dog's talcum powder that she had used. She looked around for her Yardley tin. Now where had she kept it? She had been so careful to lock up everything. Then Rachel's mother said, 'Oh I forgot to tell you – Pushpa took the Yardley with her from your dressing table. She said that you told her that you wanted her to keep it as a present, since she was leaving.'

❦ ❦ ❦

JOURNEY TO KEDERNATH

Mukesh Kumar Srivastava sat at the breakfast table, in Manjusha's house, his long legs out-stretched, while his wife knelt at his feet, a felt rag in her hand, polishing his shoes. Mukesh flicked the morning paper and had a sip of tea from the elegant bone china tea cup in his hand, as he looked occasionally at his wife's labours and muttered irritably, 'Do it carefully, look at the back as well.' Charmili renewed her efforts, panting slightly, her double chin waggling. He looked at her sourly. The sow, he thought. She was corpulent and fleshy rolls strained from her tight sari blouse. Her long hair was still black and luxuriant. But her face had taken a round, porcine appearance. Mukesh on the other hand, still looked slim and boyish and not his forty odd years.

He got up with an expression of displeasure on his face, while his wife stood submissive, a mute expression in her eyes, awaiting his next command. Just then there was a wailing noise. The baby had just soiled its diaper and it was sticky. It lay kicking its legs and bawling on the rubber sheet on the floor, where Manjusha had left it before going to the bathroom. A brown liquid oozed out of the baby's diaper. The unpleasant odour of the baby's excreta slowly permeated the room.
'Go and wash the baby's bottom and wipe the rubber sheet,' said Mukesh peremptorily.

'Surely the maid can do that,' Charmili said just a little defiantly. Hearing the baby cry, Manjusha came out of the bathroom, towelling her hair. She walked towards the infant.

'Don't pick up the baby – just after you've had your bath. Charmili will wash the baby,' said Mukesh, leaving his wife no room for escape. Charmili took the baby with bad grace and rinsed its bottom none too gently under the tap with cold water, which made it howl with the discomfort. She lay the baby on the bed and wiped it dry and gave it to Manjusha.

'Sonali,' Manjusha called out to the kitchen maid and asked her to clean up the baby's mess. Manjusha changed from her house-coat into an elegant, light blue Bengal cotton handloom sari. It had a black woven border. She picked up the hair drier from its holder on the wall, dried her hair and combed it out and came back into the dining room and sat down at the table, her shoulder length black hair falling gracefully over her oval face. She buttered herself a piece of toast and bit into it in small, elegant bird-bites.

'I'd like a cup of tea before I leave,' Mukesh said. Charmili poured out a cup for him but he took the one proffered simultaneously by Manjusha. Discomfited, Charmili drank the tea herself. Mukesh left with Manjusha in her office car to the Office of the Controller of Import and Export at Churchgate, to enquire about the status of his application for a deputation. He was sick of life in Uttar Pradesh and wanted a deputation to a central government office in Bombay. He would be able to pursue a course of studies in Business Management at the Bombay University and perhaps even wangle a posting abroad with a UN agency.

Mukesh stayed in Manjusha's house during his visits to Bombay. It was cheaper than living in a hotel and Manjusha's mild mannered husband Niranjan did not object to house guests in the small apartment. Mukesh enjoyed being in Bombay and going to music performances with Manjusha. They were going that evening to a sitar recital by Pandit Virsen Joshi. Manjusha used her own scooter when they went for late night performances, so that she did not have to bother her driver, who lived far away in Kalyan. Mukesh rode on the pillion seat behind her, with a rueful laugh, when he joined her at these events. Both Niranjan and Charmili declined to join them. Mukesh looked forward to the evenings, as Manjusha made him laugh during the intervals of the performance, with her amusing stories about the latest antics of her Minister, whose mannerisms and accent she mimicked so effectively. Mukesh often thought that unlike Manjusha, Charmili never had anything to say to him, other than that the housekeeping money was over and that the milkman had presented his bill. He was bored by Charmili's silences.

There was a time when he had been attracted by Charmili's lovely voice. She had taught Indian Classical music, at the Administrative Service Academy at Nainital. Her soulful voice and her lustrous eyes had attracted Mukesh Kumar. He was twenty-five and had just joined the Indian Administrative Service. Mukesh had a good singing voice too. Charmili's father was the Yoga instructor in the academy. Driven by the idealism from his college days in Jawaharlal Nehru University where he was a part of a Left Wing ideological movement, Mukesh scorned all class and caste barriers. He was smitten by Charmili. Only her voice mattered. They sang love duets together at the cultural evenings. They wandered about the winding roads in Nainital, hand in hand. They sat drinking hot ginger tea at Rustom's dabha. At the beginning of the month when Mukesh was flush with his pay advance, they had dinner at the Wayside Inn and ate their fill of butter chicken and hot nans. The other officers soon guffawed behind his back about Mukesh's "Singing Mistress". It was during the Diwali vacation that Mukesh and Charmili had a registered marriage in the hill station, to forestall any opposition from his parents.

But it was as his father had said. The charm of Charmili's voice faded and instead the seeds of disagreements began to grow. The other officers' wives looked down on Charmili. They knew of her humble background. Most of them belonged to families of standing – their fathers were senior officers in the army or the civil services, rich industrialists or land-lords from old zamindari families, who wanted an influential IAS son-in-law. The officers' wives did not invite Charmili to their coffee parties and they made fun of her unsophisticated ways. They commented about the lumpy unfashionable cut of her salwar kameezes. They said that she lined her eyes heavily with kohl, like a nautch girl in the old Hindi films of the sixties. They bitched about how she had cradle-snatched Mukesh who was four years younger than her.

Mukesh had sufficient time now to repent over the hasty indiscretions of his youth. He often reflected about how much more comfortable it would have been, if his father-in-law had been a Secretary to government and could ensure that he had a career graph studded with plum posts. As it was, they had a difficult time living on his salary. They were always running short of something or the other. Charmili was not a good home manager. The sofa looked ragged and their house always had an untidy appearance. Fortunately there were no children.

When Charmili's father died of a heart attack and her family had to give up their quarters at the Academy, Charmili fetched her mother home to stay with them for a while. They were both relived when after a brief visit, her mother went to live with Charmili's brother, a school master in a small village near Nainital.

Mukesh rarely came home early from work. He usually spent some time with those of his colleagues who were inclined to have a drink at the officers' club in Lucknow. He ate the delicious pakoras and chicken nuggets that the club caterer served. Charmili sat up waiting for him. When he came in, she warmed the dinner in the microwave oven and set it at the table, but he usually went to sleep without touching it.

In fact, nothing that she did pleased him now. The harder she tried to please him, the more contemptuous he became. It irritated him to see her round, brown, anxious face hovering solicitously around him. It would have been so much better to have married a sweet young beauty, with a big dowry, he thought bitterly. The girl's father would have laid out a red carpet every time he visited them.

As the years passed, Mukesh hardly ever went out with Charmili. He felt humiliated by the sarcastic smiles that her appearance inevitably evoked. He no longer wanted to sing soulful duets with her. He preferred singing them with Manjusha, whenever he was in Bombay, though she *was* a little flat. Manjusha's husband rarely went out for late night parties. He worked as an engineer in an American company and had to be at work by seven every morning. He was always at work on his computer even on weekends. He travelled to the company's New York office on work almost every two months.

Mukesh felt that he had many things in common with Manjusha and his dislike for his wife seemed to grow every day. For one thing, her eyes made Mukesh feel guilty. She had the look of an injured doe and her expression made him furious. Her air of humble servitude made him want to swat her out of his life, as though she were a tiresome insect. She was always around him, trying to gauge and anticipate his every desire and fulfil his wishes even before he asked for anything. When he reached out to get the evening paper lying on the front room table, she saw it and deposited it in his lap. When he walked into the kitchen to get a drink of water, she would hear him and pad up in her slipper less feet and pour out the water from the bottle in the refrigerator into a glass, before he could take hold of the bottle. Yet none of these services pleased him. They were the services of a slave who had nowhere else to go. A slave who was afraid of being turned out. And yet he did not think of divorce. Where would she go? With whom would she stay? Some feeling of chivalry kept him from leaving her. He just didn't speak to her unless it was to bark some command and as soon as he had heard the ten o'clock news on TV, he retired to his own bed room and Charmili to hers.

᳣   ᳣   ᳣

Charmili noticed that Mukesh's behaviour towards her had begun to change gradually after the first few years of their marriage. She was very unhappy that they did not have children. After the first wedding anniversary passed by without the expected child, Mukesh took to reading up every self help book and newspaper column about how to improve their chances of having a baby. He soaked almonds in water at night and made Charmili have them in the morning on an empty stomach. He took Charmili to several gynaecologists and even made her wear a charmed amulet from a famous Baba of Trilokchand, who guaranteed conception within three months of a visit to his ashram. However Charmili could not go for the private blessing that he gave every prospective mother, as her mother had chanced to fall very ill just then and she had to visit her instead of accompanying Mukesh to the ashram. But it was all of no avail. There was no patter of little feet in their house. Mukesh took to making excuses that he was too tired after the gruelling work day to sleep with her. He came in late and crashed into bed in the spare room.

Charmili was hurt by the long trips he began taking home to his parents, without her – something he had avoided earlier. Each time he came back, he praised his mummy-ji's cooking as something out of this world. He now had something uncomplimentary to say about the way she cooked the dal or the vegetable.

She missed his boyish adulation of everything that she did. His joyful response in singing aloud any song that she chanced to hum as she made the breakfast. Initially, he only wore the clothes that she set out on the bed for him to wear for the day, matching the shirt with trousers and socks. She had a sinking feeling as she found him increasingly wearing what he wanted to, out of his wardrobe, without asking for her opinion. He also brought back his lunch box from the office, with the food uneaten. He put the box on the kitchen table without offering any explanation and she dared not ask him why he had not had his lunch, since he flew into a rage whenever she ventured to speak to him. The times that they sang love duets together seemed another age. The sweet nothings he whispered had now turned into sharp commands. It was clear that he regretted the marriage. She had stepped into the quicksand of a failing relationship and she did not know how it had come about. What was it that had changed? Had she changed or was it he who had become another person?

She gave up trying to look attractive for him. She rarely dressed up and wore the same crushed housecoat for days on end. But he did not notice what she wore. Only when he was expecting visitors did he comment on her style of dressing. When the Ahujas said that they were dropping by in the evening to invite them to Ahuja's son's fifth birthday party, he said, 'Don't wear your usual ragged housecoat. Wear something decent looking, the Ahujas are coming this evening.' But of course they did not go to the party. It made their own childless state all too obvious. Charmili found solace in eating mithai and namkeen. She did not cook lunch the days that Mukesh was on tour, but instead she ate fried onion and potato bajjis and luscious deep red gulab jamuns in sugar syrup. Her billowing figure now made her the butt of jokes in their civil service community and made him feel debased . . .

☙ ☙ ☙

Charmili looked out of the window in the hall, watching the white Ambassador car with its amber swivel light, speed away with Mukesh and Manjusha in it, their heads close together. She wiped a single tear that had strayed out of the dull ache in her heart. She recalled that it was Mukesh who had made the first move, the first overture of friendship to her at the academy. Their meetings had rapidly turned into delicious, stolen moments of bliss. They had lain in the grass, in green meadows, the trees sighing in the wind. He had recited poetry, his head in her lap, holding her hands in his own strong, capable hands. But it was a dream that shattered – slowly, in small moments of neglect and irritation that imperceptibly gathered momentum, to ignite his anger and finally – revulsion. She turned on the TV in the living room to block out the thoughts that came beating into her head. She spent the afternoon lying on the bed in the spare room.

When Mukesh returned in the evening from the office of the Controller, he was in a bad mood. Another officer had got himself recommended to the Minister and had already been appointed by the Department of Personnel. He was expected to join any day. Mukesh flopped down on a chair and asked Charmili to make him a cup of tea. When she brought it, her fingers shook and some of the tea slopped over on to the saucer. 'Can you never do anything right?' he raged.

He asked her to go to the railway station the next morning and book two second class train tickets for their return journey home. Manjusha's peon could not be spared for the job since there was an important meeting in the office. Of course it was out of the question for a senior government official like Mukesh to stand in a long line at the smelly railway station, for a second class ticket.

The next day Charmilli set out for the VT station. Her heart sank when she saw the serpentine queue for tickets to Lucknow. She joined the line any way. But even after waiting for four hours, her turn did not come. She was thirsty and she longed for a cool drink. But she was afraid to leave her place. She finally got to the counter and bought two tickets. Her tongue was parched and she was stiff all over. She wanted to sit down at a roadside café and have a samosa and a coke. But she dared not spend any money. Mukesh was sure to check the money and ask for an account of it. She walked dispiritedly to the bus-stand and stood waiting for the bus back to Manjusha's home.

It was late in the evening when she returned. The flat was empty except for the baby and the ayah. She sat down exhausted, on the sofa. The door bell rang. It was Manjusha and Mukesh. They were joking and Manjusha's peals of laughter could be heard from outside. They were discussing the antics of the hero in the Hindi film that they had both seen. It had been a Sikandhar Khan movie. The meeting at her office had been cancelled and Mukesh and Manjusha had gone for the movie instead.

'Wish you'd been there. The movie was great,' Manjusha said idly, as she placed a box of patties on the table in the hall. The patties had an inviting aroma. Hungry and tired, Charmilli was drawn to the savouries. She opened the box and helped herself to a patty.

'Put it in a plate for god's sake and offer it to others first,' Mukesh hissed angrily from behind. Charmilli drew back, stung by the remark and dropped the patty back into the box. She stood silent. Then she slowly took out the tickets from her hand bag and gave it to her husband. He looked at them and let them fall to the floor.

'Go and get a refund on it tomorrow,' he snapped. 'There's no need for these tickets. Manjusha's PA has already booked us two tickets on the government quota.'

The door bell chimed loudly twice in succession. Someone seemed to be in a hurry. It was Manjusha's husband Niranjan. Mukesh hastily altered his expression into one of cordiality, wondering guiltily whether he had been audible in the passage outside. A white woman, with wavy brown hair, came in with Niranjan. She was slim and wore a blue pant suit. A beautiful diamond pendant hung from a thin silver chain on her neck.

'Hi, meet Lydia,' said Niranjan, 'She's come from our New York office to attend the last Board meeting of the year.' Niranjan introduced his wife and Mukesh to Lydia and they shook hands. No one noticed Charmili standing diffidently near the kitchen door. Mukesh sat on the couch in the hall, exchanging pleasantries with the others. Niranjan went into the bedroom and came back after a shower and a change of clothes, wearing a black silk kameez and off white churidars. As he left with Lydia, he told Manjusha over his shoulder not to wait up for him when she returned from her sitar recital. He was dining out with his American visitor and was likely to be late, he said.

Manjusha looked strained and did not speak as they ate their dinner of dal, bhaji and rotis. Niranjan had just assumed that Manjusha was going to a musical performance with Mukesh that evening as well. He had not bothered to ask her whether she cared to dine out with him and Lydia, because he so obviously wanted to be alone with Lydia. Though the servant had left for the day and the food was cold, Manjusha did not bother to heat up the food for her house guests. There was an uncomfortable atmosphere in the room. Manjusha did not pick up her baby when it cried in the bedroom. Charmili could not bear its wails. She looked at Manjusha's stony face and went into the bedroom and picked up the baby and held it close, crooning it to sleep again.

ॐ ॐ ॐ

When Charmili and Mukesh got back to Lucknow, Charmili found the time hanging even more heavily on her hands. She counted the long hours and unendurable minutes of each day. She was miserable. The visit to Bombay had somehow worsened her relationship with Mukesh.

One morning, her eyes fell on an advertisement in the situations vacant column of the news paper. It was a vacancy for a hostel warden for a girls' hostel in the city. Residential quarters were provided, the advertisement said. Women above thirty-five years of age, without encumbrances were asked to apply for the post. Her heart full of doubts and misgivings, Charmili applied for the job and went for the interview. However, her pleasant manner and mature appearance appealed to the interview committee. She did not tell them that she was the wife of a senior IAS officer. She was selected. As the management was in a hurry to fill in the vacancy, she was asked to join within a week.

Mukesh drove home from the office the following week. It was early November in Lucknow and there was a chill outside. Dusk had already settled in. The servant Raju opened the door to him when he rang the doorbell. He was mildly surprised not to see Charmili. It was usually Charmili who looked out for him from the window and opened the door to him. He entered the house, rubbing his hands together to warm them.

'Where is Memsahib?' he asked the servant.

'She left in the morning with a suitcase in a taxi, saab. She did not say where she was going,' Raju replied.

Mukesh found a letter from Charmili on the dining table.

"*Dear Mukesh,*" she wrote, "*I think our life together is not to be. I am trying out a new life. I hope you will find happiness. I thank you for the moments of joy you gave me.*
Yours
Charmili"

He put it down with shaking hands. It was then that he noticed another letter on the table, under the newspaper. It bore Manjusha's long sloping handwriting. Manjusha informed him tersely that Niranjan had filed for divorce. He had named Mukesh as the person with whom his wife had had an adulterous relationship and who had ruined his married life. She said that she had begged Niranjan not to divorce her. But he had remained unmoved. She wanted him to at least agree to a divorce by mutual consent and spare them both the ignominy of the long drawn out court proceedings, the washing of dirty linen. But he had proved inflexible. He had cited Charmili as a witness to the sordid events. Manjusha wrote that she wanted

Mukesh to prevail upon Charmili to refuse to give evidence in the matter.

Mukesh put a hand to his brow. Where on earth was Charmili and how was he to contact her? He did not want the embarrassment of filing a missing person's report with the police. It was sure to come out in the papers. He could see the headlines : "Top bureaucrat's wife missing. Police suspect foul play." It was so inconsiderate of Charmili to disappear on him in this manner, at this crucial juncture.

Mukesh spent a long month of waiting and indecisiveness. Then, one night, the telephone rang. It was Charmili. 'Hello, this is Charmili, Mukesh,' she said, her voice strong and self confident, quite different from the low shrinking tone that she usually adopted when addressing him. 'I called to let you know that I have taken up a job. I'm fine. So you don't have to worry. Also Niranjan has filed for divorce and has asked me to testify about your relationship with Manjusha. If you like I can refuse him. But –' There was a pause.
'Charmili – what is it? And where are you? In an ashram? A fine thing you did – just leaving me without even a hint of your intentions. These absurd charges that Niranjan is making won't told any water. I think you –' But she cut him off.
'I want a divorce by mutual consent Mukesh,' she said flatly, 'I won't give evidence in Niranjan's case, if you make me a reasonable settlement of half of what you own.'
He was shocked. 'Charmili!! I can't believe that you could –' he began, but she had already put down the

receiver. After a while his mobile beeped and he saw that there was a text message from Charmili – her advocate Dhyan Sharma would get in touch with him it said.

Mukesh spent the next few days in an agony of worry. Then he received a letter from Dhyan Sharma. Charmili demanded a payment of twenty lac rupees – half of the amount in his provident fund – and also asked that their two bed room flat in upmarket Rambaug in Lucknow be handed over to her. He could retain the bungalow that they presently lived in. Dhyan Sharma met Mukesh at a small restaurant near the market at Rambaug. He confirmed the terms of Charmili's divorce settlement and refused to whittle down any of her requirements. Mukesh found it impossible not to agree to the terms dictated by Charmili. He did not want to appear in court and be cross questioned about the nature of his relationship with Manjusha. He shrank from the unsavoury publicity, the inevitable discussion and gossip among his service colleagues. However, he actually felt a sense of relief in bringing his withered relationship with Charmili to a formal close.

In a few months Mukesh and Charmili were divorced. Charmili never came back to her marital home of bitter sweet memories. When she had left it, she had taken all of her belongings that she had wanted – her clothes and her jewellery, the few presents that Mukesh had given her – an ornate photo frame of them in their wedding finery, a jade laughing Buddha, a diamond necklace with matching earrings and a gold kada with finely embossed red and green Meena work.

Niranjan and Manjusha also obtained a quick divorce by mutual consent. Manjusha was annoyed that it was Niranjan who had sued for divorce. She should have left him long ago, she thought. He had been so absent in her life. He was so wrapped up in his work, that it was a relief to go out for an evening, even with a dull stick like Mukesh. Quite illogically she had a sense of injury and betrayal when Niranjan left for the US immediately after the divorce and married Lydia.

Mukesh tried to call Manjusha in her office, but she refused to take his calls on her mobile. She did not want to see him ever again, she told him when he rang her at her house.

'Why Manjusha? We had such a good thing going,' he remonstrated.

'I was Niranjan's wife, but he divorced me because of you,' she answered, 'But you were just a time pass for me Mukesh. Now I don't want to rehash all of that. It's best that we leave well alone and not see each other again.'

Mukesh was unable to come terms with the sudden turn of events in his life. He felt guilty remembering how he had ignored Charmili and forced her to leave him. But he could not understand why Manjusha had stopped seeing him. She had always made him feel that he was a prize matrimonial catch wasted on a village woman like Charmili. He did not feel like going to work any longer. He found his life falling to pieces. There were so many things that Charmili had attended to around the house unknown to him. Now everything seemed to be so disorganised. When he came back home one evening to find the house in darkness, it was the last straw. He had forgotten to pay the electric bill and the company had just cut the connection. The thought of living in Lucknow became unbearable. After a few weeks of indecision, he sought a transfer and took up a position in Delhi.

However, nothing quelled Mukesh's restlessness. He felt that he had to see Charmili once more. He took the Raj Kamal Express to Lucknow. It arrived at Lucknow Junction early in the morning. He went home and opened the door with his latch key and found Raju sleeping in the hall, on the couch. Mukesh roused him awake and asked him to make some tea. After a bath and a breakfast of a bowl of cornflakes, Mukesh took a taxi to Rambaug. He went up the lift to Charmili's apartment and rang the door bell. A cheerful ten year old girl, in jeans and a T shirt opened the door. He was surprised. 'Can – can I see Charmili?' he asked hesitantly.

'Amma! Someone to see you!' the little girl called out. She gestured him towards the neat sofa in the sitting room. A military looking gentleman with a bushy moustache walked into the room from inside the house. 'Yes?' he asked, 'What is it that you want?' Mukesh repeated his request.

Charmili came into the room just then. She looked a little surprised to see him. He barely recognised her. She had cut her hair in a short bob and had lost weight. She wore nylon stretch pants and a smart kurta top. She gave him a polite smile and said, 'Oh Mukesh! How are you? Subodh – this is my first husband, you've never met him.

Mukesh, meet my husband – Major Nair and Smriti – my daughter.' She asked him courteously whether he would have a cup of tea and looked at him, a question in her eyes. She so obviously wanted him to state his business. But he found that he had no business after all. He ought not to have come. Charmili had moved on. He had no place in her life. He declined the cup of tea that she offered him and stumbled out of the house. The hot April sun beat down on him as he walked the streets aimlessly. He went home late in the evening.

Confused and distraught, he lay awake all night, tossing and turning in the sweltering heat on sheets that had turned damp with his sweat. He ran over the events of his life. He had made so many wrong choices. He had messed up his life. He got out of bed early in the morning and made himself a cup of strong black coffee. He sat smoking in the bedroom, looking out of the window with unseeing eyes. Raju the servant made some dal and a vegetable and rotis for lunch and left the house. Mukesh did not notice him leave. By the afternoon Mukesh had made up his mind. He packed a few essentials into a shoulder bag and went to the railway station. He booked a ticket to Haridwar and boarded the Doon Express in the evening.

He managed to get a sleeper berth but the smelly itchy blankets provided by the train conductor kept him awake in the night. Just before day break the train reached Haridwar. There were the loud cries of tea vendors selling tea in earthenware cups. Mukesh got down at the station and had a rudimentary bath at the railway waiting room. It was dirty and messy with water all over the floor. He was hungry and found a roadside food stall outside the station. The vendor had a huge kadai filled with bubbling oil. There were potato and onion bajjis frying in it. A few flies sat on the used leaf plates piled in a corner. Mukesh stood at the stall and ate crunchy jalebis dripping with sugar syrup and salty bajjis pungent with green chillis. He also had a cup of steaming hot tea.

There were taxis going to Kedarnath. He found two college students who were travelling to the shrine. They were ready to share an Indica taxi with him. The taxi driver, a Jat called Vikram Singh, said that the road was difficult. He could take them up to Gaurikund. It was a distance of two hundred and forty kilometres. They haggled with the driver over the fare. He wanted them to pay him four thousand rupees for the journey. They finally agreed on three thousand rupees. Vikram Singh piled their luggage into the hold and they got into the taxi. He drove at a breakneck speed, taking reckless turns around sharp bends, blowing his horn loudly to warm any potential victims of his rash driving. Mukesh and his travelling companions sat clutching the door handles, their hearts in their mouths. They climbed higher and higher, up the winding mountainous terrain. Shrubs gave way to clumps of rhododendrons. Oak trees and pine appeared. They stopped for a cup of tea at a small tea stall at New Tehri. The tea vendor a Pahadi named Pratap Jogi said that the way further up was clear, but rough. They hit the road once more. It became progressively narrow and difficult. At times in the distance they sighted black bear, sambar, and musk deer in the surrounding forests. Langur came up quite close, looking out for fruit and chattering to one another excitedly, snatching bananas from passengers in the tourist buses.

Mukesh and his youthful companions reached Gaurikund by twelve in the afternoon. The road was not motor able any further, Vikram Singh said. They got down from the taxi and paid off the driver. A biting cold wind blew in the air. Mukesh shivered and buttoned up his woollen jacket and wrapped a muffler over his neck and ears. There were a few dhabas in the small settlement. Mukesh stopped at the *Dhaba Gud Luck* which had a knot of tourists standing near it. He had a quick lunch of Puri Bhaji and asked for a cup of tea. A small boy served him strong sweet tea garnished with cardamom, in a clay cup. Mukesh drank the hot tea gratefully. It made him feel warmer. He then took the road to Kedarnath with the others.

It was a steep climb of fourteen kilometres. But Mukesh felt somehow lighter as he breathed in the pure, fresh air. The pilgrims walked together in companionship. Some spoke of their life experiences. Others spoke of their ill health or worries for their children. They were all going to pray for relief from the troubles that had dragged them down. However Mukesh was silent. He did not tell the other travellers what it was that impelled him to walk to the shrine. They stopped for a meal at a dhaba in Ramwara. It was seven kilometres more to their destination.

They reached Kedarnath late in the evening. The sky was already dark. Mukesh ambled down the main road and saw a motel. The front wall had a message in bold red paint – 'Cheep rooms awailbul. Only Five Hundred rupees for double sharing room.' He checked into the motel and had a bath. He had a simple meal of Khichidi in the motel's dining hall. There were a few tourists in the hall eating pan and talking animatedly about their plans for the next day. He was tired and the loud conversation irritated him. He finished his meal quickly and walked upstairs to his room on the second floor and got into bed. The room was cold and the rough blanket provided by the motel had a few holes in it. He spent an uncomfortable night, tormented by vague fears and the cold which crept in through the chinks in the blanket.

The next morning he had an early breakfast of alu parathas and tea in the crowded dining hall. It was noisy with the sounds of people talking together. The glass windows of the hall were misted over by the steaming hot food brought in from the kitchen – idlis and sambaar, kachoris, parathas and potato baji. Hot ginger tea was served in small chipped ceramic cups. The tourists discussed the weather. It was getting to be colder. Most of them wanted a quick darshan before they walked back to Gaurikund.

Mukesh found a roadside barber outside the motel. He asked him the price of having his head tonsured and sat down on the barber's broken wooden chair. A large mirror stood propped up against a tree stump facing the chair. The barber shaved off all the hair from his head, just leaving a small tuft near the crown.

Mukesh checked the stalls selling household articles. There were pots and pans, candles, match boxes, bed sheets, readymade clothes, saffron coloured dothis, Vicks Vapo Rub, Amrutanjan pain balm, tea leaves, Bru coffee, sugar and Rudraksha malas, all piled together in disarray. Mukesh bought a saffron coloured dothi and jubba and a Rudraksha mala. He went back to the motel. He paid the room boy thirty rupees for a bucket of hot water and after a warm water bath he changed from his shirt and trousers into the orange robes. Mukesh wrapped his western clothes in a bundle in newspaper and gave it away on his way out, to a young waiter at the motel.

There were pilgrims walking towards the shrine, chanting Sanskrit slokas, occasionally breaking out into cries of, 'Bholenathji ki jai!! Ma Parvatiji ki Jai!' Some of them carried triangular saffron flags which fluttered in the breeze. Mukesh joined them and felt a little less lonely. The temple bells chimed almost unceasingly over the hills, as devotees thronged the shrine. Mukesh walked into the temple precincts, rang the bells at the entrance and bowed his head in obeisance. He sat down on the ground, his feet crossed under his thighs, in the lotus pose. The lamps flickered around the deity. Mukesh folded his hands in prayer chanting the sloka by Adi Shankaracharya – *'Praatah Smaraami Bhava Bhiiti Haram Suresham – In the early morning I remember Lord Shiva who destroys the fear of worldly existence and who is the Lord of the Devas.'* As he gazed at the lingam, it slowly took the shape of Shiva standing astride, trident in hand, his hair knotted on his head, the Ganges river flowing in a stream out of his head, a serpent adorning his neck. The Lord's eyes were resplendent and his face had a golden radiance as he lifted his right hand in a blessing. Mukesh sat transfixed, enveloped in a warm glow of light. The hopelessness in his heart receded. The churning in his mind ceased. All fear left him. He was still and a wave of contentment washed over him.

As darkness descended it grew colder. The devotees left one by one. However Mukesh did not move. The pujari signalled that it was time to shut the temple. Mukesh got up and sat outside. The priest took him home to his small one roomed hut. They shared a silent meal of rice gruel and curd. The next day, Mukesh got up before day break and opened the door of the hut. The sky was dark and a piecing cold wind blew outside. His companion was already up and was walking towards the river. He followed the priest and entered the freezing waters of the Mandakini, his teeth chattering with cold. The sacred slokas came back to his memory, as he worshipped the rising sun stealing up the slopes of the Himalayas.

Mukesh spent the days in meditation under a tree outside the temple. Devotees who visited the temple left him food on the small steel thal in front of him. He did not move from the spot that he had chosen. When it grew too cold, he wrapped himself in a blanket that a beggar had discarded.

He lived outside the temple till November. It was then time for the Lord Kedarnath to shift his residence for the winter months. Mukesh accompanied the palki carrying the idol to Ukhimath. Since he did not speak, he came to be known as Maun Baba. People asked him to bless them and tell them about what would happen next in their lives, the outcome of the difficult situations that they faced. He inclined his head in a blessing and they felt their burdens lighten.

ॐ ॐ ॐ

PRAMOD JOSHI

Pramod Joshi had requested to be posted back home to Delhi. His wife had deserted him in London for a Swiss student studying at the LSE. And so Joshi had elected to come home in order to recover from the insult. The Department of Personnel appointed him as the Private Secretary to the Honourable Minister for Coal and Mines, since he was personally known to the Minister Mr. Dagdoo Naik-Phatake who was from his home town of Nagpur. Gajapati was the Deputy Secretary for Projects and Foreign Collaborations, in the department. Joshi came to Gajapati's room in the secretariat and said, 'Hello Gajapati, I'm Joshi. I'm the new PS to M (C&M).' They shook hands. Gajapati rang for his peon and asked for a tray of coffee. They made good south Indian coffee in the department's canteen. The caterer was a Kamat who had a string of Udipi cafes in Hyderabad.

It was while he drank the coffee and Gajapati asked Joshi the usual questions about his family and which school he was getting his children admitted to, that Joshi suddenly said, 'I've come here because my wife has filed for divorce. It'll soon come through. I'm not challenging it.' There was a short uncomfortable silence after that, since Gajapati didn't know the story or know

Joshi well enough to commiserate with him. Joshi soon left, shutting the door quietly behind him.

Gajapati was a little surprised to hear the news, because Joshi was a handsome enough chap, a conservative Brahmin, and being a Foreign Service officer, a prize matrimonial catch. Most girls in India would have given their ears to have been able to marry a man like Joshi. He was tall, fair and well built, with a narrow nose and well-shaped, firm lips and a sharp chin on which he grew a distinguished beard. His straight, shoulder length hair, had streaks of grey. He often had a far away pensive look in his eye.

Notwithstanding his private grief, Joshi soon threw himself into his work energetically. Since it involved a lot of correspondence with state governments, to be followed up by visits, Gajapati saw little of him, except when he came in for a chat sometime. Joshi also accompanied the Minister on his frequent foreign trips. But Joshi's son often came to play with Gajapati's children. Mrs. Uma Gajapati befriended the poor lad and gave him a nice hot tea of puranpoli or potato bhajjis or some other savoury every evening. The boy consumed them hungrily, eating like a famished wolf cub. When Joshi's mother, cantankerous and whimsical, her nine yard sari trailing the floor, came to take him back home in the evening, the boy refused to leave Uma and cried bitterly. He clung to Uma's sari and said, 'I don't want to go with Aaji. I won't leave mummy.' The boy, Nilesh, was just seven years old and he had asked Mrs. Gajapati to be his mummy, the very first day that he had come to the Gajapati household. He had thereafter spent the night in the children's bedroom together with the two Gajapati children.

One evening just as Gajapati was clearing his desk preparatory to leaving, Joshi entered the room. His eyes were shining with excitement. 'I've just got a letter from my wife,' he said. Gajapati was rather exhausted. But he asked Joshi to sit down, all the same. It had been a hot day in May in Delhi and Gajapati had attended a daylong meeting with the association of employees. Joshi said that his wife was arriving soon for the final hearing of the divorce petition which was posted for the next week. Her Swiss boyfriend was also coming with her. Joshi was in a reminiscent mood.

'Sonali was ten years younger than me when we were married,' he said, 'she was only seventeen and I was twenty-seven. But our parents were friends and they decided that it would be a good match. Sonali didn't have a chance to go to college and when she turned eighteen, she was pregnant with our first child. When I think back now, I feel that maybe we ought to have waited, till she was little more mature. She hated the baby from the very first moment that she saw him and said, "Take him away. I don't want to see him." You see she had had such a difficult pregnancy, with a lot of morning sickness and swollen feet. Whenever she rang up any of her school friends, she found that they were away in college or going for movies, picnics with friends and involved in other interesting activities, while she was at home, cooped up with a baby. She got to hate the sound of his wails and she closed her ears with her hands saying, "I can't bear the sound of that miserable brat". It was only because my mother stepped in and looked after Nilesh that he survived at all. He was put on bottle-feed. At first, of course, he cried bitterly for his mother's milk, but he soon got used to it. We were then posted to France and I had to leave Nilesh behind with my mother.

Sonu had always been rather plump. I arranged for her to attend workouts at the local health club, in Paris, though it was rather expensive. She also learnt a few social graces. She had a typical middle class Indian upbringing – Bharat Natyam classes and playing the harmonium. She knew how to make juicy, sweet modaks and she did beautiful rangolis for Ganesh utsav and Diwali. But she didn't know how to use a fork and spoon or how to eat noodles or spaghetti, without making a mess of it. In her French finishing school she learnt how to do all that with finesse. However she was still dissatisfied that she hadn't gone to college. So when we were sent to London, after my Nepal posting, I saw to it that she got admitted to the London University for an undergraduate course in the liberal arts.

She had a lovely time at college. I was busy with my consular duties. Rather dull, of course. Except when the Ministers came on a foreign jaunt and then it was a bloody pain. You had to take them shopping and eat at curry joints. Once in a way we got a minister who wasn't a philistine – who could appreciate good wine and knew how to talk to the British Minister for the Interior on the merits of the Russian Ballet. But most of them were *gavars,* eager for cheap bargains to impress their numerous relatives.

It's true that I neglected Sonu around this time. I just didn't notice how accomplished she had become. I had spent fifty pounds a week on her swimming lessons and twenty on her swimming costume, bath robe, etc, and since I couldn't accompany her to the pool she'd always team up with a college-mate and go swimming. I didn't inquire too deeply who she spent her time with. I just assumed it was with a few girl friends.

It was when the blank calls came that I guessed that something had gone wrong. Every time I picked up the phone, it would go dead. Sometimes I actually heard someone replace the receiver. At first I said, "Funny. I wonder what *that* was." Sonu had a sort of guilty look on her face which, I initially mistook for fear.
"Don't worry, Sonu," I said, "It must be just some prankster."

However when it happened once too often, I noticed that Sonu was always rushing to get the phone. She normally lay languidly with a book, on the sitting room couch. But now she'd spring up like a lithe panther. Whenever she got the phone she'd say after a small pause, "I'm sorry, you've got a wrong number madam."

One evening I was having a shower when I heard the phone ring. I saw my chance and kept the shower going. I heard Sonu's steps near the bedroom door. Then the phone stopped ringing. She had picked up the hall extension. I got out softly and picked up the receiver in the bedroom. I heard a man's voice. He was teasing Sonu about how ravishing she had been the previous afternoon. He spoke funny, accented English.

"I'll get you a new negligee though, that stingy husband of yours doesn't appreciate what he has," he said. Sonu gave a little giggle. Then he asked her where the bear was.

"Oh he's safely in the shower," she answered. "I checked before I picked up the phone." He rang off after making a date to meet her for lunch at the Astoria. When Sonu walked into the bed room, I was still in my bath towel dripping wet, holding on to the receiver. She looked pale with fear.

"Who was that? You've been having an affair and cheating on me," I said quietly. She broke down and cried like a child.

"I'm sorry," she said, "I was so-o bored. He's just a guy I met at the swimming pool. He's two years younger than I." She promised not to see him again. I wrote to my mother and asked her to come home with Nilesh by the next flight. My mother soon arrived and together we kept a strict watch on Sonu's movements. Nilesh was admitted to a nearby school. Sonu got involved with teaching him. But she continued going for her own classes. She told me that she had broken off with her boy-friend. After six months when I felt that Sonu had got over her infatuation, *Aai* went back home. We didn't tell Sonu's parents about this incident. I just wanted everything to blow over without a fuss.

One day I came back home from the office at 11.30 in the morning. I was feeling unwell – a spot of indigestion after the previous evening's function at the Saudi embassy. I had eaten too many *Khababs*. You know it was after I joined the Foreign Service that I learnt to eat meat. My parents were horrified at first.

Then they got used to it. But my mother made me promise never to touch beef.

Sonu was usually at college at this hour in the morning and Nilesh at school. So I let myself in with my own key. As I walked in I heard a low murmur from the bed room. The door was slightly ajar. It was Sonu. She was in bed with a blonde man. When I confronted them, Sonu didn't say anything. She just dressed up and packed a few clothes into a small bag and said, "Promy I'm sorry, I should have had the guts to tell you before. I'm through with you. I'm leaving now."

I stood there speechless. The recriminations that were on the tip of my tongue died away. I just had a feeling of numbness. Her lover was tall and muscular, with a ponytail and blue eyes. He would have easily walloped me in any fight. They both went away without a backward glance. I was left to straighten out the sheets – change the dirty linen and bring Nilesh back home, since he was expecting his mother to pick him up.

It was a few weeks later that I got the divorce notice from Sonu's lawyers from India. Sonu had attached a note requesting me to release her so that she could get on with her life. "We're incompatible and we were never meant to marry," she wrote. She said that she would have liked to keep Nilesh, but since her life was a little unsettled for the present, it may be better for him if I brought him up. I then got this posting back home and now I'm on the verge of divorce.' Here Joshi broke into big, heaving sobs that shook his large frame. After a while he calmed down and blew his nose into a pocket handkerchief. He stood looking out of the window from Gajapati's room. The gleaming lights of the Oberoi shimmered in the distance.

'She's there in Room 1001,' he said looking wistful. 'Will you just come with me to the hotel?' he asked Gajapati.

Gajapati agreed. Joshi went home and changed his clothes. He chose formal evening wear – a black bund-galla embroidered at the neck and cuffs. His long hair and wire framed glasses made him look intellectual. He looked handsome and distinguished. Gajapati also wore a brown suit but it needed ironing and it looked a little worse for the wear.

When they reached the hotel, Joshi suddenly developed cold feet about going up to Sonu's room. Gajapati suggested that they first have coffee at the coffee shop. They went in and sat discreetly at a corner table in the dark coffee shop, lit with only a few incandescent bulbs. As they placed their order, Gajapati sat back and relaxed. There was a small dance floor in the restaurant. The band was playing a soft romantic number. Couples danced cheek to cheek. Then Gajapati noticed Joshi stiffen and stare at a couple at the other end of the room. Sonu was on the dance floor, dressed in a black, chiffon sari with flowery, silver embroidery. She was clinging to the blonde, young man who was her partner. He was nuzzling her cheek and whispering something into her ears. Joshi stopped drinking his coffee. He looked ahead, misty eyed and miserable. A few minutes later, he stumbled out of the restaurant. Gajapati called for the bill and paid for the coffee. He dropped Joshi and went home himself.

When Gajapati rang the doorbell, Uma answered the door herself. She had been waiting eagerly for Gajapati to get back from the hotel and she got his tray of tea immediately and sat down to cross question him. What had happened? What did Joshi tell Sonu? How did she look? Was she beautiful? Gajapati was tired and answered shortly that there had been no meeting. The poor dog should have understood that he was no longer wanted. Joshi did not appear at the office for several days thereafter.

A few weeks later Gajapati sat in his office cabin, his window open. It was a hot morning. It was only ten o'clock but the heat shimmered in the air. The Gulmohor trees in the streets outside looked brown with dust. A koel called. A soft breeze stirred ineffectually and petered out. Gajapati wiped the perspiration from his forehead as he perused an abstruse agreement to be signed with the turnkey contractors of a prestigious new mining project with Russian collaboration in Singhbumh. His private secretary buzzed him on the intercom. Uma was on the line. She told Gajapati that their neighbour John Varkey's wife, Stella Marie, had invited her for coffee in the afternoon. She had also invited Sonu. Uma said that Gajapati could use his own house key in case she was late getting back home. Gajapati thought about it for a minute.
'O.K.' he said, 'Only don't chatter away needlessly as you usually do and be careful about what you say, don't ask Sonu probing questions about Joshi.'

Uma made a sound of irritation and put down the receiver.

Gajapati was a little late home that evening. As he sat in his favourite arm chair with the evening papers, Uma brought him his tea and a plate of dal wadas. He bit into a wada, his eyes on the sports page. It was his sacred hour and Uma usually never intruded with any conversation for at least forty minutes. But today she hovered around and poured herself a cup of tea.

'That Sonu is not all to blame for the mess,' she said, after a small pause, her fingers crumbling a wada.

'Why?' asked Gajapati, turning to the crossword section.

'Joshi was so unkind to her when they were married. He told her often that she was not a beauty just because she wasn't fair. He was always counting every little thing and so suspicious, going through the household accounts every evening like an accountant, to check whether Sonu was filching the house-keeping money. And he never let her have any money of her own. He even forbade her to work. A diplomat's wife working as a shop assistant (which was all that she was qualified to be) wasn't in the interest of the country's prestige, he told her. And even when they went on home leave he counted the number of things he bought her family and kept an account of it. But if he bought a hundred pounds of gifts for her family, he always bought four hundred pounds for his own. And she never had any part in selecting the gifts. He suspected that she would buy cheaper things from the flea market, for his family members. He never really loved her. He just wanted to own her and control her entirely. And he expected to be waited on hand and foot. Though they had a servant, Sonu had to make him puris or bajjis herself. "What else are you doing anyway?" he'd shout. "I'm a busy man but you're just sitting at home enjoying yourself, dressing up for parties and wearing make-up, while I slog." He never bought her a single gift. Not even a rose. And so when Ivor Bergman just spent time laughing with her at the college cafeteria, she fell in love with him. It was only because Joshi saw a handsome young Swede fall in love with his wife that she suddenly acquired importance in his eyes. He didn't love her for herself.'

Gajapati got up and went to the flower vase on the centre table in their little drawing room and took out a single rose and handed it to Uma.

'What are you doing? Now you've spoilt my flower arrangement!' Uma protested. Gajapati surprised Uma with a kiss that muffled all her complaints.

'Let Joshi stew in his own juice,' Gajapati said, switching off the light, as he put his arms around Uma.

On a Monday morning the next week, as Gajapati went through the mail, a shadow fell across his table. He looked up. It was Joshi. Gajapati was a little irritated. He no longer felt as sympathetic towards Joshi since he remembered what Uma had told him about the man's parsimony. His story did not appear to be quite so tragic now. He seemed to be always cadging for sympathy.

'I'm going to court today. The judge will be issuing the decree,' Joshi said in funeral tones. He clenched his hands. 'The silly besotted girl can't see that he will abandon her once his passion is spent,' he said thickly. 'But I'll be waiting for her even then if she wants to come back to me. Otherwise she'll be going from man to man in Europe. Little better than a . . .' He clutched at his hair with his hands, a wild look in his eyes. Gajapati's mood changed and his attitude softened a little. Joshi wasn't such a cad after all.

Gajapati told Uma that evening about how they had misunderstood Joshi. He was actually willing to forgive his wife even if the Swede abandoned her.
'Oh ho! That's just for what he's waiting for! She'd be the biggest fool to do that, if and when that happens. Silly Gajapati dear, Lord of Elephants,' Uma said winding a finger around a lock of his hair, 'Joshi will really have his revenge on her then,' she murmured.

Gajapati did not see Joshi thereafter. Joshi had gone for the International Convention of Coal Exporting Countries at Geneva, with the Minister and he returned only after a round trip to Europe and the Middle East. All the other officers were jealous at Joshi's close proximity to the Minister, which enabled him to wangle trips abroad with ease and have two official cars for his own use. Joshi had no sympathisers for his personal tragedy. Serve him right – the chamcha, they said, while they were careful to be polite to him when they saw him in the lift, exchanging pleasantries about the weather in Denmark, Australia or where ever he had just been, as they enviously eyed the slick, slim briefcase he had bought on his trip to Italy.

Some months later, Joshi's servant Ramu came running up to Gajapati's flat, his eyes large with fear. 'Saab was not answering the door and the newspaper and milk was still on the door step. So I broke the window of the south bed room. Saab is lying down on the floor there,' he said in a voice hoarse with tension. He had got no answer when he knocked on Joshi's door at eight in the morning. Joshi was an early riser and usually picked up the milk himself from the door step. Gajapati went down with Ramu to Joshi's flat. He called the chowkidar Neelkant. Together they forced open the door. They found Joshi lying in a pool of blood in his bedroom. He had shot himself through the head with his licensed revolver. In his hand was a faded copy of his wedding photograph – Pramod in a suit, wearing a Maharashtrian bridegroom's beaded crown, with strands hanging down the sides of his face and his bride in a crimson silk, nine yard sari.

The neighbours gathered around the compound of the building, discussing what had happened in shocked voices. Stella Marie who had rushed out of her house wearing only her faded, yellow, printed nightgown, told Uma who stood next to her, that she had received a letter from Sonu the previous day. Sonali had married her Swiss lover in Geneva. She had enclosed a picture of herself looking radiant in a lacy, white, wedding dress and veil, with a white pearl encrusted coronet on her head. She didn't look at all like the plump, seventeen year old school girl from Nagpur whom Joshi had married ten years before.

ॐ ॐ ॐ

SKI HOLIDAY

Eight year old Bulbul lay in the thick black darkness, clutching her teddy bear, as sleep eluded her in the small sofa bed. The light from the street filtered in through the window and shone eerily. Menacing shadows seemed to dance in the darkness. She longed for the morning light. Bulbul wished her parents were back. They had left her at home in Geneva to go for a skiing trip.

Bulbul's parents had bought provisions to last her for the days that they would be away: three cartons of milk, which she knew how to heat on the gas stove. A dozen eggs, cheese for her sandwich lunch, a dozen apples – she was to eat one each day, cornflakes for breakfast and packets of noodle soup, tinned baked beans and sausages which she was to have for supper. She would buy bread from the local provision store on the way back from school, after the loaf in the kitchen cabinet got over. She had a thousand Swiss francs for expenses, which she kept carefully in her suitcase. She had felt quite grown up when her mother had counted out the notes and given her the money. But just now she was very scared. She wished her mother was near her and that she could nestle against her and sleep. The knot of fear in her stomach just seemed to grow.

Sarnath Ray and his wife Chikila had been selected to the training course in Switzerland, by outmanoeuvring their colleagues in the large public sector steel plant in Bhillai, where they were both senior managers. By a skilful word to the Prime Minister's Secretary, through Sarnath's cousin who was the Secretary Public Enterprises, they had both got the coveted one year's training programme in Public Administration at Geneva. They decided to take their eight-year old daughter Bulbul with them. It would broaden her outlook to study at a Swiss school for a year, Sarnath told his envious colleagues. Bulbul was the centre of attention at the Bhilai Public school on her last day. 'Don't forget to write and send us photographs when you go skiing in the Alps,' her friends told her. Bulbul nodded gravely. She was serious for her age. Being an only child she was often left to her own devices with only the kitchen maid for company, till her parents came home in the evening from work.

The Rays had hired a small, cheap apartment in a block of flats, along with the other officers, in the Carrouge district, to save on expenses. Fortunately the flats were well-furnished. There was piped gas in the kitchen. A refrigerator stood in a corner of the kitchen. A sofa-cum-bed adorned a small alcove. There was also a TV in the living area of the apartment. The only bedroom had a single bed in it. Bulbul slept on the sofa while her parents slept in the bedroom.

Sarnath and Chikila admitted Bulbul to the *British School of Geneva*, on the main road through Chatelaine. It was near the international quarter of Geneva. Bulbul soon got busy with activities at school. She made friends with a few of the Swiss boys and girls in the school, who were not intimidated by her foreign mannerisms and appearance. They were curious about the land of snakes, forests and yogis who walked bare-feet on hot coals and slept on beds of nails. Bulbul explained in a bemused fashion to her new found friends that she lived in a modern town, in a house that had electricity and a WC with a proper flush and that she had only seen a forest when she had gone on her school holiday tour to the Kaziranga wild life sanctuary in Assam. Her friends were disappointed that she had also never seen a yogi who wore a live snake around his neck. Bulbul laughed and told them that the swamaji in the Birla temple near her school was actually quite afraid of snakes and lizards and that he always got the mali to chase away any unwelcome, crawling, reptilian visitors to the temple.

When the Institute for Public Administration announced the skiing vacation at the end of four months of gruelling work, the international officials attending the course were all excited. The cold winter with its dark skies, was morbid and gloomy. They were unused to the chilly weather and being bundled up in warm clothes, moccasins and mufflers. They thought that it would be fun to learn skiing. But the dampener came when it was announced that children were not allowed. It was too much trouble to take care of children on the ten day trip.

Sarnath and Chikila were disappointed. Whatever would they do with Bulbul? They would be missing the trip of a lifetime. Two of the other participants, Meera and Raminder discussed the problem and decided against going. But Chikila was determined to find a way out. 'Bulbul is a very smart girl,' she told her husband. 'She'll certainly stay at home by herself for a week if we buy her the provisions. Remember how she went alone by air to Calcutta for the summer vacation to Mama's house?' But Sarnath was unsure.

'Suppose something happens to her when she is alone at home?' he asked worriedly. Chikila told him not to be fanciful.

'Besides we can ask Meera and her mother to keep an eye on her and visit her in the evenings and see that she is fine. May be she could even stay with them,' Chikila said. But Meera said that she had enough on her hands with looking after her son, who was sick in the cold weather. She said that she couldn't take the responsibility for Bulbul.

'Why do you have to go anyway?' she asked them, 'Bulbul may feel scared alone.'

'Not Bulbul,' declared Chikila emphatically.

They asked Raminder if Bulbul could stay with his family. But he said that they would be away during the holidays visiting relatives who lived in Berne.

Chikila was discouraged but she had set her heart on going for the skiing trip. The cost was minimal and it was not likely that they would get such a chance again. One night she sat down with Bulbul, reading *Little Women.* She remarked on how brave the young girls in the story were, keeping house while their mother was away visiting. Then she asked Bulbul in a coaxing voice, whether she could live at home by herself for a week without her parents. She explained how they may never again be able to go to a ski resort. Bulbul agreed to be brave and stay alone at home. She promised never to open the door to anyone, without checking at the peephole to see who it was. When Meera came to visit them at their apartment and expressed surprise at their decision, Chikila said that Bulbul was a clever child and that the experience would make her tough and independent. Besides they had spared no expense. She would have a thousand francs with her just in case she needed it.

Three days after her parents left, Bulbul got up from bed feeling groggy. She had a fever. She had forgotten to wear her woollen muffler around her neck when she went to school the previous day. 'If you have a temperature take a Crocin with a glass of milk,' mummy had said, she remembered. She took some milk from the fridge and had a Crocin. She decided not to go to school. She felt too weak to eat any lunch but she forced herself to have a slice of bread and milk. She was still feeling feverish the next day. She tossed and turned in bed at night, racked by nightmares of being chased by a black bear. In the morning the fever broke. She had a warm-water bath and went to school. She did not tell her teacher why she had been absent. The teacher asked her for a note from her parents. But she did not tell the teacher that her parents were away.

'Don't tell anyone that Daddy and Mummy are not at home,' her parents had impressed upon her. On no account was anyone to know that she was alone at home.

It was with a hysterical sense of relief that Bulbul met her parents when they got back. But she was quiet. She did not throw herself into her mother's arms when she saw Chikila. She was drained of all emotion. She moved away when Chikila took her warmly into her embrace. She didn't tell her parents about her illness.

In the ensuing days Chikila tried to enliven the atmosphere with amusing stories of their attempts to learn skiing at the ski resort. But the stories did not draw the expected gurgle of laughter from Bulbul. Instead she seemed tense and withdrawn. Bulbul was also quiet at school. The class teacher Edna told Bulbul that she would like to meet her parents. When Chikila and Sarnath met with Bulbul's teacher, she informed them that she found Bulbul distanced from class activities. She did not play with the other students as before. The drawing teacher had reported that at drawing class, the only thing that Bulbul drew, were black clouds and a black sea with sharp piercing waves.

Ms Edna told Sarnath and Chikila that she felt that Bulbul seemed perturbed about something. Was there anything the matter at home that could have disturbed her, she asked? Chikila and Sarnath were extra loud in their protests that everything was fine. There were no problems what so ever at home. The teacher then looked serious and asked whether they could take Bulbul to a child counsellor, so that they could find out what it was that was bothering the child. They unwillingly fixed a date in the following week for a meeting with the counsellor. But on the appointed day, Chikila called up the office of the counsellor and said that Sarnath had a course related examination on that date and so they could not attend the meeting. They set another date, for just the day before they were to leave for India. Though Bulbul's silence worried them, they thought that she would get over her "bad" behaviour when they were home in India, which was only a few weeks away after all. They did not keep the appointment with the counsellor.

When they got back to India Chikila and Sarnath were very busy getting their house in order and settling back into work. Sarnath tried to talk to his daughter at the dinner table, but she picked at her food and went back to her room in silence. They thought that Bulbul would get over her moping behaviour. It was a passing phase, all pre-teens has some adjustment problems, they told each other. They felt that she must miss her Swiss school and the interesting activities taken up in a liberal European education. Their friends who visited them, expecting to be regaled with accounts of their sojourn abroad, commented on the change in Bulbul's behaviour. She no longer came up to them and wished them with a shy smile, they said. She just ignored them. Indian schools were a hard grind for children, Chikila told the visitors, and Bulbul missed her fun lifestyle in Geneva.

Very gradually, Bulbul began talking to her parents, at first in mono-syllables and then in short sentences which were strictly functional: 'I need a new pencil,' or 'I'm not hungry,' – a sentence she often used. They showered her with toys and books. But she never touched these peace offerings. Only once when the ski trip was brought up again, did she speak a long sentence: 'Chunky told me that Raminder uncle told him that the police can arrest parents who leave their children alone at home.' Chikila and Sarnath looked guiltily at each other. Chikila said a little too hastily, 'That's not true – not if the child is not really alone. Like when you were living in the building in Geneva, so like a hostel, with all the uncles and aunties that we knew, living just next door.' But Bulbul looked away – they dared not see it – just a little scornfully.

Bulbul also refused to go back to her old school. She said that she wanted to go to a boarding school. 'What is the use of having a darling daughter like you if we cannot see you grow up?' her parents cried. But she was adamant. She wanted to go to Lovedale she said, where her best friend Carmine had enrolled. Her parents reluctantly agreed. Bulbul completed her schooling and then went on to study in the United States. She graduated with honours in Medicine from the John Hopkins University and she did her masters in surgery. She joined the State Hospital in Boston as an Assistant to the handsome Dr. Nitin Khullar. He was a widower who had lost his wife to cancer.

Dr. Khullar was patient with Bulbul. He helped her learn the ropes of working in a large American hospital. He was a brilliant surgeon but taciturn and not given to much talking. But his compassionate and gentle nature endeared him to his patients. Bulbul soon became a very competent surgeon.

The daily round of operations and hospital duties kept Bulbul busy and she scarcely had any time for herself. She visited her parents once in a couple of years for a fleeting week and then went back to her rigorous lifestyle. Sarnath and Chikila often asked Bulbul to come back home and settle down. But she was happier in the States, she told them. She couldn't bear the dust, the dirt and the poverty in India, she said. Then Sarnath and Chikila retired from their jobs in Bhillai. They hinted delicately that they were ready to be reunited with their daughter at Boston. But Bulbul did not reply to the letter. She sent them a brief e-mail occasionally, asking after their welfare, saying that she was sure that they were enjoying their retirement. She sent them a hundred dollars every Christmas. She seemed to have forgotten that there was a festival like Diwali.

Chikila wrote to Bulbul that her father had Hypertension and needed special care. When even this letter met with no response, Chikila telephoned her. Bulbul told her mother cheerfully that Hypertension was a common enough condition.
'You have to take your medication on time and cut down on fats and get enough exercise,' she said. A week later on a cold winter evening in Delhi, Sarnath had a heart attack. The neighbours helped rush him to hospital. They were just about in time. Sarnath's life was saved but the hospital bills crippled Chikila. She did not have much money left over. Chikila now looked expectantly to Bulbul with trusting eyes, confident that her daughter would not fail her now: She would come immediately and take them both to America with her. They had given her an education that most parents in

India gave a son. Instead Bulbul sent her the money that was needed and said over the bad telephone connection, that she couldn't spare the time to come home. She patiently explained her busy lifestyle in Boston to her mother. How she was up at dawn and away till midnight. And that she rarely had time to even sleep for eight hours.

The telephone call from her mother left Bulbul with a nagging sense of guilt. But there was a lump of long forgotten unhappiness in her heart that stayed like a weight within her. It had grown over long dark brooding winter nights spent alone and it rested uneasily within her.

One evening Bulbul came back from the hospital with a gripping headache. She got up in the middle of the night with a fever. The wind howled outside and there was a blanket of snow all around. Not a leaf moved nor a bird chirped. Bulbul longed for some life, some movement and the sound of her parents' voices. She had a sense of de ja vu. She groped her way to the refrigerator and poured herself some milk with shaking hands and swallowed a Crocin. But the fever did not abate. She tossed and turned in bed, in spasms of wakefulness and a feverish stupor. Her thoughts rambled. She was trapped in a long dark cold tunnel. There was no one to help her out. Somewhere dimly she heard a loud noise at the door. She roused herself to answer it.

Dr Nitin Khullar stood at the door step. He looked at her flushed face and took in the fact that she was seriously ill. He caught her as she slumped over. He rang for an ambulance and took her to the hospital. Nitin spent the next few days and nights caring for her. He took a fortnight's leave from his hospital duties. When Bulbul cried, reliving her childhood fears, Nitin held her close and stroked her face and said, 'Now that's all over and done with, Bulbul. You're a big girl now.' In a week she was able to leave the hospital. Dr. Khullar arranged for a live in nurse to help her. He visited her every evening.

When she had fully recovered and joined her hospital duties again, Nitin took her out to dinner on a Saturday evening. As they sat in a quaint little French restaurant, in a by-lane, Dr. Khullar held Bulbul's shapely fingers, in his own strong hands and asked her to marry him. They were married at the local registry office and they had a small party at Nitin's apartment.

Nitin took her for their honeymoon to a surprise destination – the Interlaken ski resort in Switzerland. They stayed at *India village*, on the banks of the river Aaree. The hotel's restaurant specialised in Indian cuisine. The food was delicious. There were nans with butter chicken and mutton korma curries and delicious sweet and creamy kulfies with falooda. They spent a blissful week, gambolling in the snow. After a quick breakfast of Swiss rolls and hot coffee every morning, they went skiing down the slopes for beginners. Bulbul fell down the first time before she had gone even a few yards. But in a little while she was able to fly over the snow with Nitin behind her. They lunched at the small cafes that dotted the main street, trying out papet vaudois, fondue with bread, and aelplermagronen, washing it down with a bottle of sparkling red wine or Champagne. They hardly knew how the week went by.

When Nitin and Bulbul came back home to Boston, there was a letter on the mat, slipped under the door by the janitor. It was written in a shaky hand by Chikila. Bulbul's father had died of a heart attack and they had cremated him, since they could not contact Bulbul in time, Chikila wrote. There was no response when she had rung Bulbul up on the phone. Chikila had sold the apartment and would be moving in a few weeks, to an old age home *Vrindavan Ashram,* on the outskirts of Delhi. The letter dropped from Bulbul's hand and she looked at Nitin, sombrely. 'Mama needs me,' she said. They both flew to India the next day.

They reached Delhi in the evening. The front door to Chikila's apartment was open. As they walked into the house, Bulbul saw workmen moving out the furniture from the house. The apartment looked desolate. The once cheerful hall with its white lace curtains, the large roomy sofa with its two arm chairs, in which they had spent cosy evenings watching the Sunday movie on Door Darshan, had vanished. Instead, there was a vast emptiness. All the furniture had been sold and there were only a few suitcases in the hall. Bulbul found her mother sitting on a chair near a window, her hair a silvery grey. Her gnarled fingers gripped a copy of the Bhagwad Gita.

Chikila looked up at Bulbul in disbelief through dim, watery eyes. She held out her shaking arms and enfolded Bulbul.

'I thought you were too busy to come to see me,' Chikila murmured through her tears.

'Ma! I'm sorry I forgot about you and Papa for so long. I'm not going to let you wither away in any old age home.' Bulbul's voice was choked, as she held her mother tight.

They sat talking in the empty apartment about how Sarnath had died of a heart attack. The neighbours – the Srivastavas were most helpful. They had come immediately and taken Sarnath to the Escorts hospital. But it was of no use. Sarnath passed away in the ICU the day he was admitted. Chikila wept silently. Bulbul gripped her mother's shoulder, torn by a sense of guilt.

Bulbul and Nitin visited the local temple with Chikila in the evening and performed a special pooja for Sarnath. When they got back from the temple, a stray cat that Chikila had adopted mewed plaintively in the corridor, asking to be let in. They opened the door to it and the cat ambled up to Chikila and rubbed itself on her sari. Chikila looked at the cat and suddenly she was worried. Who would look after the cat when she left? She walked out into the corridor and knocked on her neighbour's door. When Mrs. Srivastava opened the door, she said, 'Namasthe beti, I told you last week, that I'm leaving my apartment today. But there's this cat. You've seen it around in the apartment. I've always given it some food and milk every day. I feel bad to leave it behind when I go. Could you please take care of the cat?' Chikila was relieved when Ritu Srivastava promised to take care of the animal.

Chikila said good bye to her neighbours. She thanked them for all the help that they had rendered her. Ritu and her husband Rajnish touched her feet. Their children said, 'Gudbye Mata ji! Don't furget us when you reach Amreeka!' Chikila blessed them and left with Bulbul and Nitin. They went down to the compound. There was a taxi waiting. The cat came down with them. Chikila looked back from the taxi watching the cat as it sat on a step in the porch. Suddenly it crouched and jumped on a mouse that scurried by but missed it. It ran after the mouse. Chikila let out a long sigh and sat back in the taxi with her eyes closed. Bulbul had not let her down after all . . . Chikila had been disconsolate when Bulbul had not responded to her letters. But she was too tired to think about it now. She drifted into the easy sleep of old age. Bulbul put her arm around her mother's slight form and held her close, as the taxi sped to the airport.

ॐ ॐ ॐ

THE BRIDE IN WAITING

Harry was the life and soul of the Civil Service Academy at Mussoorie where Indian civil servants were trained. He was well built, stood six feet tall and had curly black hair which he chose to wear long, down his neck, like uneasy octopus arms. He had a sun burnt, brown, complexion. He longed to be a fair blue eyed Punjabi. Instead they had called him *Kalia* at St. Stephen's college in Delhi. Nevertheless he was popular because of his father – a powerful bureaucrat who was from the ICS – the last of the old blue blooded, civil servants, who had gone out with the Raj. Harry's father smoked a pipe, wore tweeds and had an Oxbridge accent. Harry also had plenty of ready cash, which he spent freely on booze and khababs for his friends. They spent every evening disco crawling till the wee hours of the morning.

Harry had only two regrets in life. One was his name, which was Haridasan Somashekaran Pillai. And the other was his inability to have a hip Delhi chick on his arm. While the other fellows at college were ready enough to carouse with him, the girls all fell for the handsome Chabbrias, Srivastavas and Kapoors. None of the girls wanted to date him. They danced with him once in a while out of compassion, as he danced vigorously by himself at college parties, eliciting howls of appreciation from the boys, for his unconventional contortions.

However, most of the girls were content to keep their distance. Harry had the reputation of feeling up a girl, at the very first dance. He was taken aback when at a college day jam session, he overheard Miriam say, with a toss of her long black strands: 'That Harry makes you feel so vile.' And Rupa's reply: 'Yes. He looks as though he can't wait to peel the clothes off you.' But to do him justice poor Harry had been celibate all through his university life. Though it was not from want of trying to lose his virginity.

In fact he had visited some of the brothels in old Delhi, together with a few of his more adventurous college mates. But the stink of the crumbling hovels, with their dirty sheets stained with the ardours of the previous occupants and the odour of sweat and cheap perfume on the women had put him off. The over-painted women, with their practiced coquetry disgusted him.

The male officers had done the once over of all the lady officers on the first day at the academy and summed up the ones who would be willing for a season of flirtation and set their sights accordingly. Once the state cadres were announced, those in search of a cadre change, proceeded to strike up serious relationships with girls who had been allotted a more acceptable state. North Indian men who were allotted the southern states, looked for girlfriends among the women who were allotted a northern state, while officers from the southern states allotted a northern cadre looked for a bride from among the women who had been lucky enough to get a southern state. The more enterprising young men paired up with a girl, while also going every month for the bride-viewing of girls with sizable bank balances. They enjoyed the lavish dinner and tea meetings given them at each visit to a girl's house and came away uncommitted till they reached the highest bidder for their IAS tag. The young men boasted in the officers' mess about the offers of dowry that they had received and showed off the fat diamond engagement ring, given them by the indulgent father of the bride. The other male officers who had had the bad luck to have been married before they were selected to the IAS, looked on morosely with some element of envy.

None of the women officers caught Harry's fancy. Except for Rita Chopra. Rita was tall and fair with light brown eyes and straight black, shoulder length hair. She wore leather skirts with knee-length boots and a leather jacket and she sang at every musical night, swaying seductively, mike in hand. Harry was introduced to her by their common friend Piyush. Harry asked her out to dinner at Whispering Windows. He was surprised when she accepted the invitation – she said she would also bring along two friends. But all through the evening at Whispering Windows it stung him to see her with her eyes always on Ravindar Singh from the Indian Foreign Service who sat at the opposite table in another group, cracking sardar jokes and eating butter chicken and nan. Poonam Singhania sat among them, looking graceful in a grey silk sari, with a black border woven with golden paisley motifs. Despite the back slapping and the loud laughter, Ravindar's jokes were all aimed at making

Poonam Singhania smile and turn her dazzling eyes towards him in appreciation.

The term at Mussoorie was coming to a close. The Allied Service officers prepared to leave for further training in their own departments. Rita was selected to the Customs and Excise Service and was going to the Revenue service academy at Haus Khas in Delhi. Harry was in an agony of suspense at the thought of not being able to see Rita anymore. He sat in the officers' lounge every evening and asked everyone with his palm outstretched, 'Could you read my palm and tell me – will I marry a cow?' A cow was a coy village maiden, a *nadan* malayali girl, in a white gold bordered *mundum nereathe*, mogra flowers in her long black hair, silver anklets on her feet, a sliver of sandalwood paste on her forehead, as she walked back home from the temple after the early morning puja. Harry was afraid that he would have to marry Swarna Prabha, his *morrapennu* from Kerala – his mother's brother's daughter, destined by social custom, to become his wife. Swarna was seventeen and had just passed her pre-degree and was awaiting his triumphant return home from the Academy, with shy eagerness.

One September evening Ravindar and Poonam announced their engagement. Harry noticed that Rita was absent at the Public Administration lecture the next morning. He saw her outside the academy gate around lunch time. She was getting into a cycle rickshaw with her room-mate Shubanghi. Rita's face was swollen and her nose was red. She wore her hair pulled back in an unattractive ponytail. Harry stopped near the rickshaw and asked in concern, 'Rita!! What's the matter?' But she turned her face away. The rickshaw driver cycled down the road. Stung by her response, Harry walked away dolefully to Namby's cafe at the academy gate. He ordered a cup of tea and sat down to consider his next move.

The evening shadows fell softly in the lounge at the academy. The flowing silk curtains swayed in the breeze that wafted in through the long French windows. A vintage turn table gramophone record player attended by the bearer Fernandes crooned out old melodies. The glittering lights of the chandeliers cast shadows on the walls, as couples swayed to the romantic music. Harry asked Rita for a dance. His heart spun over when she unexpectedly said, 'Yes,' and got up to dance with him. Harry was in a daze and he stamped her toes only once, during the entire dance. Rita had a glazed look in her eyes as she agreed mechanically to go out to dinner with him. In a fortnight they were engaged and Harry was delirious with excitement. They had a December wedding in Delhi much to his father's disappointment. He was a stickler for old values when it came to marriage. He said that he had no face to show his wife's brother. It had been settled between their families for ever so long that Harry would marry Swarna Prabha. But Harry was adamant about marrying the girl of his dreams. The couple left for Seychelles on a honeymoon.

Harry was sent to Uttar Pradesh. His first district posting was at Lucknow. District life was quite different from the carefree collegiate life at the Academy. Village caste ridden tensions were as real as the problems of the shortage of drinking water and periodic famines. Harry was quite busy. Rita did not get a posting with him to Lucknow. She was posted by her department to Delhi.

One evening he rang up Rita's apartment. Someone picked up the receiver. There was no answer to his request to speak to Rita. But he heard the strains of Rita's favourite song – *We had joy we had fun, we had seasons in the sun* – being played in the background. The receiver was replaced at the other end after a pause. When he rang again twice, the telephone jangled without any response. Doubts and jealous thoughts raced through his mind. He rang up again three hours later and Rita answered the phone. She said that she had been away shopping for groceries. She was surprised that Harry had thought that someone had picked up the telephone and disconnected it.
'Stop being paranoid Harry,' she said.

On weekends, when he went to Delhi, he found her distant and preoccupied. But she turned lively and animated when her batch-mates rang up. She was often late from work on a Friday evening and said that she didn't want any dinner because she wasn't hungry. He suspected that she was eating out with her friends. He found that she never responded to his sexual overtures in bed. She merely turned over and slept on her side of the bed, with a muttered excuse about a headache or stomach cramps.

Then, one Monday, after a dull week-end in Delhi, he did not dress to go back to Lucknow. He just lounged around in bed. Rita looked displeased when he said that he wasn't going back to Lucknow after all, that he could wait a few days more since there was nothing pressing at the office. In the evening the door-bell rang. Rita was in the bathroom. Harry opened the door. A tall, handsome man with wavy, black hair stood outside with a bunch of flowers. He wore blue jeans, a snazzy white t-shirt and scruffy sneakers. He looked surprised to see Harry.

'Hello I'm Digvijay,' he said, 'I'm Rita's batchmate.'

'Didn't see you at the Academy,' Harry said shortly.

'Yes, I didn't join for the course, I only went up later. Aren't you going to ask me in?'

Harry asked him to sit down. He went back to the bedroom. He found Rita sitting at the dressing table combing her hair. 'Your beau has arrived,' he announced jocularly, masking the suspicious thoughts that arose to curdle his happiness.

'Don't be silly, it's only Diggy,' she replied.

She took to staying in her mother's house in Def. Col. Harry dropped in occasionally for a meal at his mother-in-law's house. He never stayed the night however. He felt uncomfortable and unwelcome at Rita's house. A few months later, it was his old, St. Stephen's chum Piyush, who was also in the Customs and Excise, who broke him the news about Rita's love affair with Rishikesh Malhotra, a Foreign Service officer, back in Delhi from his posting as the Consular representative in Belgrade. Rishikesh was three years older than Rita. When Harry confronted Rita, she was silent. She did not deny the relationship. She merely didn't return home in the evening. She had gone to her mother's house for good.

Harry was wretched after she left. He took to drinking himself silly every evening in Lucknow as he lay sprawled in front of the TV on the couch, a cigarette dangling from his mouth and a bottle of whisky on the side table. He drained the bottle compulsively till it was empty. He often fell asleep in a drunken stupor on the couch, in his clothes and shoes, the sitting room lights on, the TV still raucous, belting out music and soap operas.

His father pulled strings and spoke to old chums who had relatives in the Department of Personnel and got Harry posted to Delhi. But Harry never went to office on time. He just sat around unwashed and unshaven and staggered into his office, bleary-eyed, in rumpled clothes, at twelve in the afternoon. The peons and clerks sniggered and whispered after him. In the end, it was his mother who took matters in hand. She consulted the best divorce lawyer in town and spoke to Rita and her parents. They had a quiet divorce by mutual consent.

Harry was drinking his third whisky in a row on a dull, Sunday afternoon in July. The monsoon had been delayed and the weather had been oppressive and hot. Swarna Prabha rang the door bell and walked in when he opened the door. She had grown taller. She was wearing a pastel pink, salwar kameez and she looked sophisticated and poised. She had cut her long hair short. She wore a lingering perfume that made her seem innocent and desirable. Harry stood silent, clutching the sideboard for support, anxious about the new feelings tumbling about in his mind.

'Cheta, drinking is bad for the liver,' she said and took away the glass from his hand.

'How long are you here? And what the hell have you done to your hair?' he asked her peevishly. She said that she was in Delhi only for a few days. Her father had received a marriage proposal for her. It was from a well-to-do doctor in Delhi.

'What are you waiting for then?' he asked. 'Go and marry your doctor.' She said that she would prefer marrying Hariettan, now that he was divorced and presumably wiser. It was only correct to follow the old tradition and marry your *morracherukan*, she said. But he was to give up drinking like a fish, she said sternly, pointing at the bottle of whisky on the side table.

They were married in the temple in Guruvayoor. He had a bare chest, a white *angavastram* on his shoulders and a gold bordered *mundu* around his waist. Swarna wore the traditional off-white and gold *mundum nereatha*, her hair covered with fragrant, white mogra flowers. She wore his wedding gift of slender, gold anklets, with tiny bells that tinkled softly as she walked behind him demurely, treading the prescribed seven turns around the sacred fire, to the chanting of the ancient mantras by the temple priest.

Harry tied the tiny gold marriage *tali* around Swarna Prabha's neck. He intoned the wedding vows in Sanskrit – *'Let us be together always. Let us love each other, with unity of thought. We will always perform the sacred rituals together. Let me be Heaven, you the Earth. Let me be the Moon and you its wearer. Let me be the mind and you*

301

its speaker. Come to me – to raise our children and have prosperity in our life.'

They were photographed wearing their heavy nuptial garlands of thickly woven mogra flowers. Then they entered the banquet hall with their guests to partake of the wedding feast served on fresh banana leaves -- fragrant steaming rice with ghee and sambaar; the mixed vegetable dish of avail, garnished with grated coconut; curd seasoned with onion and garlic; papadam and banana chips fried in coconut oil and three dishes of sweet payasam.

Every Sunday, thereafter, he accompanied Swarna Prabha to the temple and stood beside her, as with folded palms and closed eyes she made her obeisance to the gods who ruled over their destiny. He followed her meekly, as she walked around the temple, three times, after first bowing before Balaji, visiting each stone god in its corner. Ganesha, for auspicious good luck in every endeavour, Devi, in her ferocious form, astride the tiger, Hanuman, carrying the life giving *sanjivini* and Krishna the blue god with his flute. On the way home he bowed and touched the cow parked outside the temple by its enterprising owner and he paid him ten rupees for the privilege of feeding it a few blades of grass.

He also introduced himself as Haridasan Pillai, no longer as Harry. He came home every evening from his office at the dot of six-thirty. Swarna Prabha had his cup of tea and savouries ready for him. He had a bath and changed into his white mundu and jubba and sat reading the evening tabloids, spectacles on the edge of his nose, his thinning hair carefully brushed over the bald patch. Swarna Prabha sat with her large lustrous gentle eyes enveloping him in a glow of worship that nursed his broken spirit back to wholeness. From outside, came the faint music of cow bells tinkling, as the bovine animals ambled down the lane placidly on their way home.

꒱ ꒱ ꒱

OFFICE RELATIONS

It was a rainy day in July in Calcutta. The atmosphere in Writers' Building was wet and mouldy. The green bamboo matting in the long verandas of the secretariat had got unsecured and beat against the railings, spraying water on the floor and passersby. Mohan Basu walked into the clerks' hall dripping wet and headed for his small cabin at the far end. He was the Under Secretary in charge of "Innovative Methods in Nutrition", in the Food and Civil Supplies department. The rains had upset the chaotic bus service and it was twelve o'clock when he reached the office. Mohan was tall and lean, with a cadaverous face and a pencil thin moustache. He had a broad nose and thick, fleshy lips. His hair was parted down the middle and his big ears stuck out from the sides of his head.

The office was empty except for the two peons and Ram Dutta the watchman who lived in the basement. Mohan hoped that the government would declare it a "rain holiday" and so enable him to leave the office early. But he did not want to go home to his nagging wife, Parasmoni. She was a teacher in the local municipal school in Tollygunge where they lived. He would rather have gone for a cup of tea to the nearby tea house with Dolly Ganguly, his new Section Officer. Dolly was in her late twenties and had a jolly laugh. Her hair was cut fashionably into a bob. She was just a little plump. Curvy and delectable. She wore elegant salwar kameez outfits and matching costume jewellery. But Dolly had not come to the office that day.

A bell rang in the corridor. It was from the Joint Secretary's room. The peon came in and told Mohan that Mrs. Mary was asking for him. Mohan wiped his face before the cracked mirror in his room and slicked down his wet hair with a dirty comb and put it back into his trouser pocket.

He knocked at her door and entered after a short pause. Mrs. Mary was busy writing at her desk. She was short, plump and brown complexioned and she wore her curly hair in a small bun at the nape of her neck. When she did not look up, Mohan coughed slightly to attract her attention. She looked up and motioned him to sit down and continued writing.

'We have to send a report urgently to the Central Government for funds for our IEC programme,' she said at last, 'Otherwise they will not sanction us any funds for nutrition extension education. I want you to discuss the scope of the next year's programme.'

They sat for an hour discussing the various options for a mass information campaign. Posters were of no use according to Mrs. Mary. They had a very short life and people often misunderstood what you wanted to say. She narrated her experience when she was in Family Planning, how the Director of the programme had got a poster designed at a great expense from a prominent advertising agency. The poster showed a man and his harried wife with many squabbling children. The villagers, who were surveyed on the message conveyed by the poster, said that the poster projected the truism – "United we stand and divided we fall." Children should not quarrel with each other but they should learn that "many hands make light work" and help their parents in the fields. Thus much money could be saved in hiring labour. It would be advantageous to have so many children then, they said.

But Mrs. Mary was all for jingles on radio and short spots on TV. They could even launch a serial with a good sponsor so that it conveyed skilfully in between entertainment and human interest stories, the importance of eating wholesome food. They thought of possible scripts. During the discussion Mrs. Mary was distracted because Mohan's eyes often travelled to her breasts instead of occupying modestly the middle distance between her forehead and her eyebrows, as a well-trained male officer ought to, when talking to a female colleague. Mrs. Mary pulled her sari pallu around her shoulder firmly from the point where the sari border had sagged, revealing her cleavage from the deeply cut neckline of her choli. She pointedly drew his attention to some brochures that had been sent by the Ministry, so that he was forced to look away from her bosom. Mohan recalled himself guiltily and participated in the discussion with greater animation than was necessary to argue about whether they should make ten thousand nutrition information booklets or eight thousand. He justified his calculations vehemently as though his reputation depended on it.

'Alright, we can decide that later,' Mrs. Mary dismissed him, 'Now first draw up the proposal to be sent to the Ministry,' she said. She wondered whether she had been imagining that she had caught Mohan looking at her lecherously. I'm getting to be an old cat, she thought and forgot about it. Mohan was forty-five after all and had a daughter studying at the university.

Mohan left the room feeling the unspoken reproof. He was aware he ought not to have been distracted. But somehow the only thing that interested him about women, were their breasts. Even a woman as plain and on the wrong side of thirty as Mrs. Mary attracted his darting eyes which were always on the prowl. It was as if they had a will of their own. He despaired of locking them securely and fixing them on neutral ground – like the book shelf of musty books in Mrs. Mary's room or the steel Tiffin box on Dolly Ganguly's table.

He hoped that Mrs. Mary had not noticed his preoccupation. She could make an unfavourable remark in his Confidential Roll. But what could she write, he thought and laughed to himself, 'Looks at my breasts all the time, instead of attending to official discussions'?

He went and sat down at his desk and rang the bell for the peon. 'Get me a cup of hot tea and pakoras,' he told Rambhai the peon and gave him a fiver. He began writing out the draft letter to the Joint Secretary in the Government of India. It was late in the evening before the lone stenographer Pushpa Sengupta (who had come in at two in the afternoon) had retyped the letter five times, inserting each time the corrections Mrs. Mary had made meticulously in green ink. They had not yet bought a computer for the office.

He reached home before Parasmoni. He made himself a crisp omelette and ate it with bread and made himself some tea. When Parasmoni came in, a little later, he was able to offer her a cup of hot tea. 'No need for all these attentions,' she said crossly. He looked anxiously at her. What was upsetting her today, he wondered. She stomped into the kitchen after her bath and silently made the evening meal. He took the cooling milk from the kitchen table and carefully poured it into three bowls to set the curds. In the morning he would take it and keep it in the fridge so that the curds would not get too sour by dinner time. He then took the dirty clothes from the bathroom and put them into the washing-machine and ran the machine.

Parasmoni set the table and called Pooja from her room. She was studying for the Physics test, which her teacher had fixed for the next day. They ate their meal in a heavy silence. Pooja did not notice the tension in the air, since she was worrying that she had not prepared well enough for the test. Mohan and Parasmoni had brought her up carefully. She was sent to the best convent school, at a great expense at Loreto International at Park Avenue and they had taken her to see only English films. They did not speak to her in Bengali, so that she did not spoil her convent accent, gained by talking to her Anglo-Indian teachers and her classmates from upper class *Bodrolok* homes, whose parents had more often than not been educated at Oxford or Cambridge. They felt that they were justifiably proud of their accomplished daughter. Pooja played the piano and was familiar with the latest hits in English popular music. Now they would certainly be able to insert an advertisement in the Statesman matrimonial column, indicating "Bengali, Arya Samaj parents of tall, fair, convented, cultured graduate girl, seek educated, B.Tech, green Card/IAS groom for their daughter. Dowry seekers excuse."

It was Mohan's secret ambition to get Pooja married to an IAS officer. He was glad that he had been able to provide his daughter with an education that he himself had not obtained. Brought up in the colliery town of Dhanbad, where his father had been a foreman, Mohan had attended the local company school and had studied in the English medium and thereafter he had been admitted to Presidency College for a degree in Economics. But his father's sudden death in a mine accident had forced him to abandon his dream of writing the civil service examination. Instead he had to get a job in the secretariat as a clerk. He was able to rise to his present position of Under Secretary by dint of his hard work and his ability to write well in English.

Mohan and Parasmoni retired for the night. Mohan shut the bedroom door firmly, as he did when he was feeling amorous. The door had no latch. Mrs. Mary's breasts and thoughts of Dolly's plump bosom, had made desire rise in him like a sudden itchy rash, in the sweltering summer heat that needed to be assuaged at once. He made a tentative movement towards Parasmoni as she lay down, her ample body occupying three fourths of the bed. But she shoved him away with clenched fists. 'I met that Roopa Sharma from your office at the bazaar today. She told me all about this business with your new girlfriend Dolly Ganguly,' she muttered angrily. Roopa Sharma always kept Parasmoni posted with details about how Mohan ogled all the women in the office. Even the IAS Joint Secretary Mrs. Mary was not spared, she told Parasmoni.

Mohan stiffened as he listened to the familiar accusations that he was having an affair. He went out with Dolly and slept with her in strange places. He was neglecting the family, quite oblivious of the fact that he was the father of a marriageable girl. Only the names changed in Parasmoni's recitations. First she had suspicions about his dalliance with Mridula Chatterjee. Later she felt that he was having an affair with Pia Mukherjee. It was in vain that he protested that he was not at fault. He merely had to keep up office relations with his colleagues and have a cup of tea with them sometimes. It did not matter whether they were male or female, he said. They were merely office relations.

'I've had enough of your rakish behaviour,' Parasmoni said, 'I'm coming tomorrow to check up the facts. I will ask this Ganguly woman to keep her hands off you.'
He begged her not to do that. It was so unnecessary. He was innocent.
'Then I will come to know whether you are innocent and Roopa is making up lies about you,' she snapped.
They did not sleep the whole night as accusations and protestations were flung back and forth. Parasmoni reminded him how ardent he had been, when he had first fallen in love with her at college.

'And now you desert me for every young girl who flutters her eyelids at you,' she said, in a torrent of tears. He promised her that he would reform and that henceforth she would have no cause for complaint. But Parasmoni was adamant about coming to the secretariat. She would be there at three in the afternoon, as soon as school closed, she declared.

Mohan went in trepidation to the office the next day. He spent the morning with an unpleasant feeling in the pit of his stomach. He had a frequent desire to urinate. He imagined the scene created in the office. Perhaps Mrs. Mary would come out, hearing the commotion. The staff would gape at him. The peons would be grinning. He would lose all face in the office. There would be people whispering behind his back, about his lecherous ways and his vixen of a wife . . .

The office peon came in and informed him that Mrs. Mary had asked him to see her immediately. He went to her room with a sense of foreboding. Mrs. Mary waved a letter at him as soon as he entered. His heart sank. Had Parasmoni also sent her a letter of complaint? He felt profoundly relieved when she informed him that there was a communication from the Accountant General that had not been replied to by their department. Now a calamity! The AG proposed to make the insignificant draft para, a part of his annual report to parliament. He demanded an immediate reply, if the department wished to avert the unpleasant consequences of the audit para finding a place in the report of the Comptroller and Auditor General. Mrs. Mary asked Mohan to go to the AG's office that very instant. None of the excuses he offered, that he was not entirely prepared with the reply and that he would go the next day, were acceptable to Mrs Mary. Mohan left for the AG's office, fearing the worst of what would happen when Parasmoni came to the office.

Parasmoni strode into the Food and Civil Supplies Department with a pugilistic demeanour, exactly at 3 p.m. When she found Mohan missing from the office, she ground her teeth. The coward had run away. Dolly heard someone ask for Mohan Basu in a loud voice. She came out of her cabin to find out who was creating a commotion. Her face beamed when Parasmoni revealed that she was Mohan's wife.

'Oh Aunty! How nice to meet you!' Dolly exclaimed, 'Mohan Sir won't be back for some time since M'am has asked him to go to the AG's office, if you like we can have a cup of tea in the cafe across the road, while you are waiting. You know the secretariat canteen is so slow when you order tea here, you have to wait forever,' she said apologetically.

Parasmoni smiled at Dolly, a dagger hidden in her heart. So this was her competitor! She'd soon make mincemeat of her!! They sat on the plastic chairs, at a yellow sun mica topped table in the tea house. Dolly told Parasmoni that her little son was a handful, he was in play school. She said that she looked forward to the time when he would go to school. As she gave the waiter an order for elichi chai and buttered toast, she said, 'It's Mohan Uncle's favourite. And he always talks about you and your delicious cooking! He's very kind.

He treats me to tea and toast some evenings, when we have a lot of work to finish.' She pushed the plate of buttered toast towards Parasmoni. So Mohan was an 'Uncle'! Parasmoni beamed at Dolly, full of a new found bonhomie.

'Uncle is so generous!' Dolly confided, 'But he is also so strict!! Especially about spellings. My spellings are the worst. And I don't always look them up in the dictionary. I wish the department would buy computers so that we could get the spellings done from spell check.' By the time tea was over, Dolly and Parasmoni had exchanged phone numbers and promised to keep in touch. Dolly said that she could not wait much longer, as she was going for a movie with her husband. Parasmoni said that she would not wait for Mohan either as she had dinner to cook.

Mohan finished his meeting with the AG, who was quite satisfied with his explanations as to why they had spent Two out of Twenty Crores of rupees of their annual budget the last year on purchasing computers, instead of on conducting workshops on nutrition for expectant mothers. There was an intricate technical problem of programme expenditure being diverted to capital expenditure. Perhaps the department could indicate that the computers were a part of the programme implementation of nutrition education? Mohan grabbed the lifeline offered and agreed to send a suitably worded reply to the audit query. He left the AG's office and walked to the tram stop. It began raining. He had forgotten his umbrella. He raised his black, zipped Rexene bag, over his head with an exclamation of disgust, in a feeble attempt to protect himself from the rain. Fortunately a tram came by. It was empty and it reached him home all too soon.

As he trudged up the stairs to their little apartment, the delicious smell of fried fish and mutton korma wafted up to his nose. He was amazed. What was today? Wednesday? Fried fish day no doubt. But Sunday was their day for the meat curry. What was Parasmoni celebrating?

He pressed the door bell and Parasmoni opened it with a smile. Mohan's heart gave a little bound. She was wearing her pink house coat with little white paisleys. It was the garment she wore when she was ready and willing for amorous dalliance. Parasmoni scolded him for getting wet in the rain and forgetting his umbrella at home. She kissed the top of his head and took his bag from his hand. When he had washed his hands, she had a cup of steaming tea ready for him on the teapoy. He went to their bedroom. A fragrance of lavender hung in the air. Parasmoni had liberally used the room freshener that they used when they were expecting important visitors. He came out of the bathroom after a refreshing hot shower, wearing his white jubba and pyjamas. As he stood before the dressing table combing his hair, Parasmoni came up to him softly, doe eyed and demure. 'Pooja phoned to say that she will be late as she has extra classes,' she said in a low voice that sent his pulse racing. They shut the bedroom door firmly all the same. Parasmoni did not have to be coaxed or cajoled at all, this time. Mohan let out a sigh of deep satisfaction as he held all of Parasmoni. She was so soft and desirable.

It was wonderful to touch her when she was in a generous mood and they had no fear of Pooja popping in suddenly on them. This was so much better than those covert, guilty glances at Dolly and sly attempts to touch her fingers while passing her a bun maska. As he embraced Parasmoni, he dared not ask her whether she had indeed met Dolly. He did not *want* to know anything. He was just content to bask in his moment of joy.

ॐ ॐ ॐ